THE WOMAN FROM
BEAUMONT FARM

ANNEMARIE BREAR

Cece

<u>Contemporary</u>

Long Distance Love

Hooked on You

Where Dragonflies Hover (Dual Timeline)

<u>Short Stories</u>

A New Dawn

Art of Desire

What He Taught Her

THE WOMAN FROM BEAUMONT FARM

AnneMarie Brear

CHAPTER 1

*S*eptember 1914. Wrenthorpe Village, West Yorkshire, England.

BETH JACKSON ROLLED over in bed and wrapped an arm around her husband, Noah. Sleepily, she opened her eyes and watched him stir and come fully awake.

'Morning.' She ran her fingers over his naked chest, loving the feel of him.

He kissed her nose. 'Morning, beautiful.' He stretched lazily like a cat.

The pink light of dawn filtered through the net curtains as they'd forgotten to close the heavy drapes last night in their haste to get into bed and make love. Married for only four months, the novelty of being free to love each other each night hadn't yet worn off.

'I wish it was Sunday again...' Beth's fingers continued their idle journey along his stomach and headed downwards until Noah grasped her hand with a grin.

'Enough, woman.' He groaned, kissing her. 'I've got to get up and so do you.'

'It's still early. You don't have five minutes to spare?' she tempted him, knowing he'd be edgy this morning and she wanted to ease his nerves.

'No, as much as I want to, gorgeous girl. We have had the weekend to please ourselves and today is important.'

'You'll do just splendidly. I know it. You're well prepared.'

'I wish I had your faith in me.' He leapt from the bed to wash and shave.

'Haven't I always been proven right? When you doubted that you couldn't pass your exams, I knew you'd do fine.'

With a face full of foamy soap, Noah bent over the bed and kissed her. 'Let's hope you're right again today.'

Beth sighed happily, content to feast her gaze on him as he readied himself for his first day working as a qualified teacher at the prestigious Queen Elizabeth Grammar School in Wakefield, the local town only a mile up the road from their village. How had she been lucky enough to marry such a fine man?

At twenty-seven, Noah Jackson was as handsome as they come. His dark chestnut hair and blue-green eyes and strong build from years of digging for coal made her heart race. She had to pinch herself at times that this loving, devoted man was her husband. He'd been the catch of the village, and yet *she* had been the one he had chosen. She'd been Beth Beaumont, daughter of a farmer and worked on a market stall selling vegetables. Noah could have had anyone, but he fell in love with her.

Above her head, she heard Noah's three brothers who still lived at home, getting up to start their day at the coal mine. This house — a common pit house, so-called for the terrace row had been built by the mine owners to house their workers that she shared with Noah and his family — was in stark contrast to the roomy and comfortable large farmhouse she'd grown up in on the other side of the village. The two-up and two-down terrace house was home to damp and mould as well as the Jackson family. Noah's mam, Peggy, had raised five sons in the tiny rooms and each day Beth gave her credit for managing such an arduous task.

'Are you getting up, lazy bones?' Noah asked through the mirror, covering his lean body in a new dark grey suit and adjusting his tie. 'Your brother will be knocking on the door soon.'

Beth threw back the blankets. Despite being married in May, she'd seen no reason to stop working at her family's vegetable stall in Wakefield. She knew her parents were grateful for her to do it while they ran the farm, and it gave her much needed income while Noah had been studying at the teachers' college in Leeds.

'I'll make you some breakfast.' Beth donned her corset over her chemise and slipped on a black skirt and a cream blouse, knowing that soon her brothers-in-law, Albie, Alfred and James would descend downstairs grumbling they were hungry and she wanted Peggy to rest in bed for a little while longer.

Beth frowned as she brushed her shoulder-length dark brown hair and pinned it up into a bun at the back. Peggy's bad chest was sapping her strength again, and during the night, Beth had gone up to her mother-in-law to offer her a drink of water while the poor woman gasped for breath. Having spent all her life working in a cotton mill, Peggy now had what the locals called 'the weaver's chest'. Her lungs didn't work properly after years of breathing in cotton fibres.

'Your mam had another bad night,' Beth said as she and Noah left the front room, which was their bedroom, and went into the kitchen.

'Yes, I heard you go up during the night. I'll make her a cup of tea and take it up to her.'

While Noah set about filling the kettle with water, Beth raked the embers in the range and added kindling to build the heat. Her brothers-in-law, all tall, vigorous men with the good looks that had been bestowed on all the five Jackson brothers, came in and sat down at the table. Only Sid was missing, having married Meg last Christmas and who now lived with Meg's family a few streets away.

'I'm starving,' James, the youngest at twenty years old, yawned. 'Need a hand, Beth?'

'Aye, it would help.' She put the frying pan on to heat and slapped in some bacon, while in the pot she warmed the creamy porridge that had been soaking in milk during the night, no watered oats for her as was the Jacksons' custom. She'd soon changed many things once she moved into the Jacksons' house, and one of them was eating better food. She'd come from a family of farmers and fresh produce and hearty meals were what she was accustomed to, and something which she soon introduced to her new family.

All the brothers looked alike, tall and dark with differing shades of blue-green eyes, but it was her Noah who she believed held the stronger claim to being the best looking out of the brothers. He also had the most sense and intelligence. Still, she loved them all and despite their teasing and jokes, they'd welcomed her into their family with warmth and pride. She was a Jackson now, a married woman and no longer Beth Beaumont, the girl from Beaumont Farm. She was a valued member of the family and the daughter Peggy had always wanted. Beth liked that. Her relationship with her own mother, Mary, although pleasant, never reached a deeply emotional or affectionate level. Peggy Jackson gave Beth all the love Mary failed to demonstrate.

'Let me take that up,' Beth suggested, reaching for the teacup from Noah. 'You need to eat before you leave.'

'I don't think I can.' Noah sat at the table and sipped his tea, while Patch his little Jack Russell stood by his chair hoping for some breakfast scraps.

'Big day, hey?' Alfred nudged him.

'Aye. First day of the rest of my new working life.' Noah pushed away the bowl of porridge James passed to him. 'My stomach is in knots.'

Beth tutted from the doorway. 'You must have something inside you or how will you concentrate with a rumbling belly?'

She left them to it and hurried upstairs to the small bedroom. Peggy sat on the side of the bed, buttoning up her cardigan.

'What are you doing up?' Beth asked, placing the tea on the bedside table.

'It's Noah's first day. I want to wish him well.'

'I'll send him up, but you must stay in bed. You were up most of the night coughing and need to rest.'

'I'm sorry for disturbing you, lass. You've got a full day of work ahead of you, too. You don't need to be up during the night to see to me as well.'

'I don't mind.' Beth smiled gently. 'Now, have you got enough cough mixture left?'

'Aye.' She shook the little brown glass bottle on the table. 'Actually, no, maybe not.'

'I'll get some more on my way home tonight.'

'You're a good lass. I'm so pleased Noah had the sense to marry you.'

Beth kissed her thin cheek. 'Back into bed.'

Peggy sighed tiredly, pulling the bedcovers over her legs. 'I'll come downstairs later when the kitchen is warmer. I'll put a pot of stew on for our meal tonight. I can do that sitting down.'

'Lovely. There are vegetables in the box under the cupboard and Noah has brought in enough coal to last the day for you.' Beth stopped at the doorway. 'You'll take it easy, won't you? I'll see you when I get home this afternoon.'

'Right you are, lass.'

Back in the kitchen only Noah remained, the others having packed up their food and headed off to the pit. Beth quickly sipped her cooling tea and ate a slice of bread and butter. 'Go up and see your mam as she was nearly coming down and she needs to stay warm in bed.'

'I'll go up now.' He gave her a lingering kiss. 'Have a good day.'

She gently touched his shaven cheek. 'Don't be too nervous. You'll do fine. Mr Grimshaw said you'll not be teaching today but just getting a feel of the place, so don't worry.'

'What if they don't take to me, the students, I mean?' He ran a hand over his face. 'It was bad enough facing the board of governors, never mind a load of lads from wealthy families.'

'Be yourself and they will like you.' She kissed him again.

'I hope so.' He left her to go to his mam.

Beth tidied up and then pulled on her coat just as a knock came to the front door. 'I'm off now!' she called up the stairs before leaving the house.

Her seventeen-year-old brother, William Beaumont, sat up on the farm cart's seat waiting for her. 'Morning, sis.'

'Morning.' Beth climbed aboard and glanced at the crates of vegetables she'd sell today on the stall. 'Is everyone at home all right?'

'Aye.' Will flicked the reins for Snowy to walk on. 'Dad's talking about renting more fields along Beck Bottom Road at the Brandy Carr end.'

'Why?' Beth waved to Reverend Simmons as they drove past him standing outside of St Anne's Church talking to an old man.

'Dad says now a war has started, it wouldn't hurt to put more fields under plough. The government will demand it, anyway, just in case.'

'In case of what?'

'I don't know. Dad is reading war reports in the newspapers morning, noon and night. He's obsessed. He believes the country imports too much from other countries. We need to grow more of our own food, apparently.'

'But they say it'll be over by Christmas.'

'You know Dad. He's been wanting to expand the acres we have for years and put in other crops such a barley.'

'And do away with growing vegetables?' Beth said in shock.

'No, we'll do both.' Will shrugged. 'The war gives Dad a reason to do it. Mam's not happy though. She says it'll be too much work and we'll not have the manpower since every eligible fellow is enlisting.'

Beth nodded, still unable to believe the country was at war with Germany. When the government declared war last month, the country had heralded the news with joy and applause. Newspaper headlines shouted the arrogance of the German army invading Belgium and declaring war on Russia, of France rallying troops and how Britain needed every man to do their duty. War fever had gripped the nation. Army posters encouraging men to join the forces were plastered on shop walls and lamp posts. Men were signing up in the thousands, all eager to participate in the glorious adventure. No one wanted to miss out.

Beth understood the excitement to leave home and see some of the world. Unemployment was strife in the north of the country and the army offered regular payment, food and somewhere to sleep, all of which with the coming winter might be hard to find for those without jobs. So, thousands took the opportunity to fight for King and Country but also to get away from their humdrum lives.

She and Noah had joined others in town to listen to the army officers standing on stages, encouraging men to join the ranks. Along with everyone else, she'd cheered the recruits marching off to somewhere unknown to train to become soldiers.

Yet the first news reports coming in were showing it wasn't all glory and prideful marches and easy victories. The Battle of Mons had been a disaster and only now were the newspapers reporting the withdrawal and loss of life from all ranks of the British Army, and they were proper soldiers, well-trained men, the career army men. If seasoned soldiers couldn't beat back the

Germans, how were normal men, clerks, shopkeepers, labourers and such like going to do it?

Still, the news didn't seem to diminish the enthusiasm for men to 'take the shilling' as they called it, pledging allegiance to King and Country and going off to training camps that were springing up nationwide. Every conversation was about the war and the complete confidence that the British would push the German's back into their own territory and teach them a lesson for daring to invade peaceful countries.

To Beth it seemed the world had gone mad and this was reinforced as they trundled into Wakefield and passed queues of men lining up at the recruiting posts even at this early hour.

'They say the Frenchies and our lads will give the Germans a good pasting,' Will said, driving Snowy through the weaving traffic towards Brook Street and the market area.

'I hope it is over before Christmas and we can go on as before.' Beth climbed down from the cart in front of the Beaumonts' storage lock-up, where they kept the crates of vegetables when the market wasn't open.

Will helped her to load the hand cart and make the trips to their stall situated on Brook Street. Together, they set the stall up ready for trading.

'Thanks for your help.' Beth smiled at her brother. 'I'm set now, you can go home.'

'I've a few things to do while I'm in town.' He placed the handcart behind the stall.

'Anything exciting?' Beth asked, piling the apples into neat pyramids as the sun rose higher, warming the street.

'Not much. See you tomorrow morning.' He dithered for only a moment, as though wanting to say more, then with a nod of his head, he walked back to the lock-up and to Snowy.

'He's getting taller by the day, that brother of yours,' said Fred Butterworth, the stallholder beside her who sold ironmongery.

'Aye, he's nearly a man now. Seventeen.' Beth adjusted the

position of the price sign on the carrots and then inspected a brown onion to make sure it was as perfect as the others.

'He'll be joining up soon, I bet.' Fred, a large jolly man, chuckled. 'These young lads can't get into the thick of it quick enough.'

Beth's hands stilled and an icy tingle ran down her back. 'No, our Will is too young. I read the age to become a soldier is nineteen.'

Fred stacked some iron chisels on the corner of his stall. 'You can't tell me that in the rush to join up some of these lads aren't under age? Besides, the army won't care. They've been overwhelmed with new recruits. As long as they pass their medicals, blind eyes will be turned, I'm telling you.'

'Will is needed on the farm. The government has already announced that boys aged twelve can leave school to help on farms. Dad had many young lads helping with the harvesting last month as some of our regular helpers had gone to sign up. Will can't leave, Fred. He knows how busy we are. My dad wouldn't stand for it.'

'Nowt much your dad can do once the army has Will in their grip.'

'Will's a good lad. He'll not go against my parents' wishes.' She sounded more confident than she felt.

Fred nodded. 'Let's hope not, lass. Now how's your good man? First day at the posh school, isn't it?'

Beth let out a breath and thrust the war from her mind. 'Aye, he's that nervous. He couldn't eat a thing this morning.'

'It's a grand thing to see a man better himself. From a miner to a teacher, there's few who can say they've done that. You're right to be proud of him.'

'Oh, I am. Very much.' She beamed, filled with such a deep love for the man she'd married. 'Once he's settled there, we can rent a flat in town.'

'Now, wouldn't that be a thing indeed.'

'Beth!'

She turned on hearing her name being called and grinned as her sister Joanna came up the street pushing a pram. 'You're out early this morning.'

Joanna wiped a strand of hair from her eyes. 'Aye, I'm taking advantage of this one having her nap while I shop.'

Beth peered down at her baby niece, Ivy, sleeping in the pram. She had to make way for Fred to have a look.

'By, she grows more bonny each time I see her, Joanna,' he said, with the familiarity of a long-time friend. Joanna had worked on the stall alongside Beth for the last five years until she married Jimmy Shaw last year. So, Fred was like an uncle to both girls, having stood for hours in all weathers alongside them for years.

Joanna tutted. 'She's not when she's screaming at three in the morning, I can tell you.'

While Beth served a customer, Joanna chatted to Fred for a few minutes, then sat on the stool behind the stall as Beth finished.

'How's Noah then?'

Beth took a small sack of potatoes and placed them in front of the stall. 'He was nervous this morning, but I know he'll be fine.'

'Of course, he will. He's such a kind man, friendly. The kids will adore him.'

'I hope so. He'll feel better once the first day is over. He's worried that he'll not be taken seriously, being a miner and now a teacher.' Beth served another customer, weighing out a pound of apples.

'It's bound to be a big change for him. All he's ever known is the pit.' Joanna jiggled the handle of the pram as Ivy began to stir.

Beth finished with her customer and put the money in the little tin on the shelf under the stall. Her mind played on what Fred had said about Will.

'What's the matter?' Joanna asked. 'You look worried. Do you think Noah won't take to the school? Should he have stayed at the pit?'

'Oh, no. He'll be fine after he's settled, I'm sure.'

'Then what is it?'

Beth served another customer, who took her time to select some carrots, beetroot, onions and potatoes. Finally, the customer was happy and paid and Beth gave her attention to her sister. 'I'm worried about our Will.'

'Our Will? Why? What's he done?'

'Nothing.' Another customer came over, wanting apples and plums. Beth worked quickly, weighing and placing the fruit in the woman's bag.

Ivy cried, and Joanna rocked the pram. 'I'm going to have to go. She'll want feeding.'

Beth nodded and in a large brown paper bag she placed several tomatoes, a bunch of radishes, a lettuce and a handful of runner beans and then placed the bag on the wire shelf under the pram.

'I don't need all that, our Beth,' Joanna admonished.

'Nonsense. Take it. Do you want anything else?'

'No, ta. I've still got plenty from the last lot you gave me. I'll be back in a day or two, but I'd best go.' Joanna kissed Beth's cheek as Ivy's crying grew louder. 'What was it about our Will?'

'Nothing.'

'Are you sure?'

'Positive.' Beth bent over the pram and kissed the top of Ivy's head. 'Be a good girl, sweetheart.'

The stall soon became crowded with shoppers as the morning wore on. The summer had been hot and dry, providing a bountiful crop of vegetables and fruit. The stall had never looked so full, but by afternoon, the busy day had dwindled her stock and she had to make two trips to the lock-up for more produce.

As she packed away later that afternoon, Fred finished serving a customer and stepped over to her stall. 'You've had a grand day, lass.'

'I'm exhausted, Fred.' Beth loaded a half empty crate of potatoes onto the handcart.

'I wish I had half of your custom.' He shook his head. 'I'm in the wrong trade.'

'Would you rather be a farmer?' She grinned at him.

'Lord, no. Getting up before the sun each morning in all weathers, I think not.'

'Isn't that what we do now on the stall?' she joked.

'Aye, but only four and a half days a week.'

She grabbed the heavy money tin and tucked it into her bag. 'I'm off then. I'll have to go home to the farm and tell my dad we need more of everything.'

'Right you are, lass. Go steady on the tram. It's full of eager young lads who suddenly think they're soldiers.'

Beth took the handcart back to the lock-up and unloaded. She spent as little time as possible in the cold, cavernous lock-up for it was a place that held memories of when Louis Melville attacked her and cut off her hair because she refused to marry him. He'd kept her locked in the freezing room all night.

She shivered at the memory and dashed it from her mind. That had been last Christmas, nine months ago, and not worth another minute of her time thinking about it. Yet, sometimes in the crowd, if she spotted a tall thin man wearing a top hat, she'd hold her breath and hope it wasn't Melville. So far, it hadn't been. She'd not seen him since the attack. His father, Sir Melville, had ordered Louis to join him in Amsterdam and he hadn't returned.

On the tram from Wakefield to Newton, Beth sat squashed against the window as Fred's words came true and groups of young men filled the interior, laughing and messing about, holding up their signed pieces of paper which declared them now to be a part of the British Army. Their boisterousness grew a little tiring, despite the tram driver's repeated attempts to quieten them.

'It's a good job the army has them now.' An older woman sitting opposite Beth sniffed with disapproval. 'Discipline is what they need and that's what they'll get, you mark my words.'

Beth nodded and was thankful when the tram terminated at Newton and she got off. As much as she wanted to get home to Noah and hear about his day, she had to walk to the farm first.

The evening sun was low on the horizon, blinding her as she walked down the hill from Newton to the village of Wrenthorpe. The late summer weather made the walk enjoyable though and she watched the birds swooping and diving over the fields, which were in various stages of being harvested or ploughed.

Her heart skipped a beat as she saw Noah walking up the road towards her with Patch darting along beside him.

'Here she is, the love of my life.' He kissed her softly and then taking the bag from her, he tucked her arm through his.

'How was your day? Tell me everything,' Beth said as they walked into the village.

'Uneventful, really.' Noah shrugged. 'I was introduced to many of the other teachers.'

'Do they seem nice?'

'Pleasant enough. One or two looked at me funny. My history of being a miner might raise some eyebrows, but I'll deal with that should something be said.'

'You've done your training just as they have.'

'But I've not been to university, Beth.' Noah sighed. 'There will always be some people who will be prejudiced against those who haven't gone to university.'

'Then you'll have to show them that even without a higher education, you have been college trained and can teach just as well as them, probably better no doubt.'

He kissed her cheek. 'I'm a lucky man to always have such support from his wife.'

She smiled lovingly at him. 'What else happened?'

'Mr Grimshaw gave me a tour around the junior school buildings. I sat in on a few classes, that sort of thing. I'll not be teaching by myself for a week or so as I'm to shadow the other teachers for a few days to get a feel of how it all works.'

'That's sensible.'

'I think I'll like it though.' Noah pulled a golden leaf off a low hanging tree branch they passed under. 'I like the structure of the day. Everything is done to a bell. Classes, breaks, everything stops and starts at the ring of a bell. They encourage the boys to have outside activities. I can't tell you how happy it makes me feel to be outside with the sun on my face. Down the pit, depending on the shift I worked, I'd go all week without seeing daylight and in winter we didn't see daylight for weeks on end.'

'The benefits are already paying off then, aren't they? You'll have a routine in no time at all and enjoy every minute of it.' Beth stopped at the top of Trough Well Lane. 'I need to go and see Dad. I've had such a busy day. I need a larger restock in the morning than normal.'

'I'll come with you. Mam's got a stew simmering, it'll not spoil.'

'Is that all she did today?' she asked as they walked down the lane. Beth knew Peggy would try to do more than she was capable.

Noah sighed. 'No, she's in bed now, exhausted. She overdid it. She lit the boiler and did some washing and then washed the floor and ironed some clothes. When I got home from school, she was bent over the kitchen table dragging in air, trying to catch her breath. Her lips were blue.'

'I told her not to do any of that. I wish she would listen to me. I'll do it all on Saturday afternoon after I've finished at the stall.'

'Aye, that's the problem. She feels bad that you do it all and also work. It's too much for you to do, looking after all of us.'

Noah threw a stick for Patch to fetch. 'I'll get my brothers to do more to help.'

'They do their bit when their shifts allow. Alfred gets the coal in for me and Albie is helpful in preparing dinner and James makes sure they keep their bedroom tidy.' She squeezed Noah's arm. 'You help around the house, too. It's not so bad. We manage.'

Strolling down the hill, Beth stared out over the fields of Beaumont's rhubarb, which was the principal crop for the family. In November, the rhubarb that was two years old would be lifted and placed into the dark warm forcing sheds to grow over winter. The fields closer to the farmhouse where harvested of other vegetables such as potatoes and carrots and all that she sold on the stall. The fruit came from the large orchard at the back of the house and in summer she even sold bunches of flowers her mother grew in the garden or in the long glass greenhouse at the back of the barn.

Walking up the short drive, Beth saw her dad, Rob Beaumont, coming out of one of the sheds and waved. Her mam stood by the clothes line bringing in the washing. 'Want any help, Mam?'

Mary Beaumont shook her head. 'I'm nearly done.'

'I'll take the basket for you, Mrs Beaumont,' Noah offered without waiting for her to protest as Mary would. Her relationship with Noah was strained through no fault of Noah's but more because of Mary's history with his late dad, Leo. Mary and Leo had been an item before Leo threw Mary over for Peggy, who'd fallen pregnant with Noah. Mary had hated all the Jacksons for years. Only Leo's death had allowed Mary to soften towards Noah, that and Noah's devotion to Beth made her feel he wasn't like his father at all. Slowly, Mary was unbending enough to speak politely to him and welcome him into the family.

Beth went ahead into the kitchen. Her elderly Aunty Hilda, a warm-hearted woman who Beth loved dearly, stood by the oven stirring whatever was in the large black pot.

'How are you, Aunty?' Beth kissed her wrinkly cheek.

'More the better for seeing you. This is a pleasant surprise.' Aunty Hilda kept stirring. 'Grab that tray of potatoes out of the oven, will you, lass? I don't want this gravy to stick.'

Doing as she was bid, Beth helped her aunt as her mam and Noah entered.

'Thank you, Noah.' Mam took the basket of clothes from him and stowed them in the corner of the kitchen.

Not one for showing her emotions or demonstrating her affections, Mary gave Beth a nod of welcome. 'What brings you home?'

'I need restocking, more than usual.' Beth placed the tray of potatoes onto the side countertop next to a roasted chicken, the smell was divine and her stomach rumbled. 'I had such a busy day, you wouldn't believe. The tin is over there.' She pointed to the money tin she'd placed on the dresser.

Her dad came into the scullery, a room off the kitchen, and changed his boots for house slippers before washing his hands. 'Got on all right then, Beth lass?' he called through the door.

'Aye, Dad. I was just telling Mam.'

'Then wait until he's in the room, instead of shouting to him,' Mam admonished.

Dad came over to Beth and kissed her cheek. 'Tell me now, pet.' He sat down at the kitchen table and Beth took the chair next to him.

'I was rushed off my feet. I need restocking of nearly everything. The restaurants and tea rooms are doing a good trade with all the men and their families in town to enlist. They make a day of it and have a meal, which means they're coming to me to restock their kitchens.'

'Excellent. I'll have Will fill the cart in the morning. We are getting low on some vegetables. But you selling out is what we want to hear, isn't it, Mary?'

'Aye.' Mam set about slicing the roasted chicken. 'Are you staying for something to eat?'

Beth glanced at Noah, who nodded and replied for them both. 'Thank you, Mrs Beaumont, that would be lovely. My mam's got a stew on, but it'll not go to waste with my brothers about.'

'I'm sure it won't,' Aunty Hilda said with a snort. 'I bet your brothers have the appetite of giants. We find it bad enough with Will and Ronnie growing like weeds. Imagine feeding five grown men?'

'Four now remember, Aunty?' Beth smiled. 'Noah's brother, Sid, got married at Christmas and moved in with his in-laws.'

'Oh, aye. I'd forgotten.'

Ronnie, Beth's youngest brother, came running in, cheeks rosy from playing out with his mates. 'Hiya, Beth, hiya, Noah. I didn't see you at school today, Noah.'

'I don't teach at your side of the school, Ronnie. I'm with the juniors. I might see you in the playground, though.'

'Ronnie Beaumont, go into that scullery and wash your hands, ye filthy beggar.' Aunty Hilda nudged his shoulder gently. Her bark was worse than her bite.

'It was your first day at the junior school, wasn't it?' Mam asked Noah, as she placed the sliced chicken into the centre of the table.

'Yes. It was.'

'Did they like you, son?' Dad asked him.

'I think so. It's hard to tell on the first day.'

Mam drained a pan of cabbage into a bowl and placed it on the table. 'I'm sure you'll do well.'

Beth gave her a small smile. Such words coming from her mam were a compliment indeed.

'Did Will tell you, I've bought some pigs?' Dad asked Beth, reaching for his newspaper.

'Pigs?' Beth stared at him in surprise. 'Whatever for?'

'This war could mean folk going without food.'

Beth scowled. 'They say it'll be over by Christmas.'

Dad shook his head. 'I don't see it. What do you think, Noah?'

Noah took a seat opposite Beth. 'I'm in agreement with you, Rob.'

'You are?' Beth now looked at Noah. 'You never mentioned that before.'

'In the teachers' staff room today, it was all they talked about. One fellow, Mr Golding, visited relatives in Germany only six months ago. He told us that the Germans are determined to gain territory. They are a very focused race. However, so are the French. They want to regain the land they lost in the Franco-Prussian War of eighteen seventy.'

Proud of his knowledge, Beth swelled with pride at her intelligent husband, who had educated himself through years of study while working long hours down the pit.

'Well, the Germans are better prepared than us.' Dad passed the newspaper to Noah. 'Our government isn't prepared. It'll take months to organise an army large enough to compete with the Germans. Look how quickly they swept through Belgium. The Germans want Paris before winter sets in.'

Beth stood and poured out cups of tea as Ronnie took his place at the table.

Dad nodded towards the newspaper. 'All those articles about training camps and arguments over how many men are needed, and nothing about the role that us left at home must do. How are industries to survive with thousands of men gone from the country?'

'I've thought the same. The school is encouraging men to join up. Our industry isn't an essential service, not like the pit or the factories.'

Beth stared at Noah. 'They want you to join up?'

He shrugged. 'They aren't stopping anyone, and if a teacher wants to enlist, then they are assured of their position on returning home when it's all over.'

'Generous of them for sure.' Dad sounded impressed.

'Where is Will?' Mam sighed. 'He knows what time we eat.'

Aunty Hilda took Will's plate. 'I'll make him up a plate and put it in the oven to keep warm.'

'It's bad manners.' Mam huffed.

They heard the scullery door open.

'Here he is now.' Mam took the plate from Aunty Hilda. 'Sit yourself down. He can see to himself.'

Suddenly, Will stood in the kitchen doorway, clutching a piece of paper.

Everyone turned and stared at him.

'Come and sit down, lad, you're late,' Aunty Hilda said, placing potatoes on his plate. 'You've been gone all day. What have you been doing?'

Will remained where he was, his face pale, but a determined lift of his chin alerted them to something not being right.

'Will?' Mam raised her eyebrows at him.

He brought up the piece of paper and held it in two hands.

Beth's heart somersaulted in her chest. She knew what he'd done. So many lads had passed the stall holding a similar piece of paper. 'Oh, Will. No…'

Her brother focused his gaze on her, as though needing her support. 'Aye, I've done it. I've joined up.'

CHAPTER 2

'Y ou haven't.' Dad's cold, clipped words echoed around the warm kitchen. The only sound was the tick of the clock on the mantle and Patch scratching his ear where he sat by the door.

Beth closed her eyes to shut out the pain on her parents' faces.

Will straightened his shoulders. His hazel eyes, so like Beth's, swept the room. 'Aye. I have. I couldn't stand by and watch my mates enlist while I did nothing.'

'That's brilliant!' Ronnie grinned.

'Be quiet, Ronnie!' Mam stood and threw down the towel she held onto the table. 'You can jolly well march back up there and tell them there's been a mistake. You're only seventeen. They can't take you, you're underage!'

'I lied to get in. I told them I was nineteen.'

'Lied!' Dad jerked to his feet, knocking his chair over. The crack of it hitting the stone tiles sounded like a gun shot. Beth had never seen him so angry. 'You foolish boy! Do you think this is all some joke, a game?'

'No, Dad. I don't.'

'You're needed here, on the farm. I'll not have this!' Dad strode from the kitchen into the scullery, ignoring Will as if he wasn't there.

'Where are you going, Rob?' Mam ran after him.

'To tell them bloody officers that they can't have him. He's underage.'

Will spun on his heel to confront them. 'It's done. You can't undo it.'

'We'll see about that!' Dad yelled.

'I *want* to go. You can't *stop* me!' Will grew red in the face.

'Again, we'll see about that.' Dad replied, pulling on his boots.

Beth went to Will and held his arm. 'Come and sit down.'

He angrily shrugged her off and faced their parents. 'I'm joining the army and going to do my bit. You should be proud of me!'

'Proud?' Dad gasped. *'Proud!* To watch my son go off to be German bullet fodder?'

'I'm protecting my country,' Will defended.

'You're not going and that's my last word.' Dad took his coat from the hook.

'If you try and stop me, I'll only runaway and join up under a different name.'

Everyone in the room knew it to be true. Will would sneak away in the night and be gone. They'd not know how to find him.

Mam sighed heavily. 'Enough both of you. Rob it is done. We can't change it. I'll not have him disappear and spend my days not knowing where he is.'

Without a word, Beth's dad left the house, slamming the door behind him.

Wearily, Will sat down at the table and hung his head in his hands. 'I have to do this, Mam.'

'Aye, so it seems.'

Beth looked at Noah. 'I think we should go.'

Aunty Hilda wiped a tear from her eyes. 'You've not eaten yet.'

'I don't think anyone's hungry any more, Aunty Hilda. Sorry.' Beth placed her hand on Will's shoulder as she walked past his chair.

Walking arm in arm up the lane with Patch running ahead, Beth tried not to think of what was happening. How was it possible that her younger brother could now be going to war to face the bullets and bombs? He still seemed such a boy but had made the decision of a man.

Noah hugged her to him in support. 'You know your family won't be the first to feel like this. It's happening all over the country. We've seen the rallies and parades. Everyone is so excited we've gone to war. Will is only doing what so many other men are doing.' Noah took a deep breath. 'You've heard my brothers speaking about this, though not in front of Mam. I've not taken them seriously, but maybe I should.'

'Your brothers are exempt being miners. They have no need to go.'

'That's true. However, you know that's all they talk about. Pubs are filled with boasting men who have signed up. It makes other men feel left out, envious. It's the excitement of it all, isn't it? Look at Will. He lied about his age and won't listen to reason. He'll not be the only one breaking his parents' hearts.'

Beth stopped as a trickle of alarm ran down her spine. 'You'll not sign up?'

The expression on Noah's face told the story. 'I might not have a choice. I'm not exempt.'

'But it's only those who volunteer.'

'For now, yes.'

'You think they may force men to go into the army?'

'Not right away, but if it drags on, then maybe. Mr Grimshaw thinks it's a possibility if the war goes on for some time.'

An owl hooted in the fading light. Lights shone from cottages as they walked through the village.

'Do you want to go?' Beth asked, not really wanting to know the answer.

'No, I don't. My life is just falling into place nicely. I have a beautiful wife and a job I've wanted for years. I've no wish to leave…'

'But?'

'But I feel I should do my bit, too. Other men are fighting on my behalf, Beth. It's cowardly to stay at home while others die to keep me and my family safe.'

She had no response to that.

He pulled her close. 'I have a feeling my brothers might join up.'

Alarmed, she looked up at him. 'They are miners, though. They are needed here.'

'We'll have to wait and see and hope the war is over soon.'

'I wish this *war* was over already.' Beth shivered, and not just from the night air.

She thought back over the long hot summer, to their lovely wedding and the joy of spending two glorious days in Scarborough for their honeymoon, which had been a present from her parents. Those sunny days had felt the best in her life as she grew more accustomed to being Noah's wife, of the freedom she gained by being married, of the passionate love she received from Noah.

She hadn't minded moving into the Jacksons' small home while Noah studied at the teacher's college, for she knew it wasn't long term, and soon they'd have a little flat of their own in town.

Yet, now the war had come and banished the happy thoughts and memories of summer. Everything was changing and she didn't like it.

When they walked into the kitchen, Peggy was sitting at the table, darning a sock. 'Did you have a pleasant visit?'

'Not really.' Beth put the kettle over the hot plate to make some tea. 'Our Will has joined up and my mam and dad haven't taken it well.'

Peggy put down her darning. 'I expect they wouldn't.' She glanced at Noah. 'Thank God my lads are all in jobs that are exempt, except you, Noah, but you've got sense and I know you won't leave us. There's stew in the pot. Your brothers are at The Shovel having a pint.'

'I might join them.' Noah pulled his coat back on, kissed Beth and walked out.

Beth stared at the closed door. Noah rarely went to the local pub for a drink, and never on a school night.

* * *

NOAH WATCHED the class of six-year-old boys as they sat at their desks and drew him pictures of farm animals, which they had to label. Outside the classroom windows, the sun shone brightly. September was clinging on to the warm days for a little while longer.

'My pencil broke, sir,' cried one small boy at the back.

'Go and sharpen it, Roy. You know how to do it.' Noah watched the boy walk over to the sideboard and stick the pencil in the sharpener and turn the handle.

Noah peered over the shoulder of another boy. 'Very good, Bernard. Your duck looks splendid. Now write duck. D.U.C.K. Look up at the alphabet written on the board and find those four letters to make the word duck.'

Strolling between the rows of desk, Noah glanced at the drawings, some being better than others. These pupils were suddenly his alone to teach after only two weeks of him starting at the school. Their previous teacher, Mr Norris, had enlisted in the navy and resigned his position. Norris wasn't the only teacher to enlist from the school, four others had done so. War fever wasn't releasing its grip on the men in the town.

The newspapers ran thick with articles of battles and heroic deeds. The Battle of Marne had been lauded as a magnificent success at pushing the Germans back over the River Aisne. It was reported the British First Army were instrumental in the success and people read in amazement of six hundred Parisian taxis taking French troop reinforcements to the front to stop the Germans. The celebrations caused another influx of young men to join up, worried they'd miss out on being a part of the big adventure.

It was this new wave of patriotic fever that scared Noah for his brothers were swept up in it. He warned them to not speak of it at home to spare the frightened looks of his mam and Beth. But how long could he hold them back?

The school bell rang, making him jump out of his thoughts. The boys jostled their papers, eager to have a meal in the dining hall and then run about outside.

'Right, settle down. Put your names on the top of your papers and place them on my desk. We'll discuss the pictures this afternoon.'

'Will you read to us later, Mr Jackson?' A smart little boy wearing spectacles asked him as he went by. Noah tried to remember his name, but it was easy to forget who was who with twenty-five boys all in identical uniforms.

Noah stood aside so they could file out of the room. 'Perhaps. Depending on behaviour and how well you all do at writing the alphabet this afternoon.'

Two boys pushed each other in the doorway.

Noah clapped his hands. 'Charles and Fredrick, stop that. Come back here to the end of the line. I'll not have pushing in my class!'

Grumbling, the two boys plodded back to the end of the line. When at last the classroom grew silent of little boys' voices and he was alone, Noah stacked the drawings on his desk in a neat pile.

A slight knock at the door made him look up and smile at Mr Grimshaw. His dear friend and mentor came in holding a tin.

'All quiet?' Mr Grimshaw put the blue tin on the desk.

'For an hour at least,' Noah joked.

'I've brought you some fruit cake made by one of my pupil's mother, or at least by her cook. It's tasty, but too much for me. I thought you might like to take it home and share it with Beth or your mother.'

'Thank you. That's kind.'

'To be honest, I'm not a great lover of fruit cake. I'm more of a pound cake man, really.' Mr Grimshaw glanced around. 'Getting on all right?'

Noah nodded. 'There's nothing like being thrown in at the deep end, is there?' Though in truth he hadn't minded. It gave him the chance to show the school what he could do. He was determined to be the best teacher he could be, even without a university degree.

'Yes. It wasn't ideal for you. I'd hoped you'd be able to shadow Mr Norris for a month or two, but well no one thought Mr Norris had a hankering after the sea.'

'It's not the first service I'd have chosen to join, that's for sure,' Noah said.

Mr Grimshaw frowned at him. 'Is joining up something you're thinking about doing?'

Noah sighed and put down the drawings. 'If I had a choice, no.'

'But?'

'I fear my brothers will leave me no option but to enlist as they are talking about doing so and I can't let them go into danger without me. I need to watch over them.'

'Oh, Noah.' Mr Grimshaw took his glasses off and, taking a square piece of linen out of his pocket, began to clean them. 'I was anxious you'd say something like that.'

'If it happens, I can assure you, Mr Grimshaw, that it'll not be a decision I take lightly. I know I am needed here, and I don't want to leave.'

'You are needed, but your position will be safe if you enlist. You'll be treated no different to the other teachers even though you've only just begun your time with us.' He replaced his glasses. 'The board of governors are expecting more teachers to enlist. They are putting out a call to retired teachers to come back and work for the duration of the war.'

'I wouldn't go if my brothers didn't, but I can't let them volunteer without me. I couldn't live with myself. I'm the eldest. I've always looked after them.'

'I understand. What will your dear wife have to say about it?'

Rubbing his forehead, Noah shrugged. 'I dread to think.'

* * *

TWO WEEKS LATER, on a rainy Saturday afternoon, Noah was no longer kept in suspense about what his brothers were doing. While making notes on next week's lessons, Noah glanced up from where he sat at the kitchen table, expecting Beth to come home from the stall. Instead, his brothers filed in when they should have been at work. Even Sid, who married Meg and lived with her and their little boy, Walt, came in behind them.

The brothers jovial talk and scraping of chairs made enough noise to wake the dead.

'Is the teapot hot?' James asked.

'Mam's asleep. Keep it down,' Noah said, moving his books to one side. 'And no, it's not hot. Make some fresh.'

'We should go to The Shovel, a pint is more in order than a cup of tea,' Alfred grumbled. 'We're meant to be celebrating.'

Noah's heart dropped. 'Celebrating?'

'Aye, we've done it. Enlisted.' James crowed from the range where he jammed more wood into the stove.

'Tell me you haven't.' Noah stared at each of them. His worse fears had come true, and now he'd have to join up as well and leave his beautiful Beth. How would he stand it? 'You're miners, you don't have to go,' he whispered, stating the obvious and knowing it wouldn't do any good.

'We *want* to go!' Sid declared. 'It'll be a right laugh.'

'A laugh! Have you seen the newspapers?' Noah glared at him. 'You've a wife and baby at home.'

'Aye, I know it, but I'm to do my bit. Meg's always going on at me about joining up. I think she wants rid of me from underfoot.' He shrugged. 'She's no time for me now the baby is teething. All he does is scream. I'll be glad for some peace and quiet.'

Noah's eyes widened. 'You think you'll get that in a war? Are you thick in the head?'

Sid grinned. 'There are different types of peace, I can tell you. Just you wait until your Beth is yelling at you alongside a screaming baby. You can't do right for doing wrong, I tell you. France will be a lot sweeter than my current home, that's for sure.'

The hall door opened, and Mam walked in. Although thin and pale, her blue eyes came alive at the sight of her boys. 'I could hear you lot upstairs.' She sat at the table, wheezing. The stairs were becoming too much for her as the cooler autumn weather replaced the warmth of summer.

Suddenly the brothers quietened. None of them wanted to impart the news that would devastate their mam.

The front door opened and closed, and Noah tensed as Beth stepped into the kitchen. He stood and kissed her, already sorry for the pain he'd cause.

Beth stared around at the quiet men as she took off her wet coat and hat. 'What's wrong?'

Noah's stomach clenched as his mam picked up on the solemn vibe in the room.

'Aye, what's gone on?' His mam sat at the table and James poured her a cup of tea.

'Why isn't there any food on?' Beth asked, going to the stove.

Noah watched her, noticing her movements were jerky. She wouldn't look at him.

'Now, Mam, don't get upset...' Albie warned, a hand out in front of him.

'Upset?' She frowned. 'What have you done?'

'We've enlisted,' Sid supplied.

Noah continued to watch Beth. She'd become still, her back to them all. His mam's cry of anguish echoed in the room, and all at once his four brothers were on their feet and hurrying to her side to offer what comfort they could. Their jovial attitude had no place in this kitchen now.

Moving closer to Beth, Noah put a hand on her shoulder. 'Sweetheart.'

She turned and buried her face into his chest for a moment as he held her tight, then she leaned back and stared up at him. 'You're going too, aren't you?'

'I'll have to. I need to keep them out of trouble.' He smiled but knew it didn't reach his eyes.

'Well, that's that then!' Mam sipped at her tea as the brothers sat down again. She glanced at Noah. 'I expect you're off, too?'

'They give me no choice. Someone has to watch over them.'

His brothers protested strongly.

'We're old enough to take care of ourselves!' Alfred defended.

'Really?' Noah scoffed.

'We're not babies,' James said.

'You've barely left Wakefield, never mind ventured to another country.' Noah shook his head.

'We've been on the train to the coast.' James grinned.

Noah grabbed his coat from the hook on the back of the door. 'You think a day trip to Bridlington is all the preparation you'll need to travel to France and shoot other armed men?'

'No, of course,' James snapped. 'I'm not stupid.'

Noah bit back a cutting retort. 'Put your coat on, Beth. We'll go to the fish and chip shop. No one is cooking tonight.'

That she quietly did as he asked showed him how much she was hurting. How was he ever going to say goodbye to her?

CHAPTER 3

*O*n an overcast day in late October, Beth stood on the side of Kirkgate in Wakefield next to Peggy. From their spot on this road, they'd see the men marching down the street towards the train station. Her mam, dad and Ronnie stood close by, squashed in amongst the crowd. A marching band could be heard coming up the road, but as yet they couldn't see it for the swell of people blocking their view.

Beth looked up into the sky, scudded with grey clouds. A slight wind whipped the bunting, which hung from shop to shop. People leaned out of upper-storey windows, bragging to those below about how much they could see. A dog barked, wagging its tail as it crossed the street, receiving pats from children. Everyone was wearing their Sunday best, as though waving the men off was worthy of getting dressed up, and Beth supposed it was. Only inside she couldn't smile and wave. She didn't want to chat to the strangers gathered around her. Her throat was too full and her heart dissolving with cracks of pain.

The recent weeks had become a blur in her mind. Noah had enlisted to join his brothers. She understood his reasons why, not that his explanation helped to ease the ache in her chest. He was leaving her. No words could stem the agony. Oh, she tried to smile and put on a brave face. Telling all those who asked that she was immensely proud of him, and Will and her brothers-in-law. She spent hours on the stall listening to other women boast of the sacrifice their wonderful men were making, but deep inside, Beth raged at the unfairness of it all. Her husband should be at home, or at the school teaching, not firing bullets into foreign men who wanted to kill him.

Beth shuddered and goosebumps rose on her arms.

Peggy gripped her elbow. 'It'll be over soon, lass. That'll be the worst of it, sending them on their way. After that, well, they'll be at training camp for months, won't they? And we can get on with our lives in the hope that it'll be all over before they've set foot on a transport ship.'

Beth gave her a wan smile in reply, knowing Peggy suffered as much as she did.

The crowd was cheering and clapping and frantically waving British flags long before she could see the columns of men proudly marching.

Beth turned as Dad helped Joanna slip the pram into a bit of space between them.

'I didn't think I'd make it,' Joanna panted. 'I've run all the way.' She peered down at Ivy sleeping. 'She filled her nappy in such a way it went right up her back. I had to bath her before leaving the house and I was sure I'd miss Jimmy.'

'Jimmy?' Beth's eyes sprang wide. 'He's joined up, too?'

'Aye, two days ago. Sorry, I've not had time to come and tell you all.'

Mam took the pram's handle and pulled it closer to her, allowing Joanna to stand nearer to the edge of the road. 'I'm not surprised Jimmy has joined them. It's as though every man must do it in fear of missing out.'

Dad, being the tallest amongst them, craned his neck. 'Here

comes the band.' He held Ronnie by the shoulders in front of him. 'Look for your brother.'

Beth noticed the tears in her dad's eyes. Not that he'd let them fall. That wouldn't do at all. The roar of the cheering hurt her ears, nearly drowning out the band as they marched by. Hot tears ran down her cheeks as she scanned the columns of men as they filed by, all of them wearing their bests suits.

'How will I spot him?' She panicked, stepping forward, eager to see Noah.

'Can you see any of them?' Peggy asked. 'Are they together? They've got to be together, they're brothers.'

'I can't see.' Beth held onto her dad's shoulder, reaching up on tiptoe to try and search over the heads and shoulders of the crowds who waved hats and flags and blocked her view.

'I can't bear it.' Joanna sobbed beside her.

Mam put her hand on Joanna's arm. 'Be proud of him. Don't cry.'

'There!' Ronnie shouted. 'There's our Will!'

'William!' Dad shouted through cupped hands and waved his hat as Will turned and waved to them. Besides him marched Jimmy, and Joanna cried and waved her handkerchief.

Beth frantically looked for Noah. Then she saw Sid, with his lopsided grin, and Meg pushed through the crowd and ran to him to kiss him. Beth wanted to do the same, but she couldn't find Noah.

'Where are the others?' Peggy elbowed her way to the front, wheezing at the effort.

Not to be outdone, Beth shoved forward right behind her and together they searched the columns of men.

Suddenly she saw Albie. 'Albie!' she screeched, earning herself a frown from the woman stood next to her.

Peggy waved her handkerchief. 'I think that's James on the other side of Albie, do you see?'

'No...' Deflated, Beth stared after the last of the marching men and the other band that brought up the rear of procession.

'Bugger this,' Dad snapped as the crowd surged and followed the band. 'Everyone is going to the train station and so are we!'

'We aren't meant to. They said not to go to the station as it'll be too crowded.' Joanna wiped her eyes.

'I think it's time we did what we wanted, lass.' Dad took the pram's handle. 'Come on, let's hurry.'

'Not me.' Peggy stood, a hand on her chest, pale-faced. 'I can barely walk ten yards without stopping. I can't hurry to beat the crowds. You go.' She squeezed Beth's hand. 'Give them my love. I'll wait for you in that tea shop across the road.'

'I'll not go either,' Mam said. 'I'll take Ivy. You'll be quicker without the pram.' She nodded to her husband. 'Take the girls and Ronnie. I'll stay with Mrs Jackson and the baby.'

Not needing a second bidding, Beth ran, her skirts held above her ankles as she weaved through the heaving mass of people.

'Wait for me,' Joanna called, and Beth slowed enough to grab her sister's hand and they raced on with Ronnie, leaving Dad to rush after them the best as he could. It didn't help that he kept stopping to apologise to folk who he bumped into as he ran.

'Come on, Dad,' Ronnie called, running faster than them all on his spindly legs that carried him as fast as a greyhound into the station.

Barriers had tried to hold back the people wanting to see loved ones but there were too many people and the waist high barriers were no match for those wanting one last embrace.

Beth squeezed through a gap near a turnstile and pulled Joanna after her. Panting, they threaded through the boarding men, crying women and children and the harassed porters who shouted and blew whistles to no avail. Gathered like cattle at the market, families crowded the platforms, searching for their men or having found them, were having last minute words and kisses.

Beth's chest strained against her corset as she panted, out of breath. Her eyes searched everywhere at once, looking for Noah.

All the men wearing either black, grey or brown suits made it difficult to find anyone she knew.

'Jimmy!' Joanna screamed and dashed through a group of men to where Jimmy stood smoking a cigarette. He bundled her up into his arms, smiling and kissing her.

Beth pushed on, stepping over luggage and around families.

'Will!' She heard Ronnie's screech, his voice breaking between a boy and a man's.

Seeing Will step away from a group of his friends, young men he'd gone to school with at the same school Noah now worked at, Beth held back for a moment. Although eager to see Noah, she needed to speak to her brother, too.

Smiling through her tears, she reached out a hand to her tall strapping brother.

'Don't cry, Beth,' Will said, clearing his throat. 'I'm only going to training camp.'

'Aye, I know.' Nevertheless, she hugged him to her. 'Write often. Mam and Dad will expect it.' She glanced over her shoulder as Dad finally caught up with them. She kissed Will's cheek, feeling the soft stubble on her lips. Stepping back, she gave him over to Ronnie and Dad and went to find her husband.

Grouped together, the Jackson brothers stood chatting to others as they lined up to board the carriage. But she couldn't see Noah. The train's whistle blew loudly, making Beth jump. The signal given, porters encouraged the men to quickly board.

Alarmed at the surge of men between her and the Jacksons, Beth struggled to get through. She tripped over luggage, grabbing a man's sleeve to stop her from falling.

'Are you all right, love?' the fellow said, steadying her.

'Thank you.' She darted from him as the train's whistle blew again.

'Noah!' Beth yelled, dodging the men impeding her way. She saw James board and Alfred was right behind him. 'James! Alfred!'

Tears choked her throat. Where was Noah?

Finally, she reached the last carriage door where the brothers had gone through. She walked along the windows, trying to see in, but they were too high. Men leaned out, waving and smoking. Suddenly, Sid's head poked through the window.

'Sid! Where's Noah?'

'Our kid!' Sid's head disappeared for a moment as he yelled for Noah, then he was back. 'He's going to the door.'

Beth ran back to the door just as Noah jumped down the step and gathered her into his arms.

'You said you weren't coming to the station.' He held her tightly.

They kissed desperately, gripping each other, never wanting to let go.

'I love you,' she breathed, kissing him, touching his face with her gloved hands.

'I love you. I'll miss you every minute I'm away.'

'Write. All the time. Promise!'

The whistle drowned out his reply as the train's wheels squealed and nudged forward.

'No!' She couldn't let him go.

'I'll be back soon. Once training has finished.' He kissed her again and then ran with her to the door as it crept away from them. Noah swiftly jumped up onto the step, letting go of her hand.

Beth stood there and watched the train disappear down the platform and out of the station. Tears dripped off her chin.

'Let's go home, lass,' Dad said sadly, coming to stand beside her along with a sobbing Joanna and a subdued Robbie.

Heartbroken, Beth wiped the tears from her face and made a pact with herself that she'd not cry again until the war was over. While Dad held Joanna against him, Beth took Ronnie's arm and, as a fractured family, they walked out of the train station.

CHAPTER 4

November slipped into December without Beth hardly being aware. The days grew colder and shorter, and the nights grew darker and longer. With only her and Peggy in the house, the quietness became oppressive. Christmas cheer was hard to find.

The stall kept Beth busy and at her mam's request she'd started training Leah, a young woman about Beth's own age of twenty, to help her part-time on the stall. This would then free up Beth a bit more to help her mam on the farm. Aunty Hilda's arthritis was playing up again and she couldn't do as much in the house as she used to and with Will gone, Mam was helping Dad on the farm more as they grew the next crop of rhubarb in the forcing sheds and put extra fields under plough.

Beth liked Leah, a small dark-haired lass with intelligent eyes and a ready smile, and soon they were the best of friends.

Fred, from the next stall, stepped closer, his face grave as he held his newspaper. 'I still can't believe it. For the Germans to fire on our shores.'

Beth shuddered. 'I hate the thought their ships were so close to us. Firing on Scarborough, Whitby and Hartlepool is a disgrace, killing innocent people like that.'

'It's a disgrace that our own navy didn't catch the blighters!' Fred fumed. 'Makes us look foolish. Is that how we are to live now, scared German cruisers will sail up and down our coast firing on undefended towns? How will we sleep at night? What's stopping the Germans from landing on our shores?'

'Lord, don't, Fred. I can't bear the thought. But it brings it home, doesn't it? The war isn't just over in Belgium and France, but here on our coast. It scares me. What if the Germans had landed soldiers? What would we do?'

Fred shook his head. 'I dread to think.'

'Beth,' Leah called, serving a customer. 'Do we have any more pears?'

'No, we've none left at all,' Beth replied and smiled apologetically to the regular customer. 'Sorry, Mrs Beecham. I sold out yesterday.'

'She's fitting in well.' Fred nodded toward Leah who was serving Mrs Beecham with the ease of someone who'd done it years instead of two weeks.

Beth added more sacks of potatoes to the front of the stall. 'Aye, I'm pleased Mam suggested we take her on.' A cool wind blew up the street, scattering bits of paper and rubbish and sending a chill up Beth's legs as her black skirt flattened against her.

'What's the plan with her then?' Fred asked, watching Leah serve another customer.

'She'll work Saturday mornings and all day on Wednesdays for now. She has another job at one of the pubs and works there each night.' Beth repinned her hat, which was in danger of being blown off her head.

'And you'll be a lady of leisure?' Fred laughed.

'Hardly!' Beth restocked the onions. 'I'm back at home on the farm, more than I'm not. It's like I've not been married and moved out at all.'

'Your dad and mam will be thankful for your help.'

'Aye, well, it'll soon be lifting time for the rhubarb and Dad's worried they'll be no decent healthy men to hire. The school lads aren't strong enough to lift the rhubarb, they weigh more than they do! I can help planting in the forcing sheds, as well as help Mam and Aunty Hilda in the house.'

'How's Peggy?'

'She rarely leaves the house, especially now the weather has turned for the worse. In summer she can lead nearly a normal life, but in winter, especially in that damp cold house, it makes her chest worse. Even with the fire going all day, that house is as cold as ice.'

'Poor woman. At least she's not working in the mill any longer.'

'No, and Noah and my brothers-in-law are sending their army pay home to help us pay the rent and bills. We can't let her go out and work again. She'd not survive it.'

'Have you heard from your Noah lately?'

'Two days ago. He writes twice a week.' She smiled, her heart swelling at the thought of reading Noah's letters and the simple joy she felt when arriving home to see a letter from him on the table. Those letters kept her going when at times she missed him so much she thought she'd go mad with the ache of wanting him home and in her arms.

When Fred turned to deal with a customer, Beth opened the flask and poured out two cups of tea for Leah and herself.

'Thanks for that.' Leah cradled the cup and sipped. 'It's been a good morning so far.'

'Yes, let's hope it doesn't rain and send everyone home.' Beth sat on the little stool behind the stall.

'What do you do when it rains?' Leah leant against the stall post.

'Grin and bear it.' Beth laughed. 'If it gets too bad, then pack up early. There's no point staying open if no one is about.'

'Aye, right.'

'Do you think you'll stay on then?' Beth asked.

'Aye, if you're happy enough with me?'

'I am, yes. To be honest, it was becoming difficult working the stall and running a house, and then helping out at the farm. I wouldn't know what it's like to have a day to myself and do anything I please, and that's the truth.'

'Well, I'm grateful your mam offered me the chance. I wasn't happy at the mill. Since me dad died, money has been tight for us. I'm the only one working now he's gone. That's why I took on the extra pub work. It pays well but working late isn't great when you have to get up before dawn to go to the mill. I was falling asleep at my loom. Something had to give, so I walked away from the mill job. At least if I nod off on the stall, I'm not going to get injured or killed, unlike at the mill.'

Beth nodded. 'I'll talk non-stop to you to stop you falling asleep.'

Leah grinned. 'That and hot cups of tea whenever I want is a blessing. I didn't get that at the mill.'

'And you lost your mam years ago, is that right?'

'Aye, five years ago, a day after she had my baby brother Tommy. He died two days later. She shouldn't have had him so late in life. She was forty and already lost a few babies after having my youngest sister.'

'How sad.'

'So that left me, Dad and my two little sisters.' Leah drank her tea. 'Me Aunty Viv wants the girls.'

'What do you mean?' Beth ignored the crowded market noise and the hustle and bustle of distant traffic as she looked at Leah.

'Aunty Viv says she can look after Susie and Tess better than I can. She's probably right, but once they go to her, I'll be on my own.'

'How old are your sisters?'

'Eleven and nine. Aunty Viv has a lovely house on the road to Bradford. The girls would be spoilt rotten. I'm selfish keeping them with me.'

'They are your family. Of course, you want them close.'

Leah shrugged. 'I've to make a decision soon.' She put the cup down and went to serve an older woman.

Beth glanced around the row of stalls, sipping her tea, and thinking about Leah's problem. She and Peggy had a spare room at their house, but would Leah want to work and live with her?

'Beth, I mean, Mrs Jackson.' A man stopped at the side of the stall and took off his bowler hat.

It took a moment for Beth to recognise him. 'Mr Staines. How lovely to see you.' Beth smiled warmly at the butler from Melville Manor. 'Are you well?'

'I am, thank you. And you and your husband?'

'We are, or at least Noah was in his last letter.'

'He's joined up?'

'Yes, last month, alongside his brothers.'

'Good on him. I'm on my way to the recruiting office now. I'm hoping to scrape in as the recent age limit is thirty-five and I'll be thirty-five at the end of December.'

'Why would you want to leave Melville Manor?'

Staines smoothed down his oiled hair that the wind tugged. 'After reading about the attack on our coast, I can't stand by and simply watch while others fight for me. Besides, I didn't have a great deal of choice. Sir Melville is closing up the house. A closed house has no need for a butler.'

'Heavens. Closing the manor? Why?'

'Sir Melville is staying in Amsterdam permanently, and Mr Louis has joined the army. There'll be no family at the manor for the duration of the war.'

Relief flooded Beth. To not see or hear of Louis Melville for a while longer would be a blessing. 'I'm sorry you've lost your position.'

'I haven't, not really. Mr Melville has sent for me to be his batman. I'm to join him once I've passed my training.'

'I see. Is that what you want to do?'

'He said for me to either be his batman and have my old job as butler on the war finishing, or to find a new job altogether. The state of the country as it is now, finding a new job would be easy with all the men enlisting, but then I thought perhaps I should experience some excitement, too. I've spent a good part of my adult life in that manor. It feels the time to see what lies beyond Yorkshire, and I don't mean the Melville's London townhouse.' He gave a soft laugh. 'This way I'll have a job to return home to, and that's not such a bad thing even if it is for Louis Melville. When this war is over, there will be a lot of men wanting jobs and I don't want to be one of them.'

Beth couldn't help but shiver at all this talk of Louis Melville. 'I've not seen Melville since he attacked me last year. Has he been back here at all?'

'No. He's not returned to the manor. He's been either in Amsterdam with his father or in London with his sister. I've only been in contact with him through letters when he sends his instructions, and I give him a report on what's happening at the manor in his absence.'

'I see. Does Louis know of your letters to his father about his treatment of me?'

'Probably. Louis is clever, he'd have worked out it was me who informed his father about what he did to you. However, he's never once mentioned it to me in any of his letters. In fact, he has been most cordial and considerate to me and to other members of the staff. We've all received a pay rise and Mrs Handry, you remember the cook? She has been assured of a generous pension when she retires in a few years. That was down to Louis, not his father. Whatever he's being doing in Amsterdam with his father seems to have changed him somewhat. Unless he's waiting until I join him and then he'll make me pay.'

'Is it worth it, joining him, I mean? Wouldn't you be better serving in the army away from him?'

'Being a butler is all I know how to do. I might as well be a batman to Melville than any other officer. I know Melville's ways and at least then I'll know what I'm doing, unlike shooting at strangers. I've never fired a gun in my life. I doubt I could hit a barn door, never mind man who is shooting at me!' He chuckled and placed his hat back on his head. 'Good day, Mrs Jackson.' Staines paused. 'Marriage suits you. He's a good man your husband.'

'He is and thank you. Take care.'

Beth watched him walk away and then served a person waiting while Leah went on a comfort break. Her mind lingered on Louis Melville. A fleeting thought was that he could be shot and killed, and she'd never have to see him again, but then she tutted at herself for such nasty thoughts. Melville might have tormented her last year, cut her long hair off and locked her away overnight, but he didn't deserve to die. Before he became a tyrant, he'd shown her hints of kindness. The day he'd shown her around Melville Manor had been one of those times. Noah thought he had some kind of mental condition, a madness running through him. She certainly believed Louis Melville had two sides to him. A kind side and a manic side made up that man.

However, she was married to Noah and Louis couldn't hurt her now. She expected that he'd never even think of her. Once she'd hated him with a passion, but as the months passed and she was enveloped in Noah's love, she realised that Louis Melville was to be pitied. She had rejected him and that must have hurt. Gentlemen weren't used to being rejected. It had been a lesson to Melville, and he'd handled it badly.

'Can I have some carrots, please, love?' a man asked, jolting Beth out of her thoughts.

'How many do you want?' She pushed Louis out of her mind and served her customer.

When she'd finished, she grinned on seeing her best friend Jane come by the stall. 'Why are you not at work at the mill?'

Jane looked peaky, her red freckles standing proud on her pale face. 'I've been to the doctors.'

Instantly, Beth was by her side. 'Why? What's wrong? Come sit down on the stool. Do you want a drink?'

'I'm in the family way.' Jane's smile brought some brightness to her eyes.

'Oh, Jane!' Beth hugged her. 'I'm thrilled, really I am.'

'I am too, but I've been so sick, Beth. I can't tell you how awful it's been. I can barely go a few hours without something setting me off.'

'Poor you. That would be dreadful.'

'I can barely do my shift at the mill. I keep having to go outside to throw up. The foreman isn't happy.'

'When is the baby due?'

'June, apparently.'

'Alfie must be over the moon?'

'Aye, he will be when I write and tell him.' Her expression fell. 'He's gone. Yesterday. Enlisted with the rest of the fools.'

'Don't say that, Jane. They are brave men, fighting for our freedom.'

'I know, and I am proud of him and them all, but well... I'm a bit frightened now he's left. I've got to bring a baby into the world without him.'

Beth wrapped an arm around her shoulders. 'You're not alone. You have your grandparents, and Alfie's family and me.'

Jane nodded, her smiled forced. 'I'd best go. I've shopping to do for Gran.'

'I'll pop over for a visit on Sunday afternoon if the weather is good.'

'Lovely. Cheerio!'

Beth watched her go and pondered on the thought of Jane having a baby. Noah hadn't left her with a baby growing in her stomach, and she didn't know whether she was pleased or sad about it.

* * *

Juggling a box of vegetables, a bag of wool and her own bag weighed down with the stall's money tin, Beth pushed open the front door and entered the house. The neighbour from the next terrace waved, but Beth just nodded and smiled.

Peggy sat at the table, stuffing a pillow with feathers. 'How was your day, lass?'

'Not too bad. I bought you some more wool. I had to get dark blue as they had no more black.'

'That's fine, thank you.' Peggy coughed, but continued stuffing feathers into the pillow. 'I don't think the boys will care what colour their socks are as long as they're warm.'

Dumping her goods down on the table sent a flurry of feathers up into the air. Patch jumped about, trying to catch them as they floated down. Laughing at the little dog, at first Beth didn't hear the knock on the door.

'Someone's knocking,' Peggy said, scooping up the feathers. 'Look at the state of this place.'

'It's fine. I'll see who it is.' Beth opened the front door to a man she knew only by face.

'Good evening, Mrs Jackson.' He took off his flat cap and swapped his leather satchel from one hand to the other.

'Good evening. You know my name, but I don't know yours, sorry.'

'Mr Upton. Would it be convenient to speak to you and Mrs Jackson?'

'Yes. Come in.' Beth stood aside to allow him to walk down the narrow corridor to the kitchen beyond.

Mr Upton looked a little ill at ease. 'How do, Mrs Jackson.'

'Mr Upton? This is a surprise. I've not seen you about for a while. What can we do for you?' Peggy asked, tidying away her feathers and pillow case.

'Would you like a cup of tea?' Beth asked him, indicating for him to sit at the table.

He stayed standing. 'No, thank you. I'll not keep you long as I know time is getting on and my wife will have my tea ready soon.'

'What's this about then?' Peggy asked.

Slipping his finger around his tight collar, Mr Upton grimaced. 'I've come on behalf of the mine owner, Mrs Jackson.'

'Oh, aye? What does the mine owner want to do with me then?'

'It's about the house. This house.'

Peggy's eyes narrowed suspiciously. 'And?'

'You see, it's a good size and...'

Beth chuckled at the description of it being a good size. The entire house could fit in her mam's kitchen at the farm.

Mr Upton glanced between Peggy and Beth. 'You've no longer got any miners living here.'

Jerking up from her chair, Peggy glared at him. 'They're miners all right, they just happen to be serving their country, Mr Upton.'

'Aye, aye, I know that. But they didn't have to go. Miners being exempt and all that...' He swapped his satchel to the other hand. 'You see, there are many families needing houses. Miners' families...'

'And you want this house?' Peggy asked incredulously.

'It's only fair, Mrs Jackson. Two women living in a four-roomed house, well... It could be better used by a family. We've a waiting list for houses as long as my arm.'

'I don't care about your ruddy list, Mr Upton. My sons will

come back from this war and they will come back to this house, which is their home, the one they were born in!'

'Yes, but they aren't here now.'

'We're paying rent, aren't we? We're not in arrears. What does it matter to the mine owner who pays the rent?'

'The rules are the houses owned by the mine can only be rented to miners.'

'This one is! They just happen to be away at present.' Peggy's cheeks reddened and she started coughing.

Beth hurriedly poured her a glass of water. 'Mr Upton, surely you must understand that if we leave this house and then the war is over next month, my brothers-in-law will return to no home.'

'I do understand, Mrs Jackson, but we must obey the rules.'

'Stuff your rules,' Peggy panted between coughs.

Mr Upton smoothed back his oiled hair. 'We're not saying you have to leave right now. We aren't heartless. You have until the end of December.'

'Two weeks away?' Peggy spluttered.

From his leather satchel, Mr Upton pulled out an official piece of paper. 'We have to look after the miners we employ.'

'Funny that, I thought the mine still employed my sons?'

'I'm sorry. They gave up their places when they enlisted, which means they gave up this house too.'

'They were told their jobs would be safe when they returned,' Beth added.

'Aye, if the war looked to be over with by Christmas, but reading the reports that hardly seems likely, does it?' He grimaced and slid the piece of paper across the table. 'This isn't a task I enjoy doing, believe me.'

Beth glanced at the paper. 'Is there no other way to avoid this, Mr Upton? The Jacksons have lived in this house for twenty-seven years.'

'I'm sorry. Neither of you ladies are miners. It's a pit house.'

Peggy sat down with a bump, her wheezing easing a little.

'What if we took in lodgers, miners, single men who work at the mine?'

Mr Upton frowned, clearly thinking about her suggestion. 'As I see it, Mrs Jackson, as long as there are *our* miners living in this house, then that satisfies the rules. I'll leave it up to you to work out the rest, or you'll be evicted in two weeks.' He replaced his hat on his head and picked up his satchel. 'Good evening, ladies.'

Once he'd gone, Beth set about making a light meal for them both. She wished with all her heart that Noah was home.

'We could make it work, lass,' Peggy said, slowly setting the table. 'You stay in your front room and I'll stay in my bedroom. That leaves the big bedroom for a few lodgers. There are three single beds in there. We'll put the boys' things into the loft for now. That's three lodgers all paying towards the rent.'

'But it also means three strangers are living with us.' Beth didn't like the thought of living with strange men. She heated some oil and popped sliced potatoes into the pan to fry, while in another pot she boiled some eggs. Next, she buttered slices of bread while Peggy made a fresh pot of tea.

'What's the alternative?' Peggy asked. 'If we move out where will we go? A poky little flat in town? And what if in six months the war is over, and the boys come home? Where will we all live?'

Frustrated, Beth banged another pot onto the stove. 'This damned war!'

Peggy sighed. 'I've hated this house all my married life. Yet now the thought of leaving it terrifies me. I can't go without the boys. I can't give it up.'

'Ask around the village. Perhaps we can find some single men needing lodgings. It would be better if it were someone we knew.' Beth wiped a hand over her tired eyes. 'Noah isn't going to like this.'

'None of them will, but you're right. If we can find someone we know to come here and live with us, it'd be better than strangers. I'll start asking around tomorrow.'

Beth fried the potatoes, her stomach churning at the thought of strangers sitting at that table, of men sleeping above her head, of them coming home from the pub drunk. She wouldn't be able to grab a cup of tea in the mornings dressed in her nightgown like she did now. She'd always have to be fully dressed. Lodgers would change everything.

CHAPTER 5

*I*n pouring rain that blew across the North Yorkshire moors, Noah walked down the rows of white bell-shaped tents until he found the one he shared with his brothers. He was cold, soaked through and fed up.

For the last twenty-four hours the icy December wind carried rain that soaked the fields they camped in and made it difficult to keep kit dry. Their clothes and boots were always damp and freezing. His suit was ruined beyond repair, and there was still no word on when they'd get their uniforms.

Noah dried his wet hair on a damp towel that hadn't dried since he'd had his wash and shave that morning. Sitting on a canvas stool, from a slim leather wallet, his Christmas present from Beth, he brought out a piece of paper and a pencil to write a quick letter to her before they had another drill. Blowing on his stiff hands to warm them up, he began.

'My dearest love,

Merry Christmas, my darling. Thank you for my present. I am using the writing paper from it now, and it'll keep me in good stead to have something so useful. I hope everything is well at home and you and Mam are managing. Christmas isn't the same this year for any of us, but please try to be happy and make the most of the season. Apparently, we are to have a special dinner tonight. What that may be is anyone's guess. The food here, as I've mentioned in previous letters, isn't great. Yesterday we had potatoes and carrots with rice. Still, no matter what it tastes like we will eat it all as before long we are drilling again and will need all our strength.

I'm sorry we couldn't make it home for Christmas. We are being moved to other accommodation and they cancelled passes home. I think we leave tomorrow to huts, which will be far warmer than these tents.

Tell your Ronnie that we are still practising with wooden rifles. He'll find that a huge joke.

I received a letter from Mr Grimshaw yesterday. He tells me he saw you on the stall last week and had a chat with you. I am glad he comes to see you.

Your brother Will is in good health. His tent is in the next row to ours, but I've not yet managed to see Jane's Alfie yet. It's not surprising, as this camp is enormous.

I miss you terribly. The days here are the same, the routine doesn't change much and so the hours seem to trickle by. My brothers are having a time of it, enjoying every moment, even the tiresome long marches. I, however, wish only to be home with you. It's not that I'm afraid of going over to France, well, I suppose we are all concerned about that, but it's the knowing that you are only a few hours' drive away and I imagine you sleeping in our bed and I long to be beside you, holding you...

'Hey up, our kid,' Sid greeted him coming into the tent. 'Have you eaten?'

'Yes. Where are the others?'

'They're coming. Rumours are we're going on a march in an hour.'

Noah groaned. 'Another one? We did ten miles yesterday.'

'Aye, the army are enjoying knocking us into shape. It's bloody torture walking up hills for miles in the rain.' Sid laid on his cot. 'Afterwards, we're sneaking off into the village tonight for a pint or two. Are you coming?'

'I suppose so. It's better than sitting in this ruddy cold tent.'

As his brothers came in talking and laughing, Noah put away his letter to finish later.

Alfred took off his boots to change his socks for a fresh dry pair. 'I've sorted us a lift into the village tonight. Harry from the kitchen is driving the truck to get more supplies. He said we can jump in the back.'

'Excellent.' James rubbed his hands together. 'Gives us more drinking time.'

'We'll have to walk back in plenty of time, mind,' Sid warned. 'It's lights out at nine-thirty and I plan to be in bed by then.'

'You're becoming an old man,' Alfred teased.

A whistle blew outside, and they groaned, knowing they had an afternoon of drills and exercises in the rain ahead of them.

Noah followed the others out to the parade ground where they lined up and stood to attention. The rain soon wet them through. The cold made Noah shiver, and he jiggled his arms to keep warm.

'Who is moving there!' a voice bellowed.

Noah groaned and stiffened to attention and stared straight ahead.

An officer strode down the lines of men to stand a few feet from Noah.

'Who was it? I demand to know,' the officer barked.

'I moved, sir,' Noah admitted.

The officer strode to stand in front of Noah, his face inches from him. Noah quickly hid his surprise at seeing Louis Melville standing before him.

'Jackson?' Melville stepped back, grimacing. 'Good God.' He looked down the line. 'Isn't this a turn of events?'

Noah continued to stare straight ahead.

'I'm your commanding officer, Jackson.'

'Yes, sir.' Noah stared at the back of the man in the row in front of him, not making eye contact with Melville.

'This is going to be interesting, isn't it?' Melville smirked. He leaned forward to whisper. 'You're mine to do with as I like, Jackson.'

'Yes, sir.'

Melville moved to stand in Noah's eyeline. The rain dripped off the front of his officer's cap. 'This is going to be fun.'

Noah held Melville's stare. His gut clenching with hate for the man who'd treated his Beth so appallingly.

'Shall we start with a ten-mile hike with full packs?' Melville murmured. 'What do you think of that, Jackson?'

'Whatever you order, sir.'

'Whatever I order...' Melville tapped his chin. 'Oh, yes. This is going to be enormous fun. You see, Jackson, you're not so cocky now, are you? While you're in this battalion, you'll be under my charge.'

Noah remained silent.

Suddenly, Melville sighed. 'I could be an utter bastard to you, Jackson. But I promised my father I'd be a changed man, make him proud.'

Watching the conflicting emotions on Melville's face, Noah didn't know what to make of it. His heart sank that Melville was his officer. Would he and his brothers be able to transfer elsewhere?

'Why out of all the men in this camp did *you* have to be here?' Melville mumbled in annoyance, as though his thoughts mirrored Noah's. 'I suppose your dull-witted brothers are here, too?'

'Yes, sir. They are.' Noah seethed at the insult. 'So is Will Beaumont. Beth's brother, you know, my *wife*? The woman who spurned you, remember?' he goaded.

Melville stepped back as though slapped. He glared in distaste at Noah. 'Sergeant Bourke! Have these men carry full packs on a ten-mile hike, no make it fifteen miles. Then, after that Private Jackson is to be put on a working party for the rest of the week, scrubbing pots sounds good to me.'

Noah grinned at Melville's furious face.

The die had been cast.

* * *

BETH LEANED over the copper tub and squeezed out the water from the shirt she'd just washed. The steaming scullery resembled a Chinese laundry like they had in town with the amount of washing she'd hung up trying to get it to dry while outside light snow fell.

Laughter came from the kitchen and she sighed. The three male lodgers were nice men, but she couldn't get used to having them in the house. They were helpful at times and, seeing the state of Peggy, they were quick to carry buckets of water or coal for her, but their bedroom was a mess and none of them picked up after themselves.

Beth was tired of coming home to fall over boots, or to see jackets hanging on the banister rail. Newspapers had to be moved before she could sit down, and it appeared there was never enough food in the house. They ate like horses and were louder than the Jackson brothers, who'd shown some respect to others sleeping. Not these fellows. They came and went at all times of the night, making enough noise to wake the dead.

She'd escaped on Christmas Day, dragging a protesting Peggy with her, down to the farm. Although Christmas wasn't the same without Noah or Will, Mam and Aunty Hilda put on a nice spread of food. Dad collected Joanna and Ivy to spend a few hours with them, but they all agreed they were happy to see the back of Christmas Day, Peggy especially. For the first time she had spent Christmas without her sons, and she found it hard to raise a smile.

'There you are, lass.' Peggy came into the scullery. 'I've put the kettle on. Those three have gone to the pub.'

'Good. We might have some peace for a bit.' Beth added the last shirt to the rail and then hoisted it up by the pulley, so it hung suspended above her head.

'You shouldn't have taken on their washing. It's too much for you.'

'Aye, I know, but they offered to pay me and since I was doing ours, I thought why not? But I regret it now. My back is fair breaking.'

'Come sit down for a bit. You're on your feet enough behind the stall. Why don't you have a rest and write to Noah?'

'I'll write to him tonight. In his last letter he said being in winter barracks at Tring was rather boring. Their routine is monotonous, but the weather is better down south than the original camp they were in up on the Dales.'

'My poor lads. James will hate the cold.'

Back in the kitchen, Beth gratefully accepted the cup of tea Peggy made.

'Why don't you have that tea and then go down to the farm and see your mam and dad. You've not been since New Year's Day and that was over a week ago.'

'Maybe, if the snow stops falling.'

'Well, if it stops, you should go. Stay the night if need be. I'll be fine here with the lads. They don't bother me as much as they bother you.'

'I'm sorry I complain about them, but they are just so messy and loud.'

'I agree, but I'm sure I annoy them with my coughing all night. So, it's a trade off.'

'You can't help coughing in the cold bedroom, it plays havoc with your chest, but they have no excuse to not pick up after themselves.'

'Perhaps it'll be better in the summer. I don't cough so much in the warmer weather, and those lads might not be under our feet as much. Until then, we'll have to make do, but you should escape to the farm as much as you can.'

Tempted, Beth pondered on the suggestion. Tomorrow being Sunday meant she wasn't working on the stall. She could spend the day with her family. This house no longer felt like home to her, not without Noah and definitely not now three men shared it with her. Her hope of getting some village miners she knew proved useless. Most of the young men Beth had grown up with either still lived at home or had enlisted.

In the end, Mr Upton found them three fellows from the village of Stanley and when they moved in Beth felt like *she* was the stranger in the house. Even the front room, which was hers and Noah's bedroom, gave her no comfort. Without Noah it was just a room she'd slept in for six months and it meant nothing to her. They hadn't refurbished the bedroom or made it truly theirs for they thought they'd soon be moving out into a flat of their own in Wakefield. However, the war had put paid to that idea.

Suddenly, she was desperate to get out of the house and be back on the farm, surrounded by her family and sleep in the comfortable childhood bedroom that was still full of her belongings. She wanted to chat with her aunt and walk around the farm with her dad as he told her about the new improvements he'd been doing. She missed playing cards with Ronnie on an evening and having a laugh with their old farm labourer Reggie.

Patch came over and put his paws on her lap. She rubbed his little head. 'Hey, boy. Shall we walk down to the farm?'

Peggy stood and opened the back door. 'It's stopped snowing, but by it's freezing. There will be ice forming under that snow, so be careful.'

Decision made, Beth packed a small overnight bag, but left Patch with Peggy to keep her company.

'Come down to the farm tomorrow and have a meal and we

can walk back together,' Beth suggested to Peggy as she pulled on her coat.

'I don't know…'

'I insist. Mam always cooks enough to spare.'

'I'll think about it. If I'm not there for one o'clock, you'll know I'm not coming.'

'Very well. Send one of the lads to come and get me if you need me at all. It doesn't matter what time.' Beth kissed Peggy's cheek.

'Right you are, love.' Peggy cradled Patch on her lap and began sorting out wool to make more pairs of socks for her boys.

Stepping carefully on the paths through the village, the crunch of ice and snow sounded loud on the quiet streets. Most people were inside, and only some young boys were out playing snowball fights.

Beth slipped and slid down Trough Well Lane towards the farm. Snow smothered the landscape like a white blanket. A male pheasant strutted across the lane, pecking at the ruts made by farm carts before taking to flight as Beth came too close. His black and brown silhouette stood brilliant against the grey cloud-filled sky.

Smoke spiralled out of the chimneys of the farmhouse, but the yard was silent. Even the chickens were quiet as Beth trod around to the back door and into the scullery to take off her coat and boots.

Walking into the warm homely kitchen, she smiled at Aunty Hilda sitting at the large table, polishing the family's few pieces of silver. Beth kissed her paper-thin cheek.

'It's good to see you, lass, but you look sad. What's wrong?'

Beth shrugged and added more coal to the fire. 'Nothing. I'm just missing Noah, that's all. Although it has been only months, it feels such a long time since he was home.'

'Well, you're bound to miss him, newly married as you are.'

Aunty Hilda dabbed the cloth into the tin of polish and continued rubbing the silver teapot.

'Where is everyone?'

'Your dad and Ronnie are in the sheds with the men, harvesting the rhubarb to make the London train tonight. Your mam has just gone out with food and cups of tea for them.'

'What can I do to help? Do they need more hands out in the sheds?'

'No, lass. There's a dozen or so of them out there. The harvest is nearly finished. The last crop will go on the train to London on Monday morning. What's the bag for?'

Beth placed her bag by the door leading into the hallway. 'I'm staying the night.'

'Ah, that's grand. We miss you being about the place. It's not the same since you got married and then Will left. It's too quiet.'

'Even with Ronnie running about the place?'

'Aye, he's just one voice when not so long ago there used to be four of you. Have you seen our Joanna recently?'

'She stopped by the stall last week. Ivy's been sick with a severe cold, so she's staying indoors. Jimmy's parents have been doing the shopping for her.'

'I thought there must be a reason why she hasn't called this week. It'll be nice to feel the summer heat again. My old bones need to feel the sun's warmth.'

'And hopefully this war will be over by then.'

'Going by the newspaper reports it won't be. Your dad read it out to me that they're reporting a stalemate over winter. The troops can't go forward or back. They're stuck in the trenches for the winter, poor souls. A nasty situation and no mistake.'

'This is a surprise,' Mam said, coming in carrying an empty tray.

'Is it all right if I stop the night, Mam?' Beth asked, never too sure of her mam's mood.

Mam took off her coat and looked offended. 'Of course. It's still your home even if you are married.'

'Thank you. The Jackson house isn't the same with the lodgers there.'

'No, it wouldn't be,' Mam agreed, stacking the tray with the others beside the Welsh dresser. 'I'll go up and put some fresh sheets on your bed.'

'I'll do it.' Beth took a step, not wanting to give her mam more work.

'No, I'll do it. I know which sheets to use.'

'You can peel some potatoes instead,' Aunty Hilda said. 'It'll save me doing it.'

Beth went into the larder and brought out a small sack of potatoes. Her mam had gone upstairs. As she peeled the potatoes with a knife at the table, Aunty Hilda continued to polish the silver teapot.

'Have you been to the theatre lately?' Aunty Hilda asked.

'No. It isn't any fun without Noah and Peggy won't go as her cough is too loud and she's embarrassed by it. I do nothing except work the stall and come here.'

'Nay, lass. You can't put your life on hold while he's away. You've still got to live.'

'It doesn't feel like I am. I feel like I'm holding my breath until he comes home safe.'

'That could be a long time, lass. He's not even left England yet. You need to get out, have some fun. How is Jane going?'

Beth smiled, thinking of her best friend. 'She was fine last I saw her just before New Year's Day. We bumped into each other at the post office in town.'

'It was nice to see her at Christmas. It was good of her to stop by and see us.'

'I think I'll walk over and visit her tomorrow after church.'

'Get your dad to take you in the cart. You'll break a leg on that ice out there.'

'Dad's too busy. I can walk over to Alverthorpe. The roads aren't too bad if I go carefully.'

'There, your bed is made up,' Mam announced, coming back into the kitchen. 'Won't Peggy miss you being at the house?'

'Thanks, Mam and no, she's fine. The lodgers are there and one of them will come and get me should she need me. She has her medicine by her bed and there's food in the house.'

Aunty Hilda picked up a silver spoon to polish. 'You should just move back here while Noah is away.'

'I can't leave Peggy. Some days she can barely make it up the stairs, her breathing is so bad.'

'Can't the lodgers see to her?'

'I'm her daughter-in-law. I want to be there for her. The odd night here will have to do.'

'How is Leah getting on at the stall?' Mam asked, eyeing the way Beth peeled the potatoes to make sure she didn't peel the skin too thickly. Beth had grown up with her mam, wanting and expecting perfection in everything her children did.

Beth stood and filled a pot with water to put the potatoes into. 'She's great. She has a quick mind and is good with the customers. A treat to work with, really. It's like having Joanna working with me again.'

'Hardly,' Mam scoffed. 'Joanna is your sister. Leah is a stranger.'

'True, but Leah is lovely, and she's not had an easy life. I'm glad we can help her by giving her this job.'

'We'll see if she sticks it out, won't we?' Mam didn't look convinced.

'I thought you liked Leah?'

'I do, but she's not one of us, is she?'

'What do you mean? You don't trust her?'

'No, it's not that. Besides, I trust *you* to make sure *she* does her job properly.'

Beth turned away and rolled her eyes. Her mam was the main

reason why she'd never consider living here while Noah was away. They clashed too much. Mary Beaumont had a kind soul and would do anything for anyone Beth knew that, but it came with conditions, which had to be met. Beth preferred Peggy's amiable company of simple love and laughter.

Beth spent the evening playing cards with Ronnie and then wrote letters to both Noah and Will. Mam and Dad sat either side of the fireplace, Mam sewing a tear in Ronnie's trousers and Dad reading the newspaper he didn't finish at breakfast. It'd been the same routine as Beth remembered, only this time it felt different. Aunty Hilda had gone to bed early as she normally did, but the absence of funny, talkative and teasing Will affected Beth more than she realised.

The subtle change wasn't only Will not being home but herself, too. She'd grown up and really, she should be with Peggy, either ironing or knitting or reading, all the occupations she did each night sitting at the table with Peggy. She was a married woman now, not a child to go running home whenever she felt like it.

Sleeping in her own bed again was a mixture of emotions that only compounded her restlessness. No longer was she the girl who previously slept in this bed. Since leaving home, she'd married a man she adored and with him she'd become a woman who experienced physical love, something she'd only ever wondered at when she'd been living at home.

Her childhood memories of sharing this room with Joanna and being surrounded by keepsakes and girlish things no longer fitted her new life. Old diaries, clumsy attempts at painting images of farm animals, her book of pressed flowers, the penny novels, the dolls in faded dresses, even the pink flowered wallpaper she'd been so proud to have in her room, all seemed from another life, an era when everything had been innocent and easy.

Louis Melville's attack and Noah's declaration of love had changed her from being a girl to the woman she now was. Soon, if the fates and the war allowed, she'd become a mother like Joanna. Constant change was inevitable. Noah might not be back for another six months or even a year and going by the newspaper reports that seemed more likely. She shuddered at the thought of it, but it was time she accepted it.

The next morning, feeling lighter of spirit, Beth woke early and fed the chickens and Snowy, the carthorse, before starting breakfast.

Her mam, next one to come downstairs, looked at her in surprise. 'You didn't need to get up early to do all this,' she said, noticing the set table and the steaming teapot. 'It's Sunday, your day off. Ronnie would have done what was needed.'

'I want to be useful.'

Mam said no more as she helped cook the breakfast as the rest of the family slowly joined them.

'I'm going to walk over to Jane's after church,' Beth told them as they ate breakfast.

'Aww, I wanted us to go skating at the old quarry at Lindale Hill,' Ronnie moaned. 'The small lake at the bottom has been iced over for weeks and Mam won't let me go on my own.'

Mam turned the fried bread over in the pan to soak up all the bacon juices. 'No, I won't, Ronald Beaumont. The quarry is a dangerous place.'

'I'm thirteen, Mam.'

'Aye, and you'll not reach fourteen if you raise your voice to me, my lad.' She gave him a quelling stare.

'Go with your friends,' Beth answered, refilling the teapot.

'Billy's skates are broken, and Tim's lost one of his. Yours are still under the stairs. Can't you come for an hour?'

Torn, Beth didn't know what to say. 'I get little time to see Jane though, Ronnie.'

'And you never spend any time with *me*!' he argued back.

'That's not true! We played cards last night, didn't we?'

'Enough you two,' Mam snapped. 'Ronnie, I'll come with you. Let Beth go and see Jane.'

'*You'll* come?' Ronnie was astounded as was the rest of the family. Mary Beaumont didn't do activities with her children. They all knew that and had grown up never expecting their mam to be included in anything they did, for she was always too busy with the house and the farm and visiting sick friends and elderly folk in the village. When they were young Dad would go sledging with them or play cricket with the boys in the orchard or teach them all to swim in the deeper parts of the beck. As busy as he was, he made time for them and they loved him for it.

'Really, Mam?' Ronnie's voice rose in hopeful surprise.

'Aye. I'll not skate, mind you, but I'll watch.' Embarrassed, Mam looked away and quickly cleared the table. 'And we'll not be all day either. A couple of hours only.' She gave him the last piece of fried bread.

Dad smiled as he ate his bacon and eggs.

'We can all walk that way together,' Beth added, just as shocked as Ronnie that their mother was spending any time with him.

Two hours later, after sitting listening to a lengthy sermon in a freezing St Anne's Church, Beth had a quick cup of tea at the farm before kissing her dad and Aunty Hilda goodbye. She walked with Ronnie and their mam back up the lane and into the village. They waved and nodded to people they knew as they walked through the village.

Ronnie kept up the chatter as they walked and Beth felt happier as the sun poked out between white fluffy clouds, dazzling the snow and ice landscape. In her pocket were the two letters to post, one to Noah and one to Will. Her bag slung over her shoulder and her scarf tucked up against her chin, she pulled the collar of her coat higher. But the cold wasn't too bad.

'When Noah comes home, will you and he stay with Peggy

and his brothers?' Mam asked as Ronnie darted ahead, too excited to walk with them. He was still such a boy in many ways.

'No. We've talked of getting a flat in town. There's some that the school own, for the teachers, and Mr Grimshaw says we should be able to get one. We would have done that by now if the war hadn't broken out.'

'That's something to look forward to then. You'd not want to live with Peggy Jackson all your life. She has other sons to look after her.'

'But no daughter. Meg, Sid's wife, never calls. Peggy hardly sees Sid's little son, Walt. Meg is busy doing her own thing and never thinks that Peggy might like a visit.'

'Peggy Jackson is lucky to have you as her daughter-in-law,' Mam's tone was clipped and knowing the history of the two women, who years ago both wanted Leo Jackson, only for Peggy to win him, Beth didn't comment.

They turned up Potovens Road and slugged it up to the top of Sunny Hill. The snow was a little thicker on the ground in places and the ice underneath made them tread warily, though Ronnie ran ahead as sure-footed as a deer.

'Take my arm, Mam,' Beth suggested as her mam slipped on ice.

Mam hesitated, never one to admit a weakness, but then slipped her arm through Beth's.

Smiling at the contact, something she rarely received from her mam, Beth focused on where they walked, not wanting them to fall over.

'He's missing Will terribly,' Mam said, nodding towards Ronnie.

'That's understandable. They were as thick as thieves being the only boys.'

'Yes, he's a bit lost at the moment, but he's been such a good help to your dad. Before and after school, he's working hard in the sheds. It helps soften the blow of Will leaving. Your dad can't get used to the fact that Will is a soldier.'

'It's a new world for us all.'

'I hope this war is over soon and Will comes home. If he doesn't, I don't know how your dad will cope. He reads the casualty lists from the battles, and he frets that one day he'll see Will's name in the newspaper. He's not sleeping with the worry of it.'

'We have to believe that Will and Noah and them all will make it home safe.'

'I say that to your dad, but he won't listen.'

Beth chuckled as Ronnie fell over into a snowdrift as they turned onto Lindale Hill Lane and passed the terraced houses on the corner.

'That boy cannot walk when there is a chance he can run!' Mam scolded lightly. 'Thank God he's not old enough to enlist.'

Beth glanced at her mam's serious face. Will's enlistment had torn their mother's heart in two. At thirteen, Ronnie was safe from joining up for another five years and like her mam, Beth was thankful for it. 'Let us not talk of it, Mam. For Ronnie's sake, let us be happy.'

'Aye, you're right.' Mam lifted her chin as though to banish away morbid thoughts.

They passed Warren House and beyond that was the overgrown path leading into the old disused quarry. Nature had reclaimed much of the quarry and bushes grew where once men toiled, cutting sandstone for buildings. A small lake had formed at the bottom of the quarry and in winter it was often a place kids came to skate, but today it was deserted. Ronnie ran to the edge of the frozen water and quickly tied the skates to his boots.

'I've not been up here for such a long time.' Beth breathed in the clear, cold air and stared out over the rolling fields. She could see for miles.

Waving his arms like a scarecrow in the wind, Ronnie

plodded across the rocky ground to the edge of the iced-covered water which filled the bottom of the quarry.

'Go careful now,' Mam warned. 'It'll be deep in the middle. Stay out on the edges where the ice will be thicker.'

Together they watched him skate gracefully across the ice. He laughed as he wobbled a few times, but her little brother was a natural at skating.

'He is good at it,' Mam said proudly. 'I've never seen him skate before.'

The thought made Beth sad. She wished her mam had done more things with them when they were younger, but that wasn't her way. 'We are all good at skating.'

'Are you? I expect you were as you went often enough in winter ever since you were little.'

'It was always us four kids that went skating, sometimes dragging Jane along with us. She is terrible at it.'

'Dear Jane.' Mam shook her head with the slightest of smiles.

'Well, I'll get off to her.' On impulse, Beth kissed her mam's cold cheek. 'See you in a few days.'

'Aye, lass. Go steady going across the fields.'

Beth waved to Ronnie and walked away from the quarry. She crunched across the snow-covered ploughed fields to take a shortcut to Alverthorpe Road. Being on top of the hill gave her an unobstructed view of the landscape, cloaked in white. Gentle slopes flowed on all sides, farming fields, ditches and drains, lanes and roads all waited for the spring thaw when they'd be revealed once more.

A rabbit scampered out from where it hid in a rut, making her jump. It weaved and dived along the track until suddenly scooting between clumps of snow-topped ploughed earth in the field on her right.

A scream rent the air.

Beth stopped, wondering if she heard correctly. Two pheasants cried and flew up from the field. Was it a scream or a bird?

Then it came again from behind her and then another. She heard her name being shrieked.

'Mam?' Heart in her throat, Beth ran back the way she'd come. Her boots slipping and sliding on the snow-covered ground made her lose her balance and land on her knees. She scrambled up and kept running. Mud coated her boots like a second skin, making them heavy to run in.

In the quarry she paused, not seeing her mam.

'Mam!' she called between cupped gloved hands.

Movement. A black shape on the ice. Mam was on her knees in the middle of the frozen lake.

'Mam!' Beth ran towards her, skidding on the edge of the frozen water. She had no traction on the ice and her feet went out from under her and she fell hard on her bottom. 'I'm coming!'

Mam glanced back over her shoulder, her face chalk white. 'Stay back, Beth! Go for help.'

'What's happened?' She couldn't see passed her mam. Had Ronnie slipped and broken his leg?

'Hurry! Ronnie's fallen in and I can't get him out! He's too heavy.'

Like the ice beneath her, Beth's blood froze. She felt it drain from her face. 'I'll come and help you.'

'No! The ice is cracking!'

'I'll go for help,' Beth cried, turning to flee, but the sudden snap of ice breaking stopped her. She looked back over her shoulder and in horror watched as the ice splintered and shattered beneath her mam.

With a scream, Mam plunged into the water, disappearing under the surface with a splash.

Beth cried out and raced towards the widening hole. The black water crept closer to her as the ice broke and slipped under the surface like an evil menace. Cracks spread out like veins on an old man's hands, dangerously patterning the ice.

Beth skidded to a halt as a large piece of ice snapped in front of her and bobbed under the black water.

'Mam!' Beth yelled, not able to take another step. She looked around wildly, as the ice fragmented by her feet. She was going to fall in!

Panting with fright, Beth turned slowly and gently laid down on the ice, knowing she had to spread her body weight. Inch by agonising inch, she pulled herself back towards the edge of the frozen water, wondering if at any moment the ice would collapse under her and she'd fall into the freezing black depths below. Every crack of the ice sounded like a gunshot. Beth held her breath until she reached the edge.

Shaking, she gained solid ground and stood up. Spinning around, she scanned the water for signs of her mam and Ronnie.

Nothing.

The dark water rippled slightly and shattered ice gave the only hint of them being there.

'Mam!' Her knees buckled. She wanted to stay, to run back across the ice to the hole they'd fallen into, but she needed ropes. She had to get help. She knew Ronnie could swim, for they had all learnt to swim in the beck when they were little, but could Mam? And the coldness? How long could they stay in the water? And why weren't their heads poking above the ice? Where were they?

Choking back her rising panic, Beth lifted her skirts and ran back down the lane to Warren House that they'd passed on the way.

'Help!' Beth called out before she reached the front door. She banged on it with both fists. 'Help. Is anyone home? Please help!'

She peeked into the windows on either side of the door. No movement. She banged again on the front door before running around to the yard behind the house and banged on the back door. She rattled the door handle, but it wouldn't budge. She nearly cried in frustration.

Dashing back to the front of the house, she saw two young girls coming up the lane throwing a stick for a big black dog. Beth raced down to them.

'Help me, please. Where's your home? Do you have ropes? Are your dads about?'

'Aye, we lived back there.' The oldest girl pointed to the terraces at the end of the lane.

'Come with me. I need help.' Beth raced away and the young girls and the dog ran with her.

'Me dad's home.' The older girl flung open the door to the end terrace. 'Dad! Dad! A lady needs your help.'

Beth followed her into a small narrow hallway.

'What's all this nonsense and shouting?' A large older woman came out of the kitchen and up the hallway, wiping her hands on her white apron. 'Janice?'

'Mam, this lady needs our help.'

Beth twisted her hands, hardly able to get her words out. 'My brother and Mam have fallen into the quarry. They've gone under the ice. Please help me. I beg you.'

'Oh, my God.' The woman's eyes widened in horror. 'Harold!' She yelled up the stairs. 'Harold!'

A man came lumbering down the staircase, rubbing sleep from his eyes. 'Can a man not get a decent kip in this house?' he complained, tucking his shirt into his trousers. 'You know I've been on nights.' He stopped halfway down the stairs and stared at Beth and then his wife. 'Hey up, what's going on?'

'Harold, help this lass. Her mam and brother have fallen into the quarry.'

'I need rope, please,' Beth begged, wishing they'd hurry.

'Right, aye, right.' Harold dithered for a moment, then rushed down the remaining stairs and grabbed his coat from behind the door. 'Janice go next door and get young Frank and any of the other lads around. Quickly now.' He marched up the hallway and

Beth and his wife followed him. 'Edith, get some tea on, and warm some blankets.'

'Aye, yes.'

Beth was right behind him, willing him to go faster as he went outside and to his shed, which had several pigeons cooing on its roof.

Once Harold had gathered as much as he and Beth could carry, they ran back up the lane to the quarry.

Beth prayed that her mam and Ronnie would be sitting on the bank wet and cold but safe and well. Mam would be chastising Ronnie, and he'd be hanging his head saying sorry. The image was so real in her mind that when they reached the broken ice and saw nothing, she jerked to a stop in shock.

'Mam!' Maybe they had started walking home? She glanced wildly around for any sign of them. 'Mam!'

Harold had walked around the water's edge to the other side where a young tree grew out of the bushes. He tied one end of the rope around it and the other end around his waist, as a group of youths came running into the quarry and over to Harold.

'One of you go and get the constable quickly now,' Harold instructed, making his way across the ice to the water in the middle.

Like a bystander who didn't belong, Beth watched in dawning dread as Harold slipped across the ice until he fell into the lake and began swimming, cursing at the cold. The lads called out in encouragement as they tied ropes around their waists and followed him.

Puffing, Edith came to stand beside Beth, carrying several blankets and a flask of tea. 'He'll find them, pet.'

Beth stood shaking, never taking her eyes off the middle of the small lake which, really, was not much bigger than a large pond. How could Ronnie have possibly gone under? It couldn't be that deep, surely? And why hadn't Mam dragged him out?

Strange thoughts whirled around in her head as Harold dived under the water.

'Dear God, be careful...' Edith murmured, worry for her husband's safety in her voice.

Beth couldn't speak. She couldn't trust her mind to be coherent. How was this even happening?

Harold surfaced, gasping, yelling at the lads to come and help him.

One by one, they ventured over to him and a couple went under the water.

Shivering, Beth stared, scared that none of them would come back up.

Then, as if everything around her slowed down and became blurry, she watched the sturdy lads heave up a wet floppy shape. Struggling in the water and across the remaining ice, they carried their burden until they reached solid ground.

Beth ran towards them. She fell to her knees beside her mam and a pain so cutting sliced through her as she stared at her mam's beautiful white face. Her wet hair hung untidily around her shoulders. Beth knew she'd hate that.

'Lass.' Edith was beside her and covered Mam's body with a blanket.

Behind her, the sound of water made Beth turn.

They were going back in to find Ronnie...

CHAPTER 6

*B*eth couldn't get warm. She sat as close to the kitchen fire as she dared, but still the heat couldn't penetrate her bones. The ticking clock on the mantlepiece irritated her as did the low hum of voices filling the kitchen as people paid their respects after the double funeral of Mary and Ronnie Beaumont.

The cup of tea in her hands had gone cold and Beth placed it on the table. Opposite her, Peggy stood by the range making more pots of tea for everyone, while Jane cut slices of fruit cake to hand around with Leah helping her.

Beth should be mingling with their guests, but she didn't have it in her to make idle chatter. She glanced at her dad, who sat in a chair at the other end of the table. His grey skin and hollowed eyes told the same story of her own pain. Joanna stood next to Aunty Hilda's chair as they spoke in low tones to family friends.

Unable to sit any longer, Beth wandered out through the scullery to the back door. She shied away from looking at Ronnie's farm coat hanging on the hook, or his work boots…

She stared out over the yard. The sunshine, although not warm, was enough to start the thaw. Trees dripped as the ice and snow melted from the branches in the orchard. The barn, sheds and the greenhouse eves also dripped water in a rhythmic flow. In many parts of the yard, the snow had melted completely. A week of sun and higher temperatures gave the false hope of spring, but it was still a few weeks away yet.

Hugging herself, Beth leaned against the door jamb, mildly amazed that she had lasted a week since that awful day and not gone mad with grief. Not that she could cry, she couldn't. Not a tear had she shed. Even seeing her dad sob, Aunty Hilda and Joanna's tears, she still couldn't cry. The thought frightened her. She felt very alone. Unable to share in her family's grief. The funeral had been well attended and she was glad to see how many people had respected her mam. Witnessing Ronnie's friends being so sombre made the hair on the back of her neck rise. It wasn't natural to see numerous young lads quiet with sadness.

The police investigators had called at the house yesterday, declaring the deaths as accidents. A formal report would be presented, of course, but they were the findings after they'd spoken to Harold, Edith, the helpful lads and the girls Beth had first begged aid from. Talking to the quarry owners and examining old maps, the police believed an old mine shaft had broken through under the water in the quarry, and so instead of there being a shallow lake, it was, in fact, much deeper due to the shaft. The weight of mam's dress, boots and coat would have hindered her in the rescue of Ronnie, who the doctors believed had hit his head on something as bruising had darkened his forehead when they examined him.

No matter what the cause was, two people she loved were now dead and she wasn't sure how to cope with the loss.

Two men walked around the side of the house. Beth tensed, not wanting to talk to anyone. She was about to turn to go inside when her name was called.

She stilled. Not daring to hope.

'Beth, sweetheart!' Noah ran to her and gathered her into his arms in a hold so tight she couldn't breathe and nor did she care. Noah was here with her and that was all that mattered.

She looked up to see a shattered Will and she quickly held him before giving him a small smile and sending him inside to their dad, whose cry at the sight of his son rang out over the farm.

Noah cupped her face in his hands and kissed her gently. 'How are you? No, that is a stupid question.'

'How is it they have allowed you to come?' she asked, not wanting to let him go.

'Compassionate leave, sort of.' Noah shrugged. 'It helps that I get along with many of the officers. When Will and I requested leave and told them of our circumstances, they gave us a twenty-four pass. We left Tring at five o'clock this morning.'

'Only twenty-four hours?' She was dismayed, but then quickly swallowed back the disappointment. 'Forgive me. That is selfish of me. *One* hour is heaven sent. I'm grateful for every minute we have together.'

'Will and I have to be on the six o'clock train. We dare not miss it. It takes hours to get anywhere at the moment. The trains are full of enlistments.'

'Come inside. You must be ready for a cup of tea and something to eat?'

'That would be perfect. Then I'll go up and see Mam.'

'No, she's here. She came to the funeral.'

His shoulders relaxed and he smiled. 'That's saved me time going to see her then. I didn't realise she'd be here, too.'

'She came to give me support and to help with the refreshments. Aunty Hilda and Dad have taken it badly.'

'Darling.' He held her back a moment. 'You're nothing but skin and bone. How you must be suffering and I'm not here to—'

'Shh...' She placed her finger to his lips. 'It's not your fault you aren't here. I'll manage.'

Inside the kitchen, Noah was greeted warmly. Peggy hugged

her eldest son as though she'd never let him go, and Dad shook his hand, wiping away his ever-present tears.

'How is my Jimmy?' Joanna asked him and Will.

'And do you see my Alfie at all?' Jane wanted to know. 'He writes and says you've all been billeted in separate places for the winter. He's with only a couple of men from this area.'

Noah answered the questions as best he could, never letting go of Beth's hand.

As the afternoon wore on, talk grew more spirited as people asked Will and Noah questions about training and life in the army.

'Once we have our uniforms, I think it'll feel a whole lot more real,' Will said. He'd grown an inch and filled out even more in the shoulders.

'Army training suits you,' Joanna said to Will, passing Ivy to him to hold.

'Aye, it's not so bad, is it Noah?' Will looked at Noah.

'We have no choice, so we grin and bear it,' Noah answered. He sat between Beth and his mam. Beth couldn't stop staring at him. Like Will, the training camp had put more muscle on him. He'd always been lean, but strong after working down the pit, however eight months at teacher's college had softened the edge to him. Now, he appeared taller, wider in the shoulders and physically fit. He had become more handsome, and Beth hadn't thought that to be possible.

Before long, the little carriage clock on the mantle chimed five times.

Noah and Will rose as one, and Beth's heart sank.

'Can't you stay a bit longer?' Dad asked, tears welling once more.

Their guests had gone, leaving the family to spend time together, but Beth felt robbed. She needed Noah with her, not at some training camp down south.

'We should get leave before they ship us out.' Will drew on his coat.

'When will that be?' Aunty Hilda asked, packing up the sandwiches she'd made for them to take on the train.

Noah also grabbed his coat. 'None of us know. Months yet I should think. Word is they'll have us training all summer.'

With embraces and promises to write, Will and Noah left the house. Beth walked with them to the gate.

'Why can't I come to the station with you?' Beth asked as Will walked on a little way to give them privacy.

Noah pulled her against him. 'No. Not another station goodbye, Beth. It fair kills me leaving you. Besides, you need to be with your family. Your dad looks suddenly like an old man.'

She nodded. It was true. Losing his wife and son had dealt her dad a cruel blow, and she didn't know how he'd get over it.

'Go inside, my love. It's too cold standing out here.'

They kissed deeply, holding each other tightly, prolonging the moment until they'd have to let go.

Finally, after another long kiss, Noah stepped back and gave her a bright smile. 'Until next time, sweetheart.'

Her throat full, she nodded and blew him a kiss.

Alone she watched him run to catch up to Will and together the two of them walked up the lane towards the village.

* * *

BETH SERVED another customer on the stall and gazed out over the market. She and Leah had a busy morning as the brightness of the sunny day brought people out of their houses to go shopping. The talk of the town was the zeppelin raids over Great Yarmouth and King's Lynn. The newspapers were full of it, that and the rising prices of food and the demand for wages to increase.

As always, winter was a challenging time on the stall with the produce not as varied as in the summer. Brussel sprouts, cauli-flowers, stored potatoes and onions were fast being depleted. They were getting low on stock and she'd have to go to the farm this afternoon and let her dad know they needed more of every-thing. Thankfully, the greenhouse still provided some vegetables.

She'd also sold out of the jars of assorted jams her mam had made in the summer. Briefly, her heart constricted at the thought of her mam standing over a hot stove making jam. She wouldn't be doing it this summer or any summer after that.

'You can get off if you want, Beth. I can manage now the rush is over,' Leah said, placing some money into the tin.

'Are you sure?'

'Of course.'

'Well, I might then. I need to go to the farm.'

'Aye, we're getting short now.' Leah glanced over the large stall, which had several gaps in the displays.

'I'll have Reggie load the cart with whatever we have left stored in the sheds.' Beth took off her apron and dirty packing gloves and replaced them with her soft kid leather gloves. She sorted out the money tin, leaving Leah enough cash for change and the rest she took with her to hand over to her dad.

Waving goodbye to Leah, Fred and the other stall holders, Beth walked through the thinning crowds towards the tram stop. She stopped to buy a copy of the *Daily Mail* and the *Wakefield Express* for her dad from the paperboy on the corner of North-gate. Usually, Dad enjoyed reading newspapers, but he'd lost all interest in life since Mam and Ronnie's death. Beth hoped he might enjoy reading the newspapers this evening.

On the tram, Beth watched the streets and people go by without really seeing them. In the three weeks since the accident, Beth had seen her dad decline mentally and physically. He rarely ate more than enough for a bird to survive on, and the farm no longer interested him. When questioned, he took himself off to his bedroom and refused to come out.

Aunty Hilda was beside herself with worry, as she also grieved. Beth and Joanna had tried everything to get their dad on the road to normality, but he refused their support. She didn't know what to do for him.

Her heart ached whenever she thought of that horrid day. Dreams of water closing in over her head, of being trapped under ice, had become something of a frequent nightmare for her now. Her nights of broken sleep, of lying in bed missing Noah and thinking of how she might have prevented Mam and Ronnie's death gave her dark shadows beneath her eyes, and with not much appetite she was looking haggard and older than her years.

At Newton she alighted from the tram and was surprised to see Reggie driving the farm cart. 'Reggie!'

Her dad's right-hand man waved and slowed Snowy down.

She climbed into the cart. 'That's a stroke of luck seeing you here.'

'Aye. I needed to run some errands for your father.' Reggie set Snowy in motion, but the tone of his voice made Beth sit up and take notice.

'What's happened, Reggie?'

'Nowt, lass.'

'I can tell something has.' She knew this man almost as well as her own father. Reggie had been working at the farm since before she was born.

'Am I dropping you off at the Jackson house?' he asked.

'No, the farm, please, and before we get there, you're going to tell me what is wrong.'

'It's nowt to worry you with.'

She gave him a superior look. 'Let me be the judge of that.'

'You look like your mam when you're being stern.'

'Good, now tell me as you would have told her.'

He steered Snowy under the railway bridge and along the road towards Wrenthorpe. 'It's just that your dad, he's not himself.'

'I know. I wish I could find a way to help him. He's taken the loss so deeply.'

'He wanders around the farm, not saying much, not doing much, and that's fine as I can do everything. We've got some young lads who've left school and are happy to work on the farm for a few shillings.'

'I understand you must be worried about Dad, but he's lost without Mam. It'll take time. It's only been a month.'

'I can't help worrying, but not just about him, it's your aunt, too. She's an old woman and yet she's got to cope with everything now. I went into the kitchen this morning and saw she was unsteady on her feet.'

Beth stared at him in shock. 'Unsteady?'

'Aye, lass. She's taking too much on. I do what I can when I'm there and I make sure the lads do all her fetching and carrying but...'

'Don't worry any more. I'll work something out.' For the rest of the trip, Beth tried to think of ways to help at the farm. When Reggie pulled Snowy to a stop, Beth quickly entered the house, almost frightened by what she might find.

Aunty Hilda sat in a chair by the kitchen range, fast asleep. She watched her chest rise and fall just to make sure she was asleep. Beth's heart twisted at the sight of the old woman. She couldn't lose her, too.

Venturing outside, she went in search of her dad amongst the barn and sheds.

'He's not about, lass,' Reggie told her, unharnessing Snowy. 'Likely he's in his bedroom.'

'Bedroom? Why? Is he ill?'

'He stays in there a lot or so your aunt tells me.'

Re-entering the house, Beth paused by the door leading into the hallway. She didn't want to disturb her dad if he was sleeping.

Aunty Hilda stirred and blinked in surprise at seeing Beth. 'Now there's a sight for sore eyes.'

Beth gave her a kiss. 'Cup of tea?'

'Wonderful.' As she went to rise, Beth pushed her gently back.

'Stay where you are.'

'I've a meal to put on, not that your dad eats it…'

'Is he upstairs?'

'Probably. He went up a couple of hours ago. He rarely comes out of his bedroom.'

'What is he doing up there?'

'Sitting on the bed, staring at your mam's portrait. You know the little one that he got done years ago in London?'

Beth nodded and added water to the kettle. As she moved about the large room, she noticed a slight neglect of the usually polished and shining kitchen. Her mam had been a stickler for cleanliness and order. No one dare venture into the kitchen when she'd washed the stone-flagged floor, or they'd be in for it. The windows needed cleaning and Beth wondered when was the last time someone had banged the rugs outside or the curtains dusted down with a damp cloth.

In the scullery, washing mounted up, as did the ironing. In the stone sink, a large pot was soaking that needed scrubbing. Reggie was right, it was all too much for Aunty Hilda.

Setting out three cups, Beth then added tea leaves into the teapot as Reggie came in carrying a crate of supplies. 'Do you want a cup of tea, Reggie?'

'No, thank you, lass. I've got to get on.' He placed the crate onto the table. 'Now then, Hilda, I couldn't get any currants for you, nor was their much bread, but I managed to get a small loaf. I'll try again tomorrow. I got everything else on the list.'

'Bread?' Beth glanced at her aunt, who had always made the bread in this house.

'Aye, love. I can't do the kneading any more it hurts my wrists and hands now.' Aunty Hilda shook her head sadly. 'My arthritis is worse.'

'Then I'll do it. I might not be as good as you, but I'll try my best.'

'Nay, lass, you're not here enough to be concerning yourself with making bread.'

'I will be. From now on,' Beth said determinedly.

'What do you mean?'

'I'm moving back home until the war is finished. You and Dad need me to help you both.'

Relief washed over the older woman's face. 'Are you sure? What about the stall and Peggy?'

'Leah can manage.' Decision made; Beth felt calmer, focused. 'I'll go and tell Peggy. I can still call on her every day.'

At the door, she turned back. 'Me being home might help perk Dad up a bit, too.'

Walking up the lane, she was a little anxious about telling Peggy, but she knew her mother-in-law would understand. Until the war was over, and Will had returned, she'd have to help at the farm. There was no other solution. She'd make time to visit Peggy each day and Leah would manage at the stall, she was sure of it.

Beth found Peggy in bed, which at first alarmed her. 'What's happened? Your chest?'

'I'm all right, love. I just had a bit of an episode. I couldn't catch my breath, you know how it is.'

'Where are the fellows?'

'Working, I think. I'm not really sure,' Peggy sounded confused.

Beth sighed and sat on the edge of the bed. 'I can't leave you like this.'

'Why, where are you going?'

'I'm needed at the farm. Dad's not himself, and Aunty Hilda is struggling. I was going to stay there.'

'Then do that.' Peggy started coughing and it took several moments for her to stop. 'I'm fine. Go.'

Standing, Beth reached for Peggy's thick woollen shawl. 'You're coming too.'

'What? No!'

'I'm not leaving you here alone. I'll be worried sick and if I stay here, I'll worry about them lot on the farm. So, you're coming with me.'

'I'll not sleep the night at the farm.' Peggy was adamant.

'I'm not talking about just tonight, but moving there permanently.'

'Nay! Are you mad?' Peggy's shocked voice rang around the cold room. 'Not permanently. It's not my home.'

'It will be from now on.'

'Beth, no…'

'Yes. All under one roof so I can stop worrying about you and them.'

'What will your dad think?'

'My dad isn't up to thinking straight at all right now. He'll hardly notice.'

'And Hilda? She won't want me there.'

'I think Aunty Hilda will be glad of the company. Dad's a constant worry to her. She's not coping.' Beth rubbed a hand over her face, suddenly tired of the stress. 'I can't divide myself into two and be here and at the farm.'

'Lass…' Peggy tried to speak, but her coughing got the better of her.

After a sip of water and a few minutes to rest, Peggy wrapped her shawl over her nightdress. 'You mustn't worry about me. I'll come good in the summer; you know I do. Once it's warm and dry, I'll be fine.'

'Of course, I worry about you. You're like another mam to me.'

'And you're like the daughter I never had.' Love softened Peggy's face.

'That's why I want to take care of you. You're coming to the farm, at least until the war is over.'

'If I go with you, what will happen to this place?'

'Does it matter? Let the lodgers have it.' Beth glanced around the damp walls, which no amount of heat would dry out. 'I think you'll feel a whole lot better at the farm compared to this place. What's keeping you here?'

'It's the boys' home.'

'Is it? The army is the boys' home right now and will be for some time. When the war is over and they come home, they can apply for another pit house, a better one than this. Until then, let the lodgers have it. Sign the rent book over to them and we'll pack up your things and take them down to the farm. We can store them in the attic for now.'

Silence stretched between them.

'I can't do this on my own, Peggy,' Beth admitted.

Peggy gave a big sigh. 'Help me up, love. I'll come with you. I can't stand to see you so upset. Happen a change of scenery will work for me too. There's nothing left for me in this house without my lads.'

'Thank you.'

Ten minutes later, with Patch on Peggy's lap, they sat up in the butcher's cart, who Beth had run to ask if he could take them down the lane, for Peggy wouldn't be able to walk it and Beth couldn't carry the luggage and help Peggy.

Aunty Hilda's eyes widened in shock as Beth brought Peggy into the house. 'Are you all right, Mrs Jackson?'

'I've been better, thank you, Mrs—' Coughing again, Peggy let Aunty Hilda guide her to a chair by the fire while Beth brought in their bags.

'You must call me, Hilda.'

Peggy nodded. 'And I'm Peggy.'

Beth dumped the bags by the hallway door. 'Peggy is going to live with us, Aunty Hilda. I can't divide my time between two houses. She can sleep in Joanna's bed. We can store the Jacksons' bit and bobs up in the attic.'

'Aye, lass. It's probably for the best. I need you here.' Aunty Hilda smiled at Peggy. 'Welcome to Beaumont Farm, Peggy.'

'Thank you, Hilda. I'll pull my weight around the house, don't you worry about that.'

'I wasn't, but let's get you a cup of tea first, shall we?'

Beth busied herself getting a meal prepared while Aunty Hilda set the table and Peggy sat by the fire with Patch on her lap.

'Where's Dad?' Beth asked.

'Out in the sheds. He came downstairs just before you arrived.'

'Did he seem better?'

Aunty Hilda paused in laying out the knives and forks. 'I don't think anything will ever make him better again, pet.'

The following morning, Beth left Peggy and Aunty Hilda together in the kitchen while she got a lift with Reggie into town to the market. Peggy had slept in Beth's bedroom in Joanna's old bed, and with a warm fire heating the room, she'd slept better than she had in many months.

'It's good to have you home, Beth,' Reggie said as they drove along.

'It's the right thing to do. I can keep an eye on everyone now without having to go between two houses all the time.'

At the market, Reggie helped Beth to take the crates of produce down the rows to the stall. Beth found Leah serving two regular customers and Beth chatted to them for a moment as they asked after the family and gave their condolences about Mam and Ronnie.

After Reggie left to go to the wheelwright, Beth spoke to Fred for a few moments and then finally gave her attention to Leah, who seemed a little subdued this morning.

'Everything all right?' Beth asked.

'Aye. Steady trade for the first hour.'

'You look peaky.' Beth studied her friend's face.

'I didn't get much sleep. I've new lodgings and they are over a pub, so it'll take a bit for me to get used to.'

'New lodgings? Why?'

'I got a room. It's all I need now the girls are gone to live with me aunt.'

'When did that happen? Why didn't you tell me?'

'They went the day of your mam and brother's funeral. I didn't mention it as I didn't want to bother you with my problems.' Leah tucked a strand of dark hair under her hat.

'Oh, I am sorry, Leah.'

'It's fine, truly. The girls will have a better life with our aunt. She'll spoil them rotten. She bought two new dresses for them to wear as they left. I suppose it wouldn't do for her to bring home two little girls dressed in rags, her neighbours might comment.' A slight bitterness tinged Leah's tone.

'Can you visit them?'

'Oh aye. Whenever I want. And I will. I won't let me sisters forget me.'

'As if they would.' Beth tried to brighten the mood.

'I think my aunt would rather they did.' Leah shrugged.

'Well, I've come with some news.' Beth broke it gently.

Leah's face fell. 'You're not letting me go, are you?'

'Oh, no!' Beth put a hand out to reassure her. 'No, not at all. In fact, it's the opposite. How would you like to work all the days on the stall? I am needed at home. So, I won't be able to help. Do you think you can manage it?'

'Course, I can.' Leah grinned. 'I'm so thankful, Beth, really I am.'

'Good. I'll try and come once a week to see how you're going and to get the takings for depositing at the bank, but if I can't get here, you can either bring them to me at the farm or deposit them into our account yourself.'

'You trust me to do that?' Leah pushed back her blue head-scarf that held back her black hair.

Beth frowned. 'Why wouldn't I?'

'Because it's your money.'

'Actually, it's my dad's money and he and I know how much we generally make each week, so you'll not be able to hide it from us. Besides, this is your job now. You can rob us blind if you want, but if you do, my dad knows many people in Wakefield, and you'd struggle to get another job here.'

'Don't worry. I'm no thief. I'm grateful for everything you've done for me. I'd never rob a *friend*.' Leah winked, back to her old cheeky self.

Relaxing, Beth smiled. 'I never doubted you would.'

'Thank you, Beth. It means a lot to me.'

'I'll get off and do some shopping.' Beth glanced over the stall, immediately seeing what was needed. They'd brought enough to keep Leah going for a few days. 'I'll send Reggie up each day to see what you need and to restock you.'

'Right you are. And if anything ever happens where I need to speak to you, I'll catch the tram to Newton and walked down to Wrenthorpe. I'm sure I'll be able to get directions to your farm from there.'

'Yes, we are easy to find. Everyone knows Beaumont Farm.' Beth waved goodbye to her and stopped and chatted a few minutes with Fred, who said he'd keep an eye on Leah, which made Beth laugh for if Leah found out she'd be livid.

Leaving Brook Street, she noticed a group of mourners standing outside the cathedral. Pallbearers were carrying a coffin inside. Reminded of her mam and Ronnie's funeral, she turned away and hurried along Westgate to the post office to post letters to all the Jackson brothers for Peggy, plus her own letters to Noah and Will, telling them she and Peggy were staying at the farm.

Leaving the post office, Beth felt the first few drops of rain and quickly headed for the cattle market area where Reggie had taken the cart. Church bells pealed the hour of ten o'clock.

'Beth? Beth Beaumont?'

She turned on hearing her name called, ready to smile at someone she knew. However, her smile died as she stared at the officer in a khaki uniform standing before her.

Louis Melville had returned home.

Beth stared at the tall, thin man who had tormented her last year and who had cut off all her hair and locked her away for a night, threatening to come back and have some fun with her. He hadn't, thankfully, but the dread of that night had taken many months to overcome and she'd only done it with the love of her family and Noah.

'It is a surprise, a pleasant surprise, to see you.' Louis Melville took a step towards her as pedestrians walked around them. 'I couldn't believe it was you at first. You grow more beautiful every time I see you.'

'Well, my hair has grown back,' she said sarcastically. Being in the middle of town gave her courage to speak to him. They were surrounded by people walking by. Melville couldn't harm her here.

The expression on his narrow face fell, a face which seemed much older than it did last year. 'Yes... I am most sorry. Forgive me, I beg you.'

'Is my forgiveness going to change anything?' She didn't hide the doubt from her voice.

'I have already changed, I promise. My father insisted I become a better man. He has managed to do it since moving away from England, and I hope to follow his lead. Unfortunately, it is not something that can happen overnight, you understand.'

'No, I don't understand. Being decent and polite and nice isn't something most people have to work at. It seems it's a Melville trait though.'

'All I can do is apologise for my past behaviour. You do something to me… I can't explain it. I lose all reason when I am near you.'

'Do you think that saying sorry is enough?' She wanted to hit him. 'Sorry doesn't take away the memory of that night. Sorry doesn't erase the weeks of being scared and jumping at every shadow in case it was you. Sorry is just a word, Mr Melville, and it means nothing to me.'

'Nevertheless, I mean it. My actions that day were deplorable. I have no answers as to why I behaved as I did back then. But I have changed. I'm not that man, not any more. Every day I strive to control my temper, to be worthy of my family.'

'I care not, sir. I must go.' She darted away, but he was soon striding alongside of her.

'Miss Beaumont, please. I would never hurt you again.'

She spun to face him, taking him by surprise. 'I am *Mrs Jackson*!' She snapped, anger flaring.

'Yes, I'm sorry. I forgot momentarily, though I don't know how I did when your husband reminds me as often as possible.'

Beth stared at him. 'Noah? You've seen Noah?'

'I'm one of his commanding officers. Didn't he tell you?'

'No.' She pulled her red scarf up around her chin and the collar of her black coat, avoiding making eye contact with him as she walked. Why hadn't Noah told her?

He kept in step with her, his black eyes watching her. 'He's a lucky man.'

'I am the lucky one.' She hurried down Southgate, eager to reach Reggie.

'He will make a fine soldier. He has brains and is quick to pick up things.'

She couldn't talk of Noah with Melville. She was hurt Noah had kept the news from her that Melville was one of his officers.

The smell of the cattle market reached her before she could see it, and she quickened her steps. 'Good day, Mr Melville.'

He grabbed her arm and pulled her to a stop. 'Miss Beau—Mrs Jackson, please stop and listen to me.'

She glared at him. 'You haven't earned the right for me to listen to you. Leave me alone.'

'I heard about your mother and brother. I am sorry.'

She inclined her head stiffly.

'I am away to France soon. I've only come home to sort out my affairs. Melville Manor is closed up.'

'I know. Mr Staines told me.'

'Ah, Staines is also in the training camp down south. Anyway, I just wanted to say, now that I have the chance to do so, and believe me, I was going to write to you. I've tried to so many times before, but I never sent the letters.' He shook his head as though to clear his thoughts. 'I simply want you to know that I am utterly sorry for my previous actions, all of them. I behaved like a cad, a jealous, spiteful fool. I'm not proud of myself.'

She watched the emotions flitter across his face. He sounded sincere, but could he ever be trusted?

'As I said, I'm sorry and well… I don't know if I'll ever see you again. However, I am immensely grateful to have had the chance to see you in person and to apologise to you. Take from it what you will.' He shrugged. 'I'm certain in the past you have wished me dead and perhaps you may get your wish thanks to the Germans.' He smiled wistfully. 'May you have every happiness.' He turned on his heel and strode away.

Beth watched him go, unable to move. Why was it that Louis Melville always managed to get the last word? She was torn between anger and pity. Yes, she wanted to give him a piece of her mind, but soon enough he'd be facing the onslaught of bullets and bombs and nothing she said would harm him worse than that.

CHAPTER 7

*A*s the spring gave way to summer, news from the front lines in France wavered between good and bad. Zeppelin air raids created night-time light restrictions in Wakefield, and everyone was urged to reduce lighting when necessary and not to gather in large groups.

Joanna came over as much as she could to help in the house and they celebrated baby Ivy's first birthday in March and also Beth's twenty-first in April with small tea parties that were only attended by family and Jane and Leah.

In May the sinking of the passenger ship, *Lusitania*, off the coast of Ireland by a German U-boat sent shock waves across the country. Nearly twelve hundred innocent souls lost. No one could believe such a thing could happen. The rising costs of food prompted Beth to help as many of the elderly in the village as she could. Aunty Hilda and Peggy made tureens of stew to give out to those too old to look after themselves or who had little money to feed themselves.

Beth became more immersed in the running of the farm. She worked long hours in the fields and the barn as the days stayed lighter longer, and at night she wrote long letters to

Noah. The government encouraged women to work in any capacity they could, and Beth took on a few village women to help with the work on the farm. Although they were allowed to keep Snowy, due to his old age, for farm work, other farmers in the area weren't so lucky and with their horses gone to the army, they lent Snowy to neighbours to help with the heavy work.

Beth's concern over her dad's state of mind was never far from her thoughts. Rob Beaumont was a shadow of his former self. Since his wife and son's death, he barely spoke two words. He rose before dawn and worked all day on the farm, coming in at night to hardly touch his meal and then go to bed.

Beth tried everything she could think of to interest him. Aunty Hilda made all his favourite foods, but he became thinner, his hair more grey.

On a bright June day, Beth hung out washing. She'd spent the morning stripping all the beds and washing the sheets in the copper pot in the scullery. A slight warm breeze helped to dry them, and as she picked up the empty basket, she jumped on seeing her dad standing silently behind her.

'You gave me a fright.' She chuckled.

'Sorry, lass,' he said softly.

'Did you want me for something?'

'Aye.' He turned and walked into the house and she followed, intrigued.

Aunty Hilda and Peggy were in the kitchen preparing the midday meal and they looked inquisitively at Beth as she passed, but she shrugged back at them none the wiser.

In a corner of the front room, a rolled top desk and tall bookshelf was used as her father's study, after the original study had been made into a bedroom for Aunty Hilda. Numerous papers and ledgers filled the desk, and no one was ever allowed to touch it, for Rob knew where everything was and hated the women of the house touching his papers.

He sat down at the desk and picked up a piece of paper and handed it to Beth.

She read it and frowned. 'What does this mean?'

'It's a letter of authority,' Dad replied.

'For what?'

'For you to have access to my bank accounts and all legal entitlements.'

'Why?'

'In case anything should happen to me. The solicitors drew it up last week. The bank has a copy as well. It's all in my will, too.'

A shiver of fear ran down her spine. 'Nothing is going to happen to you.'

'You have full control over the farm until Will returns, then it belongs to him, as you have Noah to provide for you. If Will… if… if Will doesn't come back,' he swallowed heavily, 'then the farm is yours with a provision for Joanna. I know you'd do right by her.'

'But, Dad.'

'Listen to me!' He sounded impatient, then took a deep breath as though that spark of emotion was too much for him to bear after months of dull acceptance and grief.

Beth's legs shook and she sat down on the sofa. 'Go on.'

Dad turned to the ledgers. 'Everything you need to know about London market prices for the rhubarb, suppliers, distributors and all what goes on to run this farm are in these red ledgers. Accounts are in the green ledgers. I list crop rotation management in this brown ledger. You need to become familiar with it all. You must study it.'

She nodded, unable to take it in. 'You can teach me though.'

'Aye. We'll go through it each night for an hour.' He looked exhausted as he stood. 'I want you know it all.'

'If that's what you want, Dad.'

'It is.' He walked out of the room, head down, shoulders bowed.

Beth stood and stepped over to the desk and lightly touched the ledgers, books she'd only ever touched before to move them when dusting the room.

'What was that all about?' Aunty Hilda hobbled into the room, her swollen ankles causing her pain.

'He wants me to learn the running of the farm, it seems.'

Aunty Hilda shook her head. 'I worry about him.'

'I don't know how to make him better. Without Mam, he's lost.'

'Something will bring him back to life. The end of the war might do it and having Will home again.'

Beth walked back into the kitchen with her. 'I hope it happens quickly.'

'A note was just delivered by a young lad,' Peggy said, handing it to Beth.

Reading the note Beth smiled.

'What is it?' Peggy asked.

'Jane's had a baby boy. Born yesterday evening. Freddie, she's called him. They're both fine. Though Jane writes she's not keen to do it again in a hurry.'

'That's lovely.' Aunty Hilda nodded. 'We all need a bit of nice news.'

NOAH, lying down on the grass, fired the rifle at the target a hundred yards away. Having shot at rabbits and pheasants in the woods around his village, he knew he had a good eye, as did his brothers who were lying beside him shooting. Some poor fellows had it tough and missed the target each time, earning an ear bashing by Sergeant Bourke.

Months of training, of being in a routine that differed only slightly from day to day, was preparing them for army life. Drills seemed to go on forever, keeping kit clean and in order, marches, rifle practise, following orders, eating and sleeping and being surrounded by men all day every day was now a familiar routine. They had no other life.

Ordered to stand, Noah returned to the back of the line to let the next fellow lie down and have his practise shots. After an hour of it, they were dismissed to have their midday meal and half an hour off before more drilling.

Once he'd finished his meal, Noah returned to his tent and began a new letter to Beth.

My darling,

I hope you and Mam are all right and the rest of the family. We are as ever the same. Tonight, we go on a night-time skirmish in full kit with packs. We did the same last week if you remember me telling you in my last letter. That one was a thirteen-mile march. We expect the same tonight. We sleep out in the open and practise night warfare before sleeping under the stars for a few hours and then hike the thirteen miles back again.

This morning we were on the firing range. Apparently, we are to travel elsewhere in two days' time to practise field firing and trenching. Digging trenches is not unlike digging for coal. The body remembers and I'm once more stronger in the arms. James and Alfred have grown wider in the chest if that was possible. They've taken to army life so well. Sid, not so much, and, like me, he misses home, even the nagging Meg and crying baby. Albie is a mixture of both, I feel. Though when I say I miss home, what I mean is I miss you. It is hard for me to not think of you constantly.

Did I tell you we have a full uniform now? We feel the part at last, and it brings home that we have a role to play. My brothers instantly seemed more grown up the minute I saw them in uniform, but they only had to open their mouths for me to remember that they are still fools!

I see many of the lads from Wrenthorpe and Jane's Alfie was serving in the kitchen yesterday. He was like a dog with two tails, hearing he was a father to a boy. Give Jane my good wishes when you see her.

I met up with Will yesterday. He's on another side of the camp to me. He was laughing with his mates, so I believe he is doing fine, do not worry.

We are all tired of the waiting. I'd wish they'd either send us to France or home. This infernal waiting and sleeping in tents wears thin after months.

I hope your dad improves. I can only imagine his grief. I'm sure time will help and the safe return of his eldest son.

I'd best send this now, sweetheart, so you can have it tomorrow to read.

My greatest love as always to you,
Noah
15th June 1915
Halton Park Training Camp
Buckinghamshire

NOAH SEALED the envelope and left the tent to post his letter before his next drill.

Men were coming out of the mess tent. His brothers among them, laughing with Will.

'Hey, Noah!' James shouted.

Noah held up his hand, posted the letter in the camp mailbox and walked over to them. 'What are you lot up to?'

'Young Will here has got himself a girl.' James wiggled his eyebrows suggestively. 'Got himself caught coming back to camp after curfew and all.'

Noah stared at Will. 'Are you on a charge?'

'Nah. The sarge likes me.'

'So does the barmaid!' Alfred roared. 'The tasty piece behind the bar in the village.'

'Who's had more men than hot pies if I'm any judge of character.' Alfred snorted with laughter.

Will blushed. 'I ain't got nothing going on with anyone.'

'Love 'em and leave 'em type of fellow, aren't you, Will?' Sid grinned.

Shaking his head, Will shoulder barged him. 'There's nothing going on, I tell you!'

'Did she teach you a thing or two, Will lad?' Alfred tackled Will to the ground and James joined in.

'Get off me!' Will thumped them, laughing. 'You're only jealous as you've no lady to give you some attention.'

'She ain't no lady, Will lad!' Sid roared.

Noah rolled his eyes at their antics.

'You men there!' A shout from behind had them quickly standing straight at attention.

Melville, his peaked cap pulled low, strode up to them with another officer beside him. 'What is the meaning of this?'

Noah sucked in a breath and gazed straight ahead. 'A bit of fun, sir.'

'A bit of fun? Are we at a fun fair I don't know about?' Melville walked closer, eyeing the line up until he came to Noah and he stopped.

Noah dared to look at the face and wished he hadn't. Louis Melville stood before him with a superior tilt to his chin. Anger rose like a tide inside him. The one man he'd liked to punch into next week always seemed to be around. He treated Noah with disrespect and at every opportunity made his life hell.

'It's always you, isn't it, Jackson?'

'No, sir,' Noah ground out between clenched teeth.

'We were only having a bit of fun, sir,' Will suddenly said.

Melville walked down the line to Will. 'Did I give you permission to speak, Private Beaumont?'

'No, sir,' Will answered.

'Then don't.' Melville took another step back, a dangerous look in his eyes. 'Control your behaviour or next time you all will be on cleaning duty and confined to camp. Dismissed!' Melville strode away.

'That bloody man is always hovering around,' Sid said as they grouped together.

Alfred lit up a cigarette. 'He hates Noah and therefore hates us.'

Noah watched Melville walk towards the mess tent.

'How many times has he had you on a cleaning duty, Noah?' Albie asked.

'No more than ten times I don't think,' Noah joked, trying to lighten the mood.

'Bloody hell,' Will spoke quietly. 'I didn't know it was so many. He's a bastard who needs to be taught a lesson.'

Noah looked at Will, who stood very still, also staring at the mess tent that Melville had disappeared into. 'Don't do anything stupid, Will,' he warned.

Will said nothing and walked away.

'This is all we need.' Sid sighed. 'We can't blame young Will for wanting to thump Melville one. The swine deserves it after the way he treated Beth, but if Will touches him, he'll be in all sorts of trouble.'

'We're going to have to watch Will,' Noah told his brothers. 'He's family now. I can't have him doing something foolish regarding Melville. Beth wouldn't forgive me.'

'Do we need to watch you, too?' Albie asked. 'You've taken everything he's dished out for months. How much longer can you hold out before you punch him one?'

Noah let out a breath. 'Let's just say that if Melville sports a black eye one morning, then I was with you lot the entire night.'

They nodded and subdued went back to their tents as a whistle blew for their next drill.

CHAPTER 8

*S*traightening her back, Beth stretched out the ache from being bent over sorting through the tomatoes they were harvesting from the vegetable bed inside the long glass greenhouse. Delicate vegetables such as tomatoes, cucumbers, peas and beans were grown on trellises along the greenhouse wall and next to them grew the lettuces.

Beyond the orchard, fields grew rows of carrots, radishes, onions, turnips and potatoes. While across the lane in front of the house, acres of rhubarb grew lush green leaves.

The July sun beat down from an azure blue sky, turning the lawn behind the house brown. Fruit hung heavy in the orchard and two lambs were growing fat on the grass beneath. Her idea to purchase two lambs had been met with a frown from Reggie, who declared Beaumont Farm was a crop farm, but Dad hadn't argued and agreed to have an extra source of food would be beneficial. The panic buying of food that happened when war was first declared had slowed a little but Leah came to the farm once or twice a week to ask for more vegetables as she regularly ran low on stock.

To Beth it made sense to grow more vegetables, and the acres her dad had rented to add to their own farm now grew barley and wheat. Four lads who'd left school but weren't old enough to enlist now worked on the farm, planting and sowing. Come August, Beth expected a good harvest.

Voices filtered to her through the glass, but she ignored it. Aunty Hilda and Peggy fed the lads at midday, having set up a table in the garden when the weather was fine.

With the warmer weather and no longer living in a cold damp house, Peggy finally had colour in her cheeks. Although her chest still bothered her if she did too much, she'd put on a little weight with Aunty Hilda constantly pushing her to eat her hearty food.

Beth's stomach grumbled at the thought of food and the lads sitting at the table, no doubt eating eat bowls of delicious stew and suet dumplings.

When hands reached around and grabbed her, she screamed. Twisting, she was ready to lash out when Noah's smiling face stopped her.

He kissed her quickly and laughed. 'Are you surprised?'

'I can't believe it!' She held him tight, then smothered him in kisses. 'You're home!'

'For six long days!' He kissed her again, hungrily, demanding and receiving a passion that matched his.

Eventually they came up for air and Beth smiled lovingly. 'Six days.'

'Can you put up with me for that long?' He grinned.

'Oh, I'll try,' she joked. He looked so handsome in his uniform Beth couldn't keep her hands off him. All she wanted to do was kiss him.

Someone called out as they shared another kiss.

Noah rolled his eyes. 'They're all here. My brothers and Will.'

'Will, too? Dad'll be so pleased!' She grabbed Noah's hand and pulled him out of the greenhouse and down the yard towards the house.

Gathered around the small kitchen herb garden, the Jackson

brothers stood surrounding their mother while Aunty Hilda held Will as though she wasn't ever going to let him go.

'They're here, lass,' Peggy said to Beth, tears filing her eyes. 'What a blessed day.'

Beth hugged Will. He looked tall in his uniform and much older. 'Dad won't believe his eyes.'

'Aunty Hilda says he's in the rented fields.'

'Yes, checking the barley. We've never grown it before, and Dad is meeting a farmer from out Flockton way who has some experience growing it. Dad wants to get the harvest right or it'll be a waste of money and time.'

'Should I go and find him?'

'No,' Aunty Hilda butted in. 'Sit down and have some food. Your dad'll be home shortly.'

Beth turned to Noah. 'Patch is with him. They are constant companions now.'

'I'm pleased for both of them. Though I hope Patch hasn't forgotten me.' Noah chuckled.

They left the four farm lads to sit at the table outside while the family went indoors to sit at the kitchen table. Beth helped Peggy and Aunty Hilda to butter more bread and dish out bowls of stew followed by pudding of jam roly poly and custard. Sid didn't stay, as he had a wife and child to see, but he promised to come and spend some time with Peggy tomorrow and bring the baby.

'Did Joanna's Jimmy get leave too?' Beth asked Noah, handing him his bowl of stew and dumplings.

'Yes, and so did Jane's Alfie.'

Aunty Hilda chuckled. 'Well, we'll not see either our Joanna nor Jane for six days then.'

Beth couldn't stop staring at Noah. He looked older, fitter, and still as handsome as ever, but something else and she couldn't place it.

They'd finished eating and were chatting when Dad walked

through the back door. His stride checked as he saw Will and a smile the family hadn't seen for a long time split his face.

'My boy!' Rob Beaumont burst into tears and embraced his son.

The emotion made the Jackson brothers uncomfortable and they squirmed on their chairs.

'So, you are all staying here while you're on leave I gather?' Beth broke into the silence.

'We wouldn't want to put you out,' Albie said.

Beth smiled. 'Nonsense. We want you to stay here, don't we, Dad?'

Her dad wiped his eyes with a handkerchief. 'I insist.'

'Our old home is ours no longer, anyway.' Peggy shrugged. 'Where else would you go?'

'The pub?' Alfred winked.

'There's a spare bed in my room.' Will sat down and supped his tea.

'I'll sleep anywhere,' James said. 'We've been sleeping rough in tents for months. I'm sure we'll cope on the floor here.'

'I can't sleep in with you, Beth,' Peggy announced, 'Not while Noah's here. You two need your privacy.'

Aunty Hilda rose to her feet. 'How about you lads dismantle Peggy's bed and take it from Beth's room and bring it down to my bedroom? One of you lads can sleep in Ronnie's bed…' she paused as she spoke his name but brightened quickly, 'and one on the sofa in the front room. That leaves just one on the floor. You can take it in turns.'

With the arrangements made, the men set to dismantling Peggy's bed and setting it up in Aunty Hilda's bedroom, which had once been the study years ago until Aunty Hilda's legs couldn't make the stairs any more.

'You don't' mind?' Peggy asked Aunty Hilda.

'Of course not, you daft 'apporth.' Aunty Hilda grinned. 'After all these months living together, you're my friend, aren't you?'

'Aye, and a better friend I couldn't ask for.'

Aunty Hilda picked up an empty bowl. 'Don't be getting all soppy now. We've food to cook for this lot. Beth, take yourself and that handsome husband of yours up to the butchers. We're going to need an order filled.'

Pinning on her hat, Beth smiled at Noah and linking arms, they left the house. They'd not made it further than the gates when Noah pulled her into his arms and kissed her for a long moment.

She cupped his face. 'I can't wait for tonight.'

'Nor me, my love. How early can we leave the others? Straight after dinner?' he joked.

Laughing, she rested her head against his shoulder as he wrapped his arm around her shoulders and they strolled up the lane to the village.

As much as they joked about retiring to bed, it was gone ten o'clock before anyone headed to bed. Noah had no fears of Patch forgetting him as the little dog jumped all over him when he returned home with Dad. However, Beth noticed how during the evening Patch still went and sat on Dad's lap as he did every night now. It was as though the little dog knew Rob needed his comfort.

The Jackson brothers kept everyone entertained with stories of camp and army life. As much as Beth wanted Noah to herself, she encouraged the brothers to keep talking and making them laugh, for her dad seemed close to his old self listening to their tales. Having Will chuckling and joining in brought colour to Dad's cheeks, banishing the dullness of his eyes which had been there since the day of Mam and Ronnie's drowning. For two hours, Beth had her old dad back and she didn't want that to end.

However, eventually everyone said goodnight and Beth and Noah were alone in her bedroom.

Noah glanced at her bed as he undressed. 'It'll be a tight squeeze in that bed.' He grinned.

'It's not made for two, no.' She shrugged, not caring. She stepped closer and kissed him.

Noah groaned softly against her mouth. They finished undressing each other. Khaki uniform mixed with her cotton blue flowered dress, corset and camise fell to the floor.

Naked, kissing and touching, they climbed into the bed, hungry for each other.

'I don't think I can go slowly, my darling,' Noah whispered, nibbling her ear. 'I've been dreaming of this night for months.'

'We can go slow later,' she whispered back, feeling the taut muscles of his back as he laid over her. The hardness of him thrilled her. She opened her legs for him, raising her hips. She needed him to quench the ache inside her.

Noah's rhythm matched hers, but suddenly the iron bed springs creaked.

Noah stopped mid-thrust. 'God, that's loud!'

Giggling and embarrassed the others would hear them from across the landing, she pushed him out of her and together they pulled the mattress and blankets onto the floor.

'Where were we?' Noah laughed softly, gathering her back into his arms.

'Let me show you,' Beth replied, nibbling his bottom lip.

CHAPTER 9

*B*eth wondered if any six days had ever gone as fast as the ones of Noah's leave. For to her it felt like only hours had gone by since he'd arrived. They had packed a lot into the days and especially the nights, but it still went by far too quickly.

On the morning of his last day, she lay in his arms, sated from lovemaking on the mattress on the floor.

Noah stretched and let out a long sigh. 'I need to get up, sweetheart.'

'I know.' Emotion closed her throat, but she refused to show it. In her heart, she wanted to keep him in her bedroom forever. If only she could pause this moment and not let time tick by to the moment when they'd have to acknowledge his leaving.

Slowly, she traced the width of his chest and gently kissed him. 'Before we go downstairs and join the others, I want to talk to you about something.'

'Mmm…' He traced her hips with his hand.

'Were you going to tell me that Louis Melville is your officer?'

His hand paused. 'How did you find out?'

'Melville told me.'

Noah jerked to sit up. '*He* told you? When? How?'

'Months ago. I saw him in town and we spoke briefly. I've been waiting for you to tell me, too, but you haven't.'

'I didn't want to worry you, that's why. How come you never mentioned that you saw him?'

'I didn't want to worry you, either.' Taking a deep breath, she reluctantly pushed back the blankets and stood, reaching for her clothes. 'I expect Aunty Hilda and Peggy will have breakfast cooking. We should go down.'

'Beth, look, I'm sorry I didn't tell you.'

'It doesn't matter now.'

'Clearly it does.' Noah stood and donned his uniform. It took him longer than her to dress, so she sat before the mirror and brushed her dark shoulder-length hair before pinning it up with combs.

In the mirror's reflection she watched him wrap the puttees around the top of his boots up to his knees. He was slowly turning from her husband into a soldier again. She didn't like it.

Abruptly, she went to the door. 'I'll go down and help with breakfast.'

Downstairs the kitchen was chaotic as Reggie joined them for breakfast, wanting to wish Will and the Jackson brothers a fond farewell, and Sid had also arrived. Aunty Hilda had numerous frying pans on the heat cooking bacon and sausages, eggs and kidneys, while Peggy poured tea and made roast beef sandwiches for them to take on the train.

'I hope we get another leave like this before they send us over the water,' Albie said, eating toast.

'Maybe they'll call it all off?' James grunted.

Beth set to work on clearing away the plates of those who'd eaten. She noticed her dad had touched nothing on his plate and it had gone cold. Reggie had brought the morning newspapers, but they remained untouched on the sideboard, the headline of one mentioning battles in northern French towns. Beth quickly threw a tea towel over the newspaper.

She filled the scullery sink with boiling water from the kettle to start washing up, half-heartedly listening to the talk of the men. The knot of emotion tightened in her chest as she thought of the laughs she'd shared with them all in the last six days.

The weather had remained perfect for them and they took full advantage of it with picnics by the beck, games of cricket and walks along the lanes surrounding the farm and in Thornes Park.

Leah joined them on the Saturday night and together they all went to the theatre and watched a variety performance where a little scruffy dog dressed in a suit and riding a baby donkey wearing a bonnet stole the show.

Joanna, Jimmy and Ivy came for one picnic, as did Jane and Alfie, showing off their new baby and, being a Sunday, Leah joined them, too. For one sunny day they laughed and ate and were happy. A precious day in the midst of a war. That day would remain in Beth's memory forever.

The Jackson brothers had taken Peggy into Wakefield and bought her a new hat and soft velvet slippers for her birthday next week. Sid had brought his little son to visit them, but Meg was too busy at her new job in the mill to accompany him. Beth sensed not all was well in Sid's marriage.

Noah and Beth took the train to Leeds and he bought her a gold necklace with a heart-shaped pendant and they had high tea at a posh hotel before returning home. They called it their anniversary celebration day, as the first anniversary of their wedding had come and gone in May without them being together. Noah left her for a few hours one afternoon to spend it with Mr Grimshaw and visit the school. While he was gone, Beth had dragged the bath up to her bedroom and after many trips with hot water, she bathed and washed her hair, wanting to look pretty for him.

Most nights, after the men had returned from the pub, they all played cards and draughts. And while the others slept, Beth and Noah made love and lay in each other's arms, not talking, just simply living the moment and storing it in their minds for when they'd be apart.

Carrying clean dried plates back into the kitchen, her heart skipped a beat as the men rose ready to leave. It was too soon.

'I suppose we'd best get back to it,' Alfred said, kissing Peggy's cheeks.

'Aye, back to the drills and marches.' James sighed. 'Back to that damn Lieutenant Melville and his harassment.'

Beth nearly dropped the plate she was holding. 'Melville harasses you?'

'You fool, James!' Albie slapped James's shoulder.

'Melville harasses you?' she repeated, staring at Noah, angry that he'd not told her about any mistreatment.

'We'll walk out with you,' Aunty Hilda declared, encouraging everyone to leave the kitchen.

Alone with Noah, Beth waited for him to speak.

Noah glanced up at the ceiling and then at Beth. 'I didn't want you to know that either.'

'What exactly does Louis Melville do to you?'

'He's an officer. It's their job to bother us and knock us into shape.'

'But you. He targets you, obviously.'

'All officers will make trouble for privates if they can. They have to toughen us up, Beth. It's the army.'

'What else aren't you telling me?'

'Nothing. Nothing at all. At the start, Melville was a pain in the backside to everyone. Naturally, with our history he was always going to single me out.'

'He told me he was trying to be a better man.'

Noah sighed. 'At times, I think he is trying. His punishments for slight misdemeanours has stopped now. He's been away in London at officer training and for a while on his return he is different. I can't make head nor tail of him, and that's the honest truth. There are times when he is a maniac and other times when he is near to normal as any of us.'

'I knew there was something. I could tell. You've been a little quiet. You should have told me everything.'

'Why? Why make you worry? Officers come and go. They could draft him to France any day ahead of us, we all could go at any time. There wasn't any point in having you upset. He's always been fair to Will, even when Will has broken some rule.'

'Will?' Beth was shocked. 'Will has been in trouble? I'll have a word with him.'

Noah gave a small smile. 'Will is no longer a boy, sweetheart. He's not your younger brother who you can boss around any more. He's a man and he can look after himself.'

She wrung her hands, distraught. 'I just feel out of control with all that's happening. That Melville can cause you and Will problems, because of my history with him. What can I do to fix it?'

'There's nothing to fix. Honestly, put Melville from your mind. He's not worth a moment of thought. We are all grown men who can handle any situation.'

She couldn't reply. She felt a touch of betrayal from not only Noah but also Louis. She hated not being there to stop them from warring with each other.

'Beth, I don't want to speak of Melville in our last few minutes, please. Leaving you is hard enough as it is. I don't know how long it'll be before I see you again.' The look in his blue-green eyes crushed her.

Beth squashed down her anger and nodded. In a flash she was in his arms, holding him tight. 'Please be careful.'

'I will be,' he whispered against her hair, then he brought her face up to kiss her.

Half-heartedly, they walked out of the house to join the others at the gate. Dad held Will, his expression bleak.

Beth hardened her heart, knowing that to cry now would be the end of her. Summoning all her courage, she kissed each of her brothers-in-law goodbye and then stood next to Will, who'd just hugged Aunty Hilda.

Beth embraced him. 'Why didn't you tell me about Melville?' she demanded harshly, trying to keep her voice low. 'Write to me if Melville does anything to you or Noah. I might be able to help. He might listen to me,' she whispered against his ear.

'Don't worry,' Will whispered back. 'We can handle Melville. Take care of Dad.'

'Let's go lads,' Albie announced.

Beth stepped away from Will and gave his arm a gentle squeeze. 'Take care.'

He nodded and with a salute to their dad, grabbed his kit and headed up the lane with the Jackson brothers.

Noah gave his mam a kiss and Aunty Hilda. 'Take care of my wife.' He tried to smile, but it didn't work.

'She'll be fine, lad, strong as an oak, that one.' Aunty Hilda turned and hobbled away.

Beth grabbed Noah for a last kiss. 'I love you!'

'And I adore you!' Then he too was walking away from her.

She stood with her dad and Peggy, and the three of them watched the men trudge up the lane and turn the corner. When would they see them again?

One glance at her dad's pale face showed that he had reverted back to how he was six days ago. Beth's hopes plummeted.

* * *

Wiping the sweat from her brow with a handkerchief, Beth continued the task of hoeing between the rows of radishes. From the orchard she heard the chatter of Ronnie's three friends, who for a shilling each were picking the plums from the trees, with strict warnings not to bruise the fruit.

It squeezed her heart to see Ronnie's friends laughing and messing about, all gangly legs and knobbly knees. Their presence reminded her so much of Ronnie and made her miss him all the more, but it was a kind of comfort to have them around, as though Ronnie was with them somehow. She only had to close her eyes and listen to the boys talk of football, and she easily imagined Ronnie up the ladders with them.

Only for Dad it felt the opposite and on seeing the boys this morning, he'd whistled for Patch and gone walking the fields to check the growth of the rhubarb. The boys reminded him of what he'd lost, and he couldn't face it.

The August afternoon sun burned like a furnace. Beth finished hoeing and after inspecting the boys' haul paid them and sent them on their way. Being Saturday, Beth didn't have the help of the hired village women today and noticing that the cucumbers needed watering, she began filling buckets up from the water barrel beside the greenhouse and went along the trellises watering.

'You look busy.'

Beth spun around and grinned at Leah standing at the far end of the vegetable bed. 'I'm never too busy for a drink though. Would you like one?'

'I would, thanks. It's been a hot walk from the tram.'

Beth paused as she got closer to Leah. 'Your eye! What happened?' She peered at the bruising and puffiness around Leah's eye.

'Oh, it's nowt.'

'It doesn't look like nothing to me.'

Leah bowed her head so her loosely tied dark hair swung in front of her face. 'There was a fight in the pub last night. I got caught in it. Barely a shift goes by without some idiots brawling.'

'That must have hurt.'

'Unfortunately, it happens in that place.'

'It sounds rough. Why do you still work there? You're full time on the stall. Surely, you can quit the place now?'

'I wish I could, but the landlady has put the rent up on my room.' Leah shrugged. 'If she hadn't, I might have been able to give up the pub.'

Beth led her down the garden towards the house. 'Leave the pub. I'll cover the difference in your wages.'

Leah jerked to a stop. 'No. I'll not have you doing that, Beth. You pay me a fair wage.'

'Obviously not enough if you have to take on a second job.'

'I'll manage.' She thrust the money tin at Beth; a stubborn tilt to her chin. 'I'd best be off.'

'No, you won't. You'll come inside and have a drink to cool off. You can tell me about your week. Did Reggie take enough produce to you on Thursday?' Beth, being just as stubborn, gave her no time to walk away as she went inside the kitchen, knowing Leah would follow due to good manners.

'I ran short of everything this morning. I'll need all that you have for this week.'

'I'm surprised at that. The government is asking everyone to grow their own vegetables. Public parks up and down the country now grow vegetables instead of flowers. Allotments are developing quicker than ever.' Beth took off her sacking apron and washed her hands in the sink in the scullery before joining Leah in the kitchen.

'Aye, but not everyone is keen to garden, are they? And that's those who might have a patch of grass. There are a great many who have no yard to dig up.' Leah sat at the table and took of her battered hat to fan herself with it. 'It's a scorcher today.'

'Reggie says we'll get a storm tonight.' Beth poured them two glasses of lemon cordial.

'I hope it waits until I'm back in town.'

Sitting opposite Leah, Beth smiled. 'You can stay here tonight if you want? We can have a game of cards or something?'

'I can't. I've a shift at the pub.'

'Tell them you're finished there, please. I'll make up the difference.'

'We'll see.' Leah shrugged. 'Albie doesn't want me working there either.' Then she realised what she'd said and clapped a hand over her mouth.

'Albie?' Beth frowned. 'Albie Jackson, my brother-in-law?'

Cheeks reddening, Leah nodded. 'We've been writing to each other since he went back to camp. Do you mind?'

'Why on earth would I mind?' Beth laughed. 'I thought you two hit it off the night we all went to the theatre.'

'We did. He's nice. For some reason he seems to like me. Don't know why.'

'Oh, Leah, he sees in you a lovely person. We all do.'

'But I'm nowt, Beth. I've no family and I live in a box room in someone's house because it's either that or on the streets. Me dad was no good to anybody and we lived in the worst part of Wakefield. I can barely read or write cos I was never at school. I had to be home to look after me sick mam and me younger sisters. Now they've gone and I've not seen me sisters in weeks. Hardly a catch, am I?'

Beth reached over and gripped Leah's hand in hers. 'You're smart and decent and loyal. You're worth any man. Albie's lucky.'

'There's nowt between us. Just a couple of letters. To be honest, it's mostly him writing, as I'm not good at it. It takes me all night to read one of his letters. I have to sound out each word like a kid.' She sighed.

'Then I'll help you.'

'How?'

'You could come here each night and we'll read books together.'

'Lord, Beth, I can't be doing that. I'm fair worn out by the time I get to me room. I can't be coming to the farm every night.'

'True, I didn't think of that and in winter it wouldn't be manageable.'

'I'll just keep practising, that's all. Albie knows I'm not great at writing. He's happy with a few lines from me.'

'I know!' Beth sat up straighter. 'I'll talk to Mr Grimshaw. He's a teacher at the grammar school and Noah's good friend. He'll help you, I'm sure. He loves a project, does Mr Grimshaw.'

'I don't know, Beth...' Leah was hesitant.

'He lives in Wakefield, close to the school. So nearer for you and him to meet. He's a gentle soul, intelligent and likes nothing more than helping others. I'll call on him on Monday.'

'Beth, hang on a minute, I've not agreed yet.' Leah laughed.

'Don't you want to write lovely long letters to Albie?' She raised her eyebrows at her friend.

'Aye, I do.'

'Well then. Let Mr Grimshaw help you.' Beth glanced at the letter sitting on the mantelpiece that had arrived only that morning from Noah. 'When did you last hear from Albie?'

'About a week ago.'

'So, you know they've moved camp?'

'Aye, Albie mentioned it.'

Beth stood and picked up the letter. 'This arrived this morning from Noah. He says word around camp is that they'll be going to France any day and are unlikely to make a trip home to say goodbye.' Sadness and worry filled her voice.

'It was bound to happen sooner or later that they would go. They've been in the training camps for so long,' Leah said quietly.

'The news has rattled Peggy. It doesn't help when the newspapers are full of battles and wounded lists.'

'Five sons fighting.' Leah shook her head in awe.

'Aunty Hilda has taken her up to the village, well, Reggie drove them up to the village for Aunty Hilda's legs won't allow her to walk far nor will Peggy's chest let her. Anyway, Aunty Hilda thought they could visit people they knew, and it would distract Peggy and help ease the shock. Until now, she's been safe in the knowledge that her boys were in camps down south. Noah's letter has changed all that.'

'You must be pleased your aunt and Peggy are good friends.'

'Aye, I am. Aunty Hilda decided that Peggy would remain in her bedroom and that I would buy a proper bed for Noah and me.' Beth grinned. 'You should have seen Reggie and two lads carrying the bed upstairs with Aunty Hilda giving orders. It was funny.'

'The army should recruit your Aunty Hilda.' Leah laughed. 'At least you've got a decent bed now and a room to yourself for when Noah is home on leave.'

'I hope it's soon', Beth said wistfully, before lifting her chin. 'But it won't be so there's no point moping about.'

Leah finished her drink and stood. 'I will visit Mr Grimshaw. *If* he's willing.'

'He will be,' Beth encouraged.

'I need to write more than a few stupid lines to Albie as he's going to need comfort from home if he's to face the Germans. It's the least I can do.'

Beth grinned. 'Good. We can make a start now. I'll fetch some paper and a pen and together we'll write your letter to Albie.'

Leah's shoulders slumped. 'You're like a dog with a bone, you are. Can't it wait?'

Pausing at the door, Beth smiled. 'Absolutely not. Just think, one day we could be related by marriage.'

Leah spluttered. 'Marriage? You're getting carried away, aren't you? I'm only writing a few letters!' But she couldn't hide the light in her eyes.

CHAPTER 10

*I*n the dark night where rain clouds covered the moon and a slight cold wind blew, Noah marched with his fellow men to a mind-numbing chorus of artillery. Ahead, the black sky lit up at intervals as the shells exploded.

The battle had been going for hours, and as Noah's unit was a part of the reserve, they were following behind the attacks around the French village of Loos. Noah couldn't feel the individual blisters on his feet any more. Instead, the burning sensation of pain started from his toes and went up his shins. For days they'd been marching. Since landing in Le Havre, in the first week of September, they'd been given orders to head for Loos to be held behind the lines in reserve for the major battle about to take place.

For three weeks they'd been marching with full packs. Optimism had kept the men cheery on starting out, but that energy had dismissed with every mile they trudged on dirt roads in ill-fitting boots and sleeping rough where ever the officers told them to drop.

As they moved up the trenches that littered the Loos valley, a whole unknown world opened up before them. The ear-ringing sound of the shells and canons had been their companion for over twenty-four hours, but now they were being called up to attack and to do so they had to cross enemy trenches already taken.

Recent rain filled the trenches and waterlogged the rutted fields, shell holes and craters. The mud made for slow going, but the worst experience was their first sight of seeing dead and mutilated soldiers, British and German alike.

At first, Noah simply stared in horror at the corpses lying exposed on the ground, or half buried in shell holes or hanging from rolls of barbed wire. However, after hours of wading through narrow muddy trenches, where stepping on bodies was the only way to get through, his senses dulled enough for him to only concentrate on the task at hand.

He hadn't looked back to gauge the reaction of his brothers, he dared not. He couldn't speak of the destruction surrounding them. The mud, the bodies, the destroyed buildings and fields were inconceivable and that was only what he could see by the light of the artillery flashing in the night sky. How would it look by day he dreaded to imagine.

Noah focused ahead, his rifle in his hands and a mindless fascination of walking towards the bright bursts of light that brightened overhead like fireworks in the distance while the rain fell, adding to their misery.

Dawn came and went and a weak light in a muted grey sky gave Noah's battalion their first proper glimpse of the battle-fields. First aid casualty clearing stations had been hastily set up and wounded soldiers sat on broken walls or lay quietly on stretchers. Those that could, smoked cigarettes, but many lay with eyes closed, white-faced wearing bloody, filthy and wet uniforms. A line of blindfolded soldiers, holding onto the shoulder of the man in front, staggered past Noah and the men.

'What's wrong with them, Noah?' Sid asked.

'They've been gassed,' Noah replied quietly. 'Chlorine gas canisters are our secret weapon, or so the officers say.'

'It's not that good then if our lads are blinded by it.'

'It depends on the wind. Don't hesitate to put your mask on if you see a greenish haze. Remember your training. Put your mask on before helping others.'

They marched on, reaching beyond the village of Loos, which had been pulverised into rubble. What surprised Noah and his brothers was the area was a mining community. Slag heaps and winding towers dominated the skyline.

'Bloody hell,' Alfred stared. 'We've come all this bloody way to stop at a mining village that looks like home. We can't get away from coal even in France!'

James gazed around. 'Miners just like us,' he said in awe. 'Poor bastards.'

Under orders, they picked their way through the ruined buildings, around dead horses and damaged transports that filled the streets running out of the little village.

'Look at the state of it,' Sid whispered beside Noah.

'They've had a rough time of it and no mistake,' Noah replied.

Beyond the village, battles continued; the noise of the artillery deafening, the ground shaking beneath their feet.

Sergeant Bourke ordered them into the trenches to rest and wait for further orders.

'So, this is war,' Albie snorted as he moved the body of a dead German to one side so he could sit down.

As a sombre, exhausted group, the brothers, including Will and some others, gathered in the trench to eat some of their rations.

Surrounded by the debris of battle and the corpses of mutilated Germans, Noah gritted his teeth, trying to control his mind at the sheer incredibleness of it all. How had he gone from being a teacher of small boys to this incomprehensible horror?

He lifted a sandbag to a better position for him to sit on it, glancing at Will to make sure he was doing all right after the tiring march through the dark and the rain. Thankfully Will seemed fine.

'What's the name of this place again, Noah?' James asked, gulping his water down.

'It's Loos, apparently.' He gazed back at the burning remains of a building. 'Go easy on that water, James. We don't know when we can get a refill.'

'Right, ladies, let's be having you, it's not a picnic you know,' Sergeant Bourke ordered them back to their feet. Noah liked Bourke. The stocky man in his mid-thirties was one of them, working class, but more importantly he was sensible and knowledgeable. He didn't ask them to do anything he himself wouldn't do.

In narrow, waterlogged muddy trenches they inched forward. Soldiers were coming past them, their uniforms covered with dirt and faces telling silent stories of the hell they'd just endured.

Squeezing between stretcher-bearers carrying their heavy loads and the able-bodied soldiers who were being relieved, Noah concentrated on putting one aching foot before the other.

They'd lost the daylight by the time the order came for them to stop and man the trenches. Tremendous explosions and constant shelling blunted the senses. The barrage of allied and enemy artillery thudded their bodies like a drumbeat.

'We are to defend this trench all night,' Sergeant Bourke yelled. 'Stay alert. Be silent. No fires, no lights.'

Exhausted, Noah flopped onto a sandbag. In turns the men stood on the step of the trench to keep watch, giving the others time to sit and eat or try to sleep despite the horrendous noise.

Throughout the night, Noah stood his turn on the step. His sight narrowed onto the murky terrain in front of him, searching for any movement of the enemy through the smoke haze. At times he wondered if his eyes were playing tricks on him and he had to peer into the dark, praying they weren't about to be attacked. He'd glanced back into the trench at his sleeping brothers and young Will and knew he had to keep them safe. How would he live with himself if anything happened to them? How would he face his mam and Beth?

At first light, all the men were on alert and ordered to 'stand to' onto the step. Dawn raids were a tactic used by both sides, and Sergeant Bourke bawled at them to be vigilant. They heard battles raging to the north and south of them. However, after an hour of no movement, they were allowed to step down with only few men on lookout as breakfast came up the trench. The tea wasn't very hot, and it tasted slightly of the kerosene tins it was transported in, but the men welcomed something warm especially as there was bacon to accompany it.

Although the rain had eased, the overcast dullness and wet conditions made the men cold. Despite being so tired his eyes stung, sleep was impossible for Noah, but Alfred managed to nod off and James sat with his eyes closed but his fingers tapped on his thigh.

'Men.' Sergeant Bourke came along the trench, frowning as he stepped over the body of a dead German. 'We are to attack in three hours at eleven hundred hours. Get some rest and eat, sleep if you can. Check your weapons.' He handed out packets of cigarettes as he went along. 'Be ready for the order to move up the forward trenches in an hour.'

Sergeant Bourke stopped in front of Noah and gave him two material chevrons. 'Jackson, you're now lance corporal.'

'I am?' Noah's eyebrows rose. 'Why?'

'Because you are. Don't ask me stupid questions I don't have the time. I follow orders, and my orders were to make you a lance corporal. A higher officer would have given them to you, but they are busy in HQ readying for this attack. Sew these on before battle. Do it now.'

Noah inspected the material stripes.

'I'm surprised at that,' Albie said when Bourke walked further along the trench. 'I wonder what Lieutenant Melville will have to say about it?'

'He's not here. So, who cares?' Noah searched through his kit for the small sewing tin. His relief that Melville had not joined them so far was immense. Melville had left them at Le Havre for more officer training, and Noah had felt a weight lifted off his shoulders the moment the man walked away. In camp Melville had made sure Noah received the worst of the duties and on kit inspection Melville always found something wrong with Noah's equipment even though he made it spotless and without fault. To Noah it seemed Melville was two sides of one man. The kinder man he was trying to be when he spoke to Beth never quite replaced the nasty piece of work he was to Noah. Melville would never accept his marriage to Beth. Would never accept he'd lost her to Noah, a man from a lower class than himself.

Noah shook off thoughts of Melville and moved over to sit next to Will. 'How are you feeling? All right?'

Will gave a half smile. 'No idea.' He shrugged, looking suddenly very young. 'How are you meant to feel? This is like another world, a nightmare.'

'I don't think there is a right or wrong answer.' Noah dug the toe of his boot into the mud. 'It's all right to feel afraid, uncertain, eager to get it over with. None of us have ever experienced something like this before. Today we will kill other men and it will forever change us.'

'Have you written home?' Will's look was so similar to Beth's.

Noah heaved a long sigh. Will reminded him of Beth so much. He had her cheeky smile and some of her facial expressions. 'I'm just about to write to Beth.'

'What do we say?'

'Whatever you want to.'

Will looked uncertain. 'Are you going to be honest to Beth about all this?'

'Yes. I owe it to her. God willing, we shall return home and those at home won't understand what we've seen or been through unless we tell them because, I think, after today, all of us might never be the same again and they need to understand that in some way. Write to your dad.' Noah patted his shoulder and moved away to pen a few lines to Beth.

Dearest love,

Sorry I've not written for a few days. We have been marching for some time and we fall asleep wherever we drop at the end of each day. Recent rain has turned the countryside into a quagmire as the roads are all churned up by military movement. Last night we were in the reserve trenches in readiness to go forward shortly. We're to be tested at last. I wonder how we will stack up against the enemy? All around us brave men have fallen on both sides. My hands shake, but I must be brave, though I find it madness that soon I will be killing strangers – men who wish to do me harm. I wonder if they feel the same?

Will sits opposite me. He is well and writing to your dad as I write to you. My brothers are all fine, too. But we are cold and wet.

I will write again as soon as I can if the fates allow.

Your loving husband,

Noah.

26th September 1915

WHEN THE ORDER CAME, Noah took a deep breath and with a nod to each of his brothers and Will, he moved off. Knowing his brothers had his back gave him confidence, but as they moved along the sap, the shallow trench leading into no man's land, his gut clenched.

Artillery pounded the forward positions of other battalions as the fighting intensified. Mist swirled over the landscape, obliterating landmarks, though the sergeant said they were to take the wood and that could be seen as a faint outline in the distance.

Suddenly the eerie sound of bagpipes filled the air as the Scottish Highlanders advanced.

'Bloody hell, talk about letting them know they're coming!' Sid said in amazement as they crawled out into the churned mud of no man's land.

The whistle blew and instinctively Noah leapt forward and ran in the direction of the wood. Machine gun fire spluttered into the ground around him as he ran across uneven ground. He tripped and fell into a hole as a shell burst close by, showering him with dirt.

Scrabbling up, he kept going, vaguely aware of the men running with him. Bullets whizzed past his ears, making a zipping noise. A cry from a fallen man was drowned out by artillery peppering the field with shells.

Their objective didn't seem to be getting any closer. Noah's chest heaved with the effort of running over churned up mud and dodging holes and fallen soldiers.

He dived into a crater as another shell burst to his left. An officer was in the hole, peering over the other side. He turned as Noah crawled up beside him.

'Jackson?'

'Melville?' Shocked, Noah stared at the one man he hated more than anything else.

'*Lieutenant* Melville!' Melville spat, peering over the edge of the crater.

'I thought you were at some training facility?'

'I arrived at HQ at dawn and address me as sir or lieutenant, you ignorant oaf!'

Noah swallowed back a cutting retort. Melville had given him every harsh duty he could think of while in training camp, delighting in the fact he could order Noah around. It was just Noah's luck that the bloody bastard had to be an officer in his platoon.

'Well, what are you sitting around here for, Jackson? Get out there!' Melville ducked as gun fire splattered into the dirt by his head.

'Are you coming with me, *lieutenant?*' Noah gave him a sarcastic lift of an eyebrow. 'Let's face the bullets together, yes?'

A devilish gleam entered Melville's dark eyes. 'Yes, why not? The winner gets the spoils of victory!'

'Which are?' Noah said, not caring as he inched up to the top of the shell hole.

'The beautiful Beth, of course.'

Noah jerked and spun around, slipping down the side a little. 'Beth is already *mine*. She is my wife!'

'And may soon be a widow!' Melville laughed and scrambled up the side and over the top. He was soon lost in the haze and smoke.

Taking advantage of the smoke cover, Noah ran forward, eager to catch up with Melville.

Out of nowhere, a trench gaped before him. Jumping down, he fired on the German who twisted towards him. The trench was full of men fighting. Vaguely he was aware of Alfred further along. Another German came around the corner of the trench and fired, missing Noah's head by inches. Angered, he fired back, hitting the man in the shoulder. Noah rushed forward and shot him in the head as Sid and Albie jumped down into the trench behind him.

They followed the trench along until they found steps to climb up and out onto the field. Bullets whizzed over their heads. Noah flattened onto the grass. Machine guns firing to the right pinned them down.

'We can't stay here!' Albie yelled. 'Come on!'

Noah sprinted after him, ducking and weaving until the gunfire overwhelmed them and they fell into a large shell hole, the bottom of which was filled with murky water.

Crawling up to the rim of the shell hole, Noah aimed his rifle at the enemy in the trench only twenty yards away, but who were firing at an advancing unit on their left. Taking aim, Noah targeted the man operating the machine gun and pulled the trigger. The German fell over his machine and quickly his companion pushed him aside and took control of it himself, swinging it about to shoot at Noah.

'Get down,' Noah screamed at Albie as a hail of bullets flew over their heads and smashed into the dirt behind them.

'Wait for him to reload,' Noah warned Albie.

Judging they'd heard the pause correctly, they popped up over the edge of the shell hole and did a round of rapid fire.

They killed the machine gunner and after a moment to check they could escape, Noah scrambled up. 'Come on!' he yelled to Albie.

The haze of smoke and the ear-splitting noise of battle disorientated Noah. He ran ahead, not knowing where he was going, but he wasn't alone. Scottish Highlanders, distinct by their kilts, were running with him. Where the rest of his section was, he didn't know.

The wood was a blaze of sparks and fire as shells landed, cutting down trees that speared the ground. Enemy fire brought down the man running next to him, before Noah jumped into a trench among British and German soldiers embroiled in hand-to-hand fighting.

Noah bayonetted a German who was strangling a British soldier. He turned to fight the man behind him, before realising it was Sid.

Further along the trench Noah recognised Will, who thrust his bayonet into the stomach of his opponent.

'Where have you been?' Sid panted, crouching low as they trod along duckboards, rifle at the ready.

'Trying to get across to here. What did you think I was doing?' Noah snapped.

Suddenly a wave of German soldiers came over the top of the trench and landed amongst Noah and the British soldiers.

Knocked sideways, Noah thrust his bayonet upwards into the

face of a German. Blood spurted over him. The German's shocked eyes stared at Noah before he crumpled to the ground.

'Retreat!'

Noah glanced around. Who said that? Was it an order?

Sid jerked him by the collar and heaved him up over the trench. 'Hurry. More are coming!'

Glancing wildly over his shoulder as he ran, Noah saw the wave of grey-clad soldiers yelling and shooting as they reinforced the trench.

Noah ran as fast as he had ever done. Sid ran beside him. They fell into the previous German trench they'd claimed and sucked in a lungful of air.

'Stop! Wait here, lads. We'll make a stand here!' Sergeant Bourke demanded, gasping for breath as he fell in beside them. He'd lost his hat and his brown hair was oiled flat to his head. He straightened, a determined stare in his eyes. 'Stand to!'

As one, the group of men turned and slammed themselves against the trench wall, rifles ready, facing the other trench they'd just retreated from.

They watched with bated breath as the fighting continued ahead of them. Some British soldiers managed to make it back to them, but others were shot as they ran. The vast number of Germans filling the other trench meant any allied soldiers in there were either shot or taken prisoner.

Noah and the others cover-fired any British soldier who crawled across the grass, trying to make it back as the Germans shot at them.

'Come on!' Sid yelled to a soldier twenty yards away from them who was crawling on his elbows through the grass and mud towards them.

'You can do it,' Noah urged, his gut clenching as the soldier, his expression one of pain and effort, focused on reaching them.

'I'll help the poor sod,' Sid said, pulling himself over the edge.

'No!' Noah yanked him back down as bullets thudded into the dirt near their heads.

Abruptly, the soldier jerked and spasmed as bullets riddled him. He lay dead only five yards from Noah and Sid.

Sid swore long and hard.

Noah dropped his chin to his chest.

Throughout the night, Noah and Sid remained together, keeping each other alert in the darkness as they defended their part of the trench. Two Scottish Highlanders held the next section of the trench and beyond them, Noah had to hope were his other brothers and Will.

Sergeant Bourke, keeping low, moved his way towards them just before dawn. 'Look lively, lads. It's the perfect time for the Boche to come at us.'

'Do we attack again?' Noah asked without taking his gaze from the field in front of him.

'No. We wait for reinforcements.'

'And if they don't arrive?'

'They will. Never fear of that, Jackson.'

Sid hunkered down on the step and cupped a cigarette in his hand to show no light to the enemy. 'Have you seen our brothers, sir?'

'Aye. James and Albie are two bends along. I've told them you two are fine.'

'And Alfred or Will Beaumont?' Noah glanced at him.

'I've not seen either of them. Probably they are in some other trench elsewhere.'

'Lieutenant Melville?' Noah asked.

Sid frowned. 'Is *he* back?'

Sergeant Bourke nodded. 'He arrived in the trench just before the whistle. He's about somewhere. I saw him giving orders to a runner about an hour ago. Now have you any rations left?'

Both Sid and Noah shook their heads.

'No food will be brought up here. You'll not eat until you're back in our trenches. Just hold your positions, lads. I'll be back shortly.'

'Him mentioning food has me guts rumbling like thunder.' Sid grinned, taking up his position beside Noah.

Noah remained silent. Movement caught his eye. Was there something out there or was tiredness playing tricks on his sight?

'Holy shit,' Sid whispered, slightly moving his rifle. 'I think they're coming, our kid.'

Noah swallowed. Now he was sure the grass and mud moved like a sea of ants were crawling over it, but it wasn't ants. 'Christ, there are so many.'

'We ain't got enough ammunition to keep them off us.' Panic filled Sid's voice.

'We hold off as long as we can and then we make a run for it, understand?' Noah flexed his shoulders and trained the rifle onto a German's helmet he could see poking over a mound of mud. 'Stay true, Sid. Like shooting rabbits back home. Lock on one at a time. Pick them off.'

'Aye.'

In a heartbeat the dawn was lit up by gunfire. Noah and Sid stood side by side in the trench, carefully picking their targets off.

One of the Highlanders was hit and his cry sent a shiver through Noah. The onslaught grew. The Germans edged closer. The hail of bullets never seemed to stop.

'We can't keep them back on our own,' Sid shouted.

Noah ducked down and ran to the remaining Highlander. 'We can't hold them. Without reinforcements, they'll mow us down!'

'It's time to go then!' The Scotsman fired one last shot and then ducked down. 'Come away. We cannae hold them any longer!'

'Sid!' Noah beckoned.

The three of them, bent double, hurried along the trench into the sap leading back to no man's land and the British-held trenches. Wounded and dead soldiers lay scattered about, but they couldn't stop to offer help or comfort.

'We're going to have to run for it,' Noah said as they knelt for a pause to catch their breaths.

'Loos is our only hope,' the Scotsman said, pointing to the fleeing allied soldiers who were also running for their lives across open land. The ruined village and the valley it sat in would give them some protection if they could make it back.

'Surely in the village there would be the reserve units?' Noah said.

Bullets thudded into the sandbags lining the top of the sap. The whistle for retreat sounded.

'Let's go!' Noah didn't wait for an argument and raced away across no man's land just as he had done the day before only this time in the opposite direction.

Behind him, he heard a yell, and glancing back saw the Scotsman fall.

Sid ran past Noah, always being the fastest of the two. 'Leave him!' Sid shouted as bullets pinpricked the dirt around them. 'Run!'

CHAPTER 11

*W*hen Beth didn't get her monthly show in early October, she knew she was pregnant. Her breasts were tender and the smell of frying meat turned her stomach.

'What's up, lass?' Aunty Hilda asked, flipping the piece of liver in the frying pan. 'You're looking peaky.'

Beth swallowed back the nausea as she sat at the table buttering toast. Morning sun filled the kitchen and outside they could hear the lads greeting each other as they started a new day.

Peggy frowned as she poured out cups of tea. 'Are you having a baby, love?'

Beth stared at Peggy and nodded. 'I think so. How did you guess?'

'You're green around the gills.' Peggy laughed.

'Well, that's the grandest piece of news I've heard in a very long time,' Aunty Hilda declared, giving Beth a smacking great kiss on the cheek.

Peggy's eyes filled with tears. 'I'm to be a grandma again and this time I'll see more of my grandchild than I do with Sid's little 'un.'

'Aye, this time you'll be sick of the sight of it!' Aunty Hilda joked. 'Especially at two in the morning when the little scrap is screaming its head off.'

'You look worried, love.' Peggy gave Beth's arm a squeeze.

'I am a bit and I wish Noah was here, too.'

'Write to him today, lass,' Aunty Hilda commanded. 'Let him know he's to be a dad. He'll be made up with the news.'

'I will, later.' Beth stood, taking the toast with her. 'I'll go out and tell Dad, happen it'll make him feel better.'

'Aye, do that. Tell him to come in for his breakfast, too, not that he'll listen.' Aunty Hilda tutted.

Pulling on her coat, she pushed her feet into farm boots and walked outside into the weak late October sunshine. Fallen leaves of red and gold scattered across the lawn and the flowers, which had looked so beautiful in the summer, were now dying back into the soil. She hated the thought of winter coming, but at least she would be in a nice warm house, whereas she dreaded to think where Noah and the rest of the boys would be.

She found her dad in the forcing sheds, where he oversaw the village lads forking out manure in preparation for the rhubarb planting next month.

'You're to come in for your breakfast,' she told him.

A slight lift of his lips was as close as she got to a smile these days. 'Aye, in a minute.'

Beth knew that could mean five minutes or two hours. Her dad was no longer the man he used to be. Before the war and her mam's death, he'd been a strong, well-built man full of good humour and in the best of health. Now he was too quiet, thin and stoop backed. Since the double deaths in January, he'd aged considerably.

'I've got some good news to tell you, Dad. Will you not come inside for a bit?'

'I've too much to do but tell me your news.'

'I'm to have a baby.'

For a moment happiness filled his eyes and he smiled properly, then the light faded and his face grew sad. 'That's grand, lass. Your mam would have been over the moon.'

'Are *you* happy for me though, Dad?'

'Aye, lass. I am.' He patted her hand and walked to the back of the shed, the conversation over.

Beth went outside, partly annoyed, and partly upset. Before the grief, her dad enjoyed life and adored babies. When Ivy had been born, he'd gone to the pub with Jimmy and bought all the patrons a drink. He'd bought Joanna a thin gold chain as a present the day Ivy was born. Yet Beth knew none of that would happen for her and her baby. Rob Beaumont no longer resembled her dad. He wasn't the man she once adored, she barely recognised him.

Returning to the kitchen, Beth waved away Peggy and Aunty Hilda's protests to sit down and have some tea and instead began sweeping the floor ready to scrub it.

'Nay, you'll not be on your hands and knees scrubbing a floor now,' Aunty Hilda admonished.

'Who else is to do it? If I'd done this yesterday, you'd have been none the wiser. Besides, are we to have a mucky floor until the baby is born?'

'We'll get a lass from the village to come and do it.'

'No, we won't. I can do it perfectly well. I'm pregnant, not an invalid.' Beth ignored them and for the rest of the day she washed the floor, dusted the furniture, cleaned out the ashes from the fireplaces, banged the rugs and even black-leaded the range before Aunty Hilda shouted at her to get herself into a hot bath and then rest.

Beth had the hot bath, but instead of resting, she turned to the account books and opened the mail as the sun set and the lamps were lit.

With the fire glowing and the curtains drawn against the night, Beth stared around at her small family gathered in the front room. Aunty Hilda sat knitting socks, as did Peggy. Her dad stood gazing into the flames and she knew any moment he'd say goodnight and go upstairs.

The ticking of the mantle clock seemed loud in the room, the only other noise was the soft clicking of the knitting needles and the odd shift of a log in the grate.

Such quietness. Beth hated it. 'I might visit Joanna in the morning and then Leah at the stall, and while I'm out I'll stop by Jane's and have a cup of tea with her, too.' Her voice sounded louder than expected.

'Aye, good idea, lass.' Aunty Hilda nodded, puffing away a strand of grey hair that had fallen into her eyes. 'Can you pick me up some more wool? I thought to have a rest from making socks for the lads and instead make a little jacket for your baby. Noah was home in July, so by my reckoning the little 'un should be here by April.'

Smiling at the thought, Beth toyed with the pen she held. 'Yes. I think so, too.'

'White wool and yellow ribbons,' Peggy announced. 'I'll make some booties and a little bonnet to go with it, shall I, Hilda?'

'Grand.' Aunty Hilda nodded. 'I'll get one of the lads to go up into the attic, Beth, and bring down the trunk of baby clothes your mam used. Joanna didn't want it as Jimmy's parents bought her all new clothes. But I'm sure they'll be some blankets and useful items up there.'

Beth smiled. 'We can sort through it all and then make a list of anything we're short of.'

'Good night all,' Dad suddenly said. He pressed a hand to Beth's shoulder and left the room.

Aunty Hilda watched him go. 'I'm right annoyed with him. He could at least pretend to be happy about the baby.'

'It's like he doesn't even care,' Beth murmured.

'He's just missing your mam, that's all.' Peggy started coughing. 'My chest can tell when the weather has turned. It's going to be cold tonight. I hate to see the summer finish.'

'We've had a good run of it this year,' Aunty Hilda said. 'Happen you should knit yourself a winter vest, Peggy.'

'Happen I might.' Peggy sighed.

'At least when the spring comes the baby will be here.' Beth grinned. 'That'll make the winter not so harsh.'

Peggy reached over and grasped Beth's hand. 'I can't wait for it, love. It'll be smashing to have a little 'un to cuddle and spoil.'

'I'd best tell its father then!' Beth grinned and, feeling better in spirit, took a fresh piece of paper from the desk drawer and wrote to Noah.

Dear darling husband,

I hope this letter finds you safe and well. I have the most wonderful news, my love. We are to be parents in April.

Are you surprised? I know I am.

We've been married for eighteen months or so, and I didn't fall in the months before you enlisted, but I wasn't too worried about it as I knew we had all the time in the world. Only we weren't to know that the world would change, and we would be apart for months on end, and for how much longer, who knows?

I understand that the news will worry you, but please don't be concerned. I have Peggy and Aunty Hilda here, and Joanna and Jane. I shall be fine. Perhaps by April you will be home? I hope so, but if not, I'm in good hands.

Did you get the box of comforts I sent last week? Do you have enough socks? I'll make up another parcel next week when Aunty Hilda has finished knitting your scarf and I'll remember to put all the food in tins this time so the rats can't have a feast of it. I never thought about that, my darling, and feel terrible that ugly rats ate your fruit cake. I feel bad they ate your chocolate as I know how much you were looking forward to having it.

Do you need more Harrison's Pomade? In Will's last letter he said it was the only thing to help get rid of the lice. I'll include some more anyway, for you can share it if you have too much.

I'll post this letter in the morning when in town. Everyone sends

their love and I hope you're happy about the baby news. I want it to be a
little boy who looks just like you.

Take care, my darling.
With all my love,
Beth
Beaumont Farm
27th October 1915

THE FOLLOWING MORNING, Reggie took Beth in the cart to Joanna's house in Stanley. She'd have caught the tram, but she always wanted to give her sister a box of vegetables and didn't fancy carrying it all the way on the tram.

'You've just caught me,' Joanna said, giving Beth a hug as she opened the door.

'Where are you off to?' Beth placed the box in the hallway.

'They've set up a Red Cross centre in the village hall. I go twice a week to roll bandages and pack comfort boxes to send to our boys. I did tell you.' Joanna manoeuvred Ivy's pram down the front steps. 'Morning, Reggie.' Joanna waved to Reggie seated up in the cart.

'You're looking well, Joanna,' he said.

'Aye, I'm not so bad. Ivy's been teething, but we're doing all right.' Joanna turned to Beth. 'Want to come with me to the village hall for an hour?'

Beth dithered. 'I was wanting a chat with you, but not surrounded by a group of women. I've to see Leah as well.'

'Is it urgent?' Joanna pushed the pram down the small path to the roadside. 'Shall I come to the farm tomorrow and spend the day?'

'Would you? That'd be lovely.' Beth hugged her sister goodbye. 'I'll send Reggie to come and collect you.'

'Champion.' Joanna waved as she walked away, as did little Ivy.

'The market then?' Reggie asked as Beth climbed back up onto the cart.

'Yes, please. Will you come and get Joanna and Ivy tomorrow for me, please?'

'Course I will.' Reggie set Snowy walking.

'I don't know what I'd do without you, Reggie, none of us would.' She gave him a smile of genuine gratitude.

'Well, you Beaumonts are like family after all these years of me working at the farm. I've only got me old mam and when she goes, I'll be alone except for the friendship I have with your dad and the rest of you.'

'You'll always be a valued part of our family, Reggie. Dad depends on you more each day.'

'It's a good job I'm too old to enlist then, isn't it?' Reggie grinned as he steered Snowy through the merging traffic into the town centre. 'Did your dad send off the letter about Snowy to the army?'

'No, I did it. I'm waiting on a reply.'

'Why do they keep asking for Snowy when they've already decided we need one horse for the farm? Have they no sense?'

'I feel it's more a case of the army is losing horses rapidly and they need replacing.'

'And how are we supposed to feed people without horsepower?' Reggie tutted. 'We can't farm without at least one horse.'

'Well, that's why I've written another letter. Hopefully, it'll do the trick and they'll leave us alone. Shall I speak to Dad about buying one of those motor agricultural tractors?'

'They are expensive and I doubt if your dad would be interested, lass.'

'No, probably not.' Beth sighed. Getting her dad to be interested in anything was hard work lately.

Reggie halted Snowy at the end of the market near the Beaumont's lock-up and carried the crates of vegetables to store there for when Leah runs short of supplies.

'I'll see you at home, Reggie.'

'Aye, see you then.'

Beth made her way through the rows of stalls, stopping to chat with stallholders she'd known all her life. Many asked after Noah and the family and it took her a full twenty minutes before she could get away to Leah, who was busy bagging up some apples for a customer.

'Are you doing all right?' Beth asked, immediately serving another waiting customer.

'I've been run off my feet.' Leah gave the woman her change.

With a glance at Leah, Beth frowned at the bruise on her jaw. 'Is that a fresh bruise?'

'Aye.'

'What happened this time?'

'A patron got a little amorous, nothing to worry about. I soon sorted him out.'

'Oh, Leah.' Beth finished serving and gave Leah her full attention after saying good morning to Fred next door. 'You need to give up working at the pub. You said you would!'

'I have. Last night was my last night. I don't have time now anyway as Mr Grimshaw is happy to teach me three nights a week.'

'That's brilliant he's giving you so much of his time, and I'm pleased you're finished with the pub. How's it coming along, your reading and writing?'

'Good enough.' Leah shrugged. 'I'm reading better than I was, and I'm better reading than I am writing. Some days the letters just don't make sense to me.'

'You'll improve with time.'

'She's been reading me newspaper every morning, has that one.' Fred nodded, his hands resting on his large stomach as he stood behind his stall. 'I'm lucky to see me own paper first, the cheeky beggar.'

Leah laughed. 'Get away, Fred. You like me reading to you as you set up. I make us a cuppa and read the headlines while he unpacks as he's always late, aren't you?'

Fred raised an eyebrow in mock severity. 'I'm not as young as I once was. Getting out of bed on a frosty morning is becoming harder to do. Don't you start complaining, lass, you get a free newspaper each day to read.'

Leah chuckled and turned to serve another customer. Beth stayed with her for another ten minutes and helped her with more customers.

'Right, I'm off.' Beth wiped her hands on a rag from under the stall. 'I've shopping to do and a visit to the post office.'

'Will you post my letter for me if you're going?'

'Is it to Albie?' Beth teased.

'Aye, who else would I be writing to when I hate picking up a pen?' Leah took the letter out of her bag. 'I've money for the stamp.'

'Leave it. I'm posting at least eight letters so another one won't matter.' Beth waved away her money. 'Peggy writes to her boys every day in rotation, and I've my letters to Noah and Will and business mail to send. I feel I live at that post office!' Beth picked up her bag and popped Leah's letter inside to join the others. 'Reggie has dropped off the crates in the lock-up. Come for tea on Sunday if you've a mind to.'

'Thank you, I will.'

With her shopping done, Beth caught the horse omnibus from town down to Alverthorpe to visit Jane.

As usual, the Taylor household was chaotic and full of children not of school age. Jane welcomed Beth inside and shoved a young lad off a chair so Beth could sit.

'Where's your mother-in-law?' Beth asked.

'At the mill. She's taken on more shifts now I'm home with the baby and can look after this brood.' Jane mashed the tea, her eyes downcast.

'What's wrong?' Beth stood and put an arm around Jane's thin shoulders.

'Nowt, it's just me being an idiot.'

'Why?'

'I received a telegram this morning saying Alfie has been wounded.'

'Oh, Jane!' Beth gasped.

'He's fine,' Jane hurriedly added. 'He's not in any danger, they say, but they have sent him to an army hospital on the coast of France. The wound is slight apparently.'

'Still, a telegram would still make you anxious.'

'When it came this morning, I couldn't open it for half an hour. I took the kids for a walk to Henderson's Dairy to get some milk, even though the milkman had dropped our bottles on the doorstep. I just couldn't sit still. I fed Freddie gazing at the telegram the whole time.' Jane smiled lovingly over at her sweet baby boy who slept contentedly despite the noise from four other children in the room. 'I was shaking like a leaf when I did finally open it.' Tears gathered on her gold lashes and her freckles stood out stark on her pale skin. 'I expected the worst.'

'You're bound to.' Beth rubbed Jane's arm in comfort. 'But a wound that isn't serious, well in my opinion that's a good thing.'

'How so?' Jane quizzed.

'Because while ever he's in a clean hospital bed then he's not being fired at.'

Jane let out a deep sigh. 'I never thought of it that way. I was too busy thinking he'd die of his wounds and Freddie and me would have to live without him.'

'Instead,' Beth said brightly, 'I bet he's sitting up in bed, eating his head off and enjoying the peace and quiet and the soft hands of a nurse.'

'Aye, he would be.' The concern left Jane's expression and she smiled. 'In hospital he'll have the best of care, won't he?'

'Of course, he will.'

Relaxing her stiff shoulders, Jane poured out the tea. 'I'll write to him tonight. They gave me the hospital's address. I'm so pleased you've come, Beth. I've felt sick all morning. You've cheered me up no end.'

'That's what friends are for.' From her bag, Beth took out a lemon cake. 'I bought this from the bakery. I thought we could have it with our tea.'

'Lemon cake, my favourite,' Jane gushed.

'I know.' Beth grinned and was suddenly swarmed by the Taylor children, all hoping for a slice of cake.

As she cut the cake, Beth glanced at Jane. 'I was wondering if you'd like to be a godmother?'

Jane picked up Freddie from his basket as he began to fuss. 'Godmother? What are you on about?'

'A godmother to my little one when he or she is born next April?'

'No! You're having a baby?' Jane's mouth dropped open in surprise.

'I am.'

'Oh, Beth, that's the best news. Aye, I'd be honoured to be its godmother.' Jane hugged Beth with one arm while holding Freddie. 'Just think Freddie and your baby will be best friends too.'

Emotional, Beth nodded. 'Wouldn't that be something?'

CHAPTER 12

$\mathcal{B}$y the light of the moon at the end of February 1916, Noah walked down the snow-white main street of a little Belgium village south of Ypres. Tiredness made him yawn. Allied soldiers lingered, either coming from or going to the little public house on the left, the same place Noah headed for. It was the only establishment in the village that sold alcohol, and he knew that's where his brothers would be. Despite wanting his bed, he knew they'd be expecting him to join them on their first night off in weeks.

Squinting through the cigarette smoke, Noah made his way through to the bar. Close by his brothers sat at a table well under the influence of alcohol and enjoying themselves.

A soldier played the piano in the corner, and the sound of laughter and easy chatter filled Noah's ears instead of gunfire and bombs exploding.

'Noah!' Albie wrapped an arm around his shoulders. 'Wine or beer?'

'Beer, please.'

Albie tapped the bar top and an older Flemish woman gave a smile and nod of welcome as she poured a beer for Noah.

Noah passed over some coins and took a long sip. 'By, that's good.'

'Isn't it?' Albie turned and leaned his elbow on the bar. 'This night is due reward for suffering through a freezing winter.'

'Hey up, our kid,' Sid said to Noah. 'Have you only just finished?'

Noah drank some more and then nodded. 'You know what a bastard Melville is. He finds every duty he can for me.'

'What was it this time?' James asked as he and Alfred left a group of men they'd been talking to and ordered another round of beers.

'He had me and Mr Staines running errands for him.'

'Poor Staines. How does he stand it?' Albie muttered.

'No idea. He has the patience of a saint, that's for sure. Every time Melville looks at me, I want to shoot him.'

'Hey enough of that,' Albie warned, lowering his voice. 'There are ears everywhere here.'

'Well, the French are always up in arms over their officers, why shouldn't we, too?' Alfred spat.

'Melville needs teaching a lesson,' James added. 'Look what he had me do yesterday before we came out of the line.'

Noah's jaw clenched at the thought of the event yesterday when Melville ordered James and Noah to go over the top of the trench in the early hours of the morning after being on watch for four hours. They were to help the stretcher bearers bring back the dead and wounded stuck out in no man's land after that day's assault. The entire time they were scrambling about in the mud, enemy snipers took shots at them. The task was not only dangerous but soul-destroying when trying to drag dead men through churned up mud and over a landscape full of craters filled with water. A wrong slip and you could fall into the crater and drown before anyone knew you were gone.

Noah finished the rest of his beer and signalled for another one. 'I can understand and put up with him targeting me, but he should leave you lot alone.'

'We're your brothers so he's going to target us to get to you,' Sid said. 'The only one he leaves alone is Will because he's Beth's brother. Melville won't touch him.'

'Why for God's sake, though?' Albie asked. 'Beth is married, and he can't have her. He needs to let it go.'

'How can he when he sees Noah every day reminding him of what he's lost?' Albie said.

'She was never his to lose,' Noah muttered.

'Melville is a typical toff. He wants everything he sees and usually no one says no to him.'

'Where is Will?' Noah asked, glancing around the taproom filled with British soldiers and a few Australians.

'Over in the corner behind the piano, sitting with those two Australian fellas. He's right chumming with them,' James said. 'He's met them before. They were on the transport cattle train with us a few weeks ago.'

'The day it took all of eight hours to go three miles?' Sid snorted.

'Aye, sitting in cow shit all day. What a way to run a war.' Alfred sighed and drunk more beer.

Noah eyed the Australian soldiers, men known for their bravery and friendliness, but also for the lack of respect to British officers and a tendency to gamble. The ones he'd encountered always made him laugh with something outrageous they said.

'Apparently,' James added, 'those two Aussies are farmers. They've vast properties so large it takes days to ride a horse from one boundary to another.'

'They'll be pulling his leg.' Sid chuckled.

James frowned. 'It doesn't seem so. Will has seen a map they keep with them, and one fellow has a photo of a shearing shed with thousands of sheep around it. The photographer stood on water tank twenty feet in the air and took the photograph. Will said it was impressive.'

'It is a big country,' Noah said, realising he'd drunk his second glass of beer while listening to James. He yawned again, weary. Weary of being singled out by Melville and weary of being in this war.

'Let's have a sing along!' Sid abruptly demanded. 'Get that fool off the piano unless he agrees to play something livelier than the grave-digging music he's playing, for God's sake!'

James bounded over to the piano player, who nervously pushed his glasses up his nose. 'Can you play something better, man?' James demanded.

'What like?'

'Anything! Something to sing to.'

As if possessed by another person, the nervous private suddenly began banging the keys in an upbeat tempo and the men recognised the song and started singing to 'It's a long way to Tipperary.'

Relaxing, Noah laughed as Alfred and James started dancing with each other and swinging themselves about like young lads. More soldiers got up and started clapping and stomping about.

Sid roared with laughter as Albie swept the madame from behind the bar out into the centre of the room and danced with her as though she was a queen.

The music drew in more crowds and Noah took a seat at the table with Sid, for once feeling light-hearted.

Noah wasn't sure when it happened, but suddenly the music stopped and the private playing the piano stared at the officer in the doorway.

Noah craned his neck to see who was there, and his spirits plummeted as Melville walked in with Sergeant Bourke behind him.

'So, this is what my men get up to when they have a pass for the night?' Melville stepped to the bar as the soldiers realised why the music had stopped.

Melville smiled grimly at the madame as she tided her hair and quickly came back behind the bar. 'A bottle of your finest wine, madame,' he said in perfect French.

He turned to the men. 'At ease, fellows, relax and enjoy your pass.' Then his gaze caught Noah's and he stiffened and walked to the table the Jackson brothers returned to.

As one, all the brothers and Will stood and saluted.

Melville saluted. 'Sit. Sit.' His eyes roamed over them all. 'You'll need all your energy for tomorrow men, for we are going on a training exercise at six hundred hours.'

'But we thought we were off duty, sir?' Alfred groaned as they took their seats.

'You are, but even so, we will be still be doing exercises each day. It wouldn't be right for my men to become lazy now, would it?' Melville smiled. 'And rumour has it that some of you had lighter kits last time we performed a training exercise, so in the morning I will be personally inspecting all kits before we start.' His gaze bored into Noah's. 'You especially, Jackson. I hear you had a lighter weight than the others.'

'You heard wrong, Lieutenant Melville,' Noah said, knowing the other man was lying through his teeth.

Melville leaned down closer and tipped Noah's glass of beer into his lap. 'Well, you'll be lighter by a pair of trousers now, won't you? Perhaps I'll place an extra ten-pound weight in your kit.'

Noah stiffened, his groin soaking wet with cold beer. Rage filled him, but he fought it back. 'If that pleases you, lieutenant.'

'It does, very much.'

'Bastard,' Alfred mumbled.

'What was that?' Melville straightened. 'Sergeant, what did that man say?'

Sergeant Bourke took a step forward. 'I didn't catch it, sir.'

'I said hurray, sir,' Will lied, lounging in his chair to take the heat off Alfred. 'I like a good training exercise.'

'Smarten yourself up, Beaumont,' Melville snapped, 'and I suggest you all stop drinking and get some sleep.'

'I believe we have a pass until ten o'clock, lieutenant,' Noah mumbled, every ounce of him hating the man who'd done his best to break him since training in England eighteen months ago.

'Don't play clever with me, Jackson. Your passes are revoked. Get out all of you.'

They stood, moaning under their breaths.

Noah stepped closer to Melville. 'I wanted to go to bed, anyway. I've my beautiful wife's letter to read,' he taunted.

'Noah.' Albie held Noah by the elbow.

Melville flinched. 'You don't deserve such a wife, Jackson.'

'No, I don't but she's mine and every day she gets bigger with my child growing in her belly.'

A dead light entered Melville's eyes. 'You'd best hope you survive this war then, hadn't you?'

'Oh, I intend to.'

'Ah, but strange things happen in battle, Jackson,' Melville warned.

Noah grinned. 'That they do, but I can assure you that should anything happen to me, my brothers will find the person responsible and put a bullet through their head.'

Melville blanched. 'Is that a threat?'

'No, not at all, Lieutenant Melville. It is merely a fact.'

Will slipped in between Noah and Melville. 'Lieutenant, my sister writes that Melville Manor has been taken over by the army as a small convalescent home. You must be pleased your home is being put to good use?' he said in a rush.

Taking a step back, Melville straightened his officer's cap. 'I am pleased, Beaumont. I'm also pleased your sister has taken an interest in my home.' He gave Noah a smug look.

'Well, the farm is supplying the vegetables for the house,' Will finished lamely.

'We must all do our bit, Beaumont.' Melville flicked one last glance at Noah and grabbed the bottle of wine from the counter and threw French notes down. He turned at the door. 'Six hundred hours. Be ready or you'll all be on a charge.'

* * *

IN THE LONG glass greenhouse behind the forcing sheds, Beth sat on a wooden stool planting lettuce seedlings into trays. She'd been up since dawn and already planted radishes and tomatoes into trays, and they sat in the sunshine streaming through the glass. The end of February was a busy time for early seed sowing to be ready for spring planting, but the rhubarb harvest needed to be finished first and with that done, she could now turn her mind to other tasks.

While Dad, Reggie and the hired lads worked in the fields, preparing the soil for summer planting, Beth enjoyed being in the glasshouse, which had always been in her mam's domain, but was now hers alone.

The warmth of the sunshine through the glass made her a little drowsy as the morning passed. Her large stomach made it awkward for her to sleep well, but feeling the baby kick beneath her ribs brought a smile to her face each time. The wonder of carrying Noah's baby gave her such joy. She couldn't wait to meet the little one. The new baby had also given Peggy a new lease on life, too. Although her cough still tormented her throughout the winter, she looked healthier than Beth had ever seen her and she was so pleased she'd been able to give Peggy a better life.

With the lettuce planted, she moved onto the onion seeds and sowed those into trays. She had many days ahead of sowing, but it was easy work she could do without breaking her back being bent over. She needed to get as much done as she could before the baby arrived in about eight weeks. Her list of jobs never seemed to diminish, but with the worst of the winter over and March fast approaching, now was the busiest time on the farm.

'Mrs Jackson.' Davey, one of the lads working on the farm came into the greenhouse.

'Yes?'

'Reggie told me to come and see you and ask if you had any jobs for me, as they don't need me in the fields at the moment as Snowy's thrown a shoe. Us lads are to come back here and help you.'

'Right, where are the others?'

'Coming now.'

Beth walked out with Davey to meet the four other lads, all ranging in age between fourteen and sixteen, as they came into the yard.

'Davey, you can clean out the nest boxes in the chicken shed and lay them with fresh straw. The chickens will start laying soon now spring is coming. Ollie and Wilf, you two can harvest the last of the leeks. You'll find them in the first two rows of the field on the other side of the barn. Richard and Tom, you two can ask Aunty Hilda or Peggy for some buckets of hot soapy water and wash down the outside of the greenhouse. I noticed the glass is mucky with mould from winter.'

With nods, the lads went off to do their tasks, while down at the bottom of the drive Beth watched Reggie lead Snowy through the gates. She walked down to him as he placed the extra harness into the barn.

'Is Snowy lame?' she asked in the doorway.

'No, just a loose shoe. I'll walk her over to Mick Ferguson's place and he'll put some new shoes on.' Reggie came back out and stroked Snowy's white nose.

'I've set the boys to work. I've plenty for them to do today.'

'Good. I thought you'd have jobs for them.'

'Where's Dad?' She walked with Reggie, leading Snowy back down to the gates.

'Still in the field cleaning out a bit of the ditch that's clogging up with muck from last week's rain.'

Beth glanced up the lane as the postman rode his bicycle down from the village towards them.

'I'll be off then.' Reggie clicked his tongue for Snowy to walk on, passing the postman who slowed to a stop and handled Beth a bundle of post.

'Thank you.' She smiled and he peddled away.

Staying by the gate, Beth sorted through the mail, groaning at the amount of mail addressed to her dad and which she'd have to deal with. The last envelope was bluff coloured, and her heart dropped alarmingly. It was from the War Office and address to her dad.

It could only be about Will.

A trickle of fear ran over her skin and she shivered in the weak February sun. In the distance she could make out her dad digging at the edge of a field where the drain ran between the largest of the rhubarb fields.

Should she go to him or wait for him to come to the house? Would he want to read whatever was inside the envelope while out in the mud, or inside sitting at the kitchen table?

Beth didn't know what to do. The baby kicked as though spurring her on to make a decision.

Swiftly, she walked back up the drive around to the back of the house.

Peggy, bent over in the kitchen herb garden, straightened as she came down the path. 'I've put the kettle on, love.' Peggy paused. 'What is it?'

'A telegram for Dad. It's Will...'

'Oh, love. Come inside.'

In the kitchen, Aunty Hilda sat at the table mixing the batter of a sponge cake. 'Beth, your boots!' She frowned, then seeing

Beth's expression, she dropped the wooden spoon, spraying batter over the tablecloth.

'It's for Dad.' Beth placed the bundle of post on the table except the buff envelope.

'Right...' Aunty Hilda stared at the offending envelope Beth held. 'You'd best take it to him.'

'Or wait for him to come inside?'

'He might not be in for hours. He's been taking to walking the lanes and fields with Patch inspecting the crops.'

Beth bit her lip, undecided. 'I'll go to him then, shall I?'

Aunty Hilda nodded.

'Will might be wounded, that's all,' Peggy quickly spoke. 'Like Jane's husband, Alfie. Nothing serious. Alfie was back with his unit within two weeks, Jane said.'

A knock on the kitchen door made them jump. Davey stood there.

'What is it, lad?' Peggy asked sharper than needed, which started a bout of coughing.

'I've brought the eggs...' He held out two eggs in each hand. 'I didn't want them to get broken as I cleaned out the boxes. Looks like they've started laying again.'

'Put them in the scullery, please,' Beth told him.

'Davey,' Aunty Hilda stopped him from leaving. 'Go and tell Mr Beaumont that he's needed in the house. Hurry now.' Aunty Hilda looked at Beth. 'Your dad needs to read it here, with us, just in case...'

Feeling light-headed, Beth slumped into a chair. 'Let him only be wounded, please,' she whispered. The thought of Will being killed made her breath short. The baby kicked again, and she rubbed her stomach as though to soothe it. How would they cope if Will was taken from them also?

No one spoke or moved until Rob Beaumont came into the house with Patch trailing at his heels. 'Is the baby coming?' he asked, slightly out of breath, staring at Beth. 'Have your pains started? Do you need the midwife?'

'No.' She held out the envelope to him.

He stepped back in alarm, his eyes widening in horror. 'No...'

'Please read it, Rob,' Aunty Hilda begged. 'The unknown is too frightening.'

'I can't.' He shook his head. 'I can't.'

'Beth, give it to me.' Peggy held out her hand and Beth gladly gave her the ugly envelope and all it contained.

For several moments no one moved or spoke as Peggy read the note. 'Will has been reported as taken by the enemy as a prisoner of war.'

Beth let out the air trapped in her lungs. 'Prisoner. He's alive!'

CHAPTER 13

'Write again!'

Beth took a deep breath and faced her dad in the front sitting room. 'There is no point, Dad. For the past week I've written every day to the War Office, to Will's commanding officer, Lieutenant-Colonel Radley, and to the Red Cross. They have no more information other than what we already know from Lieutenant Colonel Radley. Will was taken while during a difficult battle near Ypres, along with four other men. The Red Cross are doing all they can to gather information. They are in communication with the other side and are trying to find out about Will and let us know.'

'It's not enough! Why hasn't Noah written? He might know what actually happened.'

Tired, Beth rubbed her stomach where the baby lay in an uncomfortable position. 'I don't know, Dad. Do you not think I want to hear from him, too, or Peggy does? We've had no letters all week. We're worried sick!' She swallowed back the emotion building, desperate not to cry. A week without any letters from anyone caused such turmoil within the family after Will's capture. Usually not a day went by without some letter or postcard from one of the lads over there, and to receive nothing wore on their nerves.

'I ask you to write again, Beth,' he pleaded.

She closed her eyes at the look of utter devastation on his face. His skin had turned as grey as his hair and in the week since that awful missive arrived, he'd barely eaten or slept. 'Yes, Dad. I'll write again.'

'To all of them. Ask the Red Cross if they know of other organisations we can contact. Write to the Queen Mary at Buckingham Palace, she's been known to be sympathetic to families wanting information. King George has been reported in saying she is overrun with letters begging for help. She might help us, too.'

'I will.' She turned on the chair and took another piece of paper from the desk's drawer. How was she ever to get her other jobs done when her dad wanted her chained to the desk writing useless letters all day? Write to the Queen Mary indeed. As if that would work?

'The post!' The cry came from outside the window where Reggie had the lads weeding the flower gardens and turning the soil over to plant more vegetables.

'Post!' Dad dithered on the spot. 'Go out and get it, Beth.'

'Dad, Reggie will bring it in or one of the lads will do it,' she snapped. Her dad forgot that she was not as fast as she once was. Sometimes he forgot altogether that she was heavy with child and kept her up late each night with demands to write many letters, to scour the newspapers for any hint of prisoner of wars lists.

Peggy came in, followed closely by Aunty Hilda. Peggy held two letters. 'One from Noah for you, love, and I've got one from James.'

'Open them!' Dad urged. 'Quickly now!'

Giving her dad a furious look, Beth opened Noah's letter and read it out loud.

. . .

MARCH 3ᴿᴰ 1916.

Dearest darling,

Just a brief note to let you know I am in good health. We've been in several battles and well, the toll has been high. By now you'll know that Will was taken prisoner, at least we hope that is what happened.

BETH LOOKED up at her dad and what little colour he had drained from his face.

'Noah thinks he's dead?' Dad whispered.

'Let her read, Rob!' Aunty Hilda cried.

MY DARLING, I wish I could be more certain. This morning when we came out of the front line for a rest, I was given your letter dated yesterday. I know you must be worried. I am, too. Will was with another group of men ahead of me as we made our way through a small wood. The enemy ambushed us. We fought gallantly but had to retreat or be wiped out. I lost sight of Will and the leading group. Some were cut down that we know of, but reports of prisoners being taken seem to be true.

Later, we proceeded back to the wood after the artillery had been let loose on it. Nothing much remained, but we were able to claim some of the bodies of our men. Will wasn't among them. A stretcher-bearer I spoke to said when he went out to retrieve the wounded and dead, he'd seen British soldiers walking with their hands on their heads behind enemy trenches. We all pray Will was one of them.

I hope this gives you some small hope and peace of mind. If I hear more information, I'll let you know as soon as I can. Unfortunately for us, we seem to be in a hot spot at the moment.

I hope you are doing well and as always you have all of my love.

Noah.

. . .

BETH STARED down at the written words. Her beloved sounded tired.

'Read your letter, Peggy.' Dad's dull voice filled the room.

'Rob,' Aunty Hilda clenched her fists, 'that is Peggy's business.'

'It's all right, Hilda.' Peggy held up her hand. 'I don't mind reading it to you.'

Peggy gave a small cough and opened James's letter.

DEAR MAM. I hope you're all right. I am fine at the moment, though I sprained my ankle a bit in the last battle as we retreated. We've been having it rough lately.

All your sons are well as of writing this letter. We are in a support trench waiting to go back up soon. Will Beaumont has been taken prisoner or killed, we don't know which and are waiting more news. If Will has been taken prisoner, then he is lucky to be out of it. I'm thoroughly sick of war and fighting and can't wait to be home.

Can you send another pair of socks, please? I've holes in both my pairs and some toffee if you can afford it.

Your loving son, James.

PEGGY FOLDED the letter back into the envelope.

Beth watched the emotions play on her dad's face. 'As a prisoner he's safe from being killed in battle, Dad.'

The look he gave her was of utter contempt. 'What do you know? You know nothing, girl. As a prisoner of the Germans, they could shoot him at any time. If he's wounded, will they tend to him or let him suffer and die? What is he to them but a mouth to feed? They are starving over there, apparently. The newspapers report that the Germans don't feed prisoners. The Red Cross have reported them for their harsh conditions and treatments. Will isn't important to them. He holds no value. He's not an officer, so he'll not be treated well. They can shoot prisoners as easily as snapping their fingers. Will is no more safer with them than he was in a battle! He's as good as dead!'

'Dad, we have to hope!' Beth gave into her anger. 'We have to believe he is all right.'

'I don't believe in anything any more and you're foolish to do so!' Her dad gave a mocking laugh.

'Rob,' Aunty Hilda reprimanded.

'What was it all for? What was all my years of hard work on this farm for when both my boys are dead?' Head down, he left the room.

Seated at the desk, Beth felt battered by her dad's harsh words. 'Will isn't dead.'

'Take no notice of him, lass.' Aunty Hilda came to her and patted her cheek tenderly. 'He's out of his mind with worry. He doesn't mean to speak so nasty to you.'

Beth nodded. 'I'll write some more letters to the War Office and Lieutenant Colonel Radley asking for any additional information.'

'I'll put the kettle on.' Aunty Hilda kissed the top of Beth's head.

Once she'd left the room, Peggy stepped closer to where Beth sat. 'You all right, love?'

'Oh, Peggy. I wish this war would end.'

'Me, too, love. Me, too.'

'Both Noah and James sound like they've been through it lately.'

'Aye, well, although James writes about all the times they play football and cards and the training exercises they do when not in the trenches, I can tell it's wearing them down a bit. It's not all laughs as he often makes it out to be.'

'And James can always find the fun in any situation.'

'That he can.' Peggy smiled. 'He's a scamp and no mistake.'

'Will is strong. I'm certain he'll survive the German camp.'

'He will. We know the Germans don't treat the prisoners as well as the allies do theirs, but they wouldn't shoot them for no reason, surely?'

A gunshot sounded and Beth frowned. 'Those lads aren't out rabbiting, are they? I've told them not to. Old Mr Barnsdale at the bottom of the lane said they shot at his cat the other day, though they denied it. Silly fools.'

Peggy looked out of the window. 'They're meant to be weeding the garden beds and fixing a hole in the roof of the larger forcing shed.'

Sighing, Beth rose from the chair. 'I'd best go and see what they are up to. I haven't time for this.'

Walking into the kitchen, Beth was about to speak to Aunty Hilda when Davey came racing in, his face white, eyes large.

'What is it now, lad?' Aunty Hilda snapped. 'Who is firing that gun? Was it Tom? I'll tan his backside for him as big as he is!'

'There's been an accident. You're to come quickly. Tom's gone for the doctor!'

'Gracious, has one of you fallen off the ladder or something?' Aunty Hilda tutted. 'You lads will be the death of me.'

'I'll go,' Beth said.

'No!' Davey screeched. 'Reggie said you're not to come.'

'I'm having a child, I'm not an invalid or squeamish.'

'I'll go,' Peggy said, shaking her head. 'I'll take the bandage box out with me. Really, those lads would get a lot more done if they didn't mess about so much.'

From a cupboard in the Welsh dresser, Beth took the tin box that held bandages, small scissors and a bottle of iodine and gave it to Peggy as she left the kitchen.

'I'll heat the irons,' Beth said. 'There's a mountain of ironing to be done. Do you need use of the table for a while?'

Aunty Hilda stirred the mutton and vegetable stew in a large pot on the range. 'No, I've got this stew on and the dumplings are made. I was saying to Peggy earlier that I'm running low on wool again.'

'I'll get you some tomorrow when I go into town. I need to see Leah anyway and give her the last crates of cauliflower and cabbages. The lads' first job in the morning when they arrive is to pick the daffodils in the orchards. The snowdrops are finished but the daffs are flowering well. We should get many bunches this year to sell on the stall.' Beth placed the irons on the range to heat up.

Aunty Hilda placed a board on the table and then a cloth over it for Beth to iron on. 'I might ask Rob or Reggie to see if they can get us a pheasant from the butcher. We've not had pheasant for a month or so.'

'I know we are having mutton tonight, but I fancied some lamb the other day, but it's too soon for lamb,' Beth said, laying out a white blouse on the table. 'Oh, the ribbon on this blouse has frayed.'

Peggy staggered back into the kitchen, her face the colour of putty.

Beth looked up from the blouse. 'Peggy?'

Tears streamed down the other woman's cheeks. 'Oh, love…'

'Good God, what's happened?' Aunty Hilda stared.

'Peggy?' Beth couldn't move.

'It's your dad, love.' Peggy cried harder. 'He's shot himself, love. He's dead.'

Beth felt herself slip sideways before the world went black.

ON A DULL GREY MARCH DAY, Beth walked down the lane with Patch at her heels, leaving the house and its occupants of mourners. She was tired of conversation, of hearing people's sincere condolences and telling her what a kind and good man Rob Beaumont had been.

That morning St Anne's Church in the village had been over-flowing with friends and acquaintances. Rob Beaumont had known so many people, and those people had come in droves to pay their respects. Many had come to the house after the funeral, to drink tea and eat fruit cake.

After an hour, Beth had let Joanna see to them, and slipped away, needing air, needing somewhere to go before she screamed out her anger.

She carefully made her way down the bank to the edge of the beck, the one place she loved to be. The beck held happy child-hood memories of her and Jane paddling and enjoying picnics, talking of pretty dresses and what it would feel like to be kissed by a young man. Such innocent summer days.

While Patch sniffed in the grass, hunting rabbits, Beth gently eased herself down onto the grass and watched the water flowing over the rocks.

She recalled the day Noah first joined them on a picnic, and how she'd been in awe of such a good-looking man wanting to spend time with her. Then their lovely picnic had been spoilt by Louis Melville and his damn dog that bit Noah and Patch. How angry she'd been then, just as she was now.

A hot fury burned through her with such intensity it scared her. Its power blinded her to the swallows swooping and diving above her head and deafened her to the thrushes singing in the hawthorn hedge bordering the lane and which was just showing new leaf. The awakening of spring was lost to her today.

Instead, she wanted to rage at the selfishness of her dad.

Hearing friends talk of him as a wonderful man drove her nearly insane. Rob Beaumont, a leader in the farming commu-nity, a successful farmer, a man to admire and aspire to. That's what they said.

Beth thought him to be a coward.

The happy loving dad she grew up with died the day her mam

and Ronnie drowned. The man that remained had been a stranger.

'I knew you'd be here,' Jane said, coming down the bank. 'Though why you'd want to come outside on a such a cool day is anyone's guess.'

Patch ran up to Jane and licked her hand before dashing back into the bushes near the water.

'I couldn't stay there.'

Jane plucked a piece of grass. 'I don't blame you. Too many people. Joanna and Aunty Hilda are holding the fort well enough. Peggy is in charge of Ivy and Freddie with help from the other women there, so I thought to come and find you.'

Beth gave her a small smile.

'This also arrived.' Jane handed her a letter as she sat on the grass. She'd left her black hat at the house and her red hair shone brightly.

Letting out a deep sigh, Beth opened it and read the few lines from the Red Cross, before screwing up the letter in her hand.

'What does it say?'

Beth stared across the fields. 'It's been confirmed that Private William Beaumont is listed as a German prisoner. More information to come.'

'So, Will isn't dead as your dad thought,' Jane whispered.

'He was never dead. My dad was too selfish to wait and find out.'

'Your dad was in pain, Beth.'

'He believed the worst without waiting to find out the truth.'

'I think he thought the idea of Will being dead was too terrible to live with, especially after losing your mam and Ronnie.'

'I lost them, too.'

'That's different,' Jane defended.

'How so?' Beth asked, anger bubbling.

'Will being taken only a month after the first anniversary of their deaths. It's going to make him think there's nothing to live for.'

'But there is! There's me and Joanna and Ivy and my new baby! We matter, don't we?'

'He wasn't thinking straight.'

'Oh, don't give me that, Jane. I'm sick to death of hearing it. I lost my mam and brother, as did Joanna, as did Will. Have we gone to pieces?'

'That was his wife and his child. It's different.'

'Be quiet, for God's sake.'

'I know you're angry.'

'I have a right to be!' Beth fumed.

'You do, yes, I agree. But think of the baby.'

'A baby my *dad* will never get to see because he chose to leave us!'

'Beth...'

'Don't, Jane. Words are useless.' Struggling to stand with her round stomach, Jane quickly helped her up.

'What are you going to do now?' Jane asked as they walked back up the lane.

'I have to keep the farm going for Will. He needs something to come home to, doesn't he?'

When they returned to the farm, the funeral guests had gone. Reggie came out of the house as Beth walked down the path between the herb gardens.

'Ah, you're back,' he said, dressed smartly in his best suit. 'I'll feed Snowy, check the sheds and then be off home. I'll be back at six in the morning.'

'Thank you, Reggie.' Beth placed her hand on his arm. 'I feel I'm going to depend on you a great deal in the future.'

His expression sad, he nodded. 'Well, lass, I'm always here, aren't I? This is my second home and you're all my family. Rob was like a brother as well as my boss. I've known him since we were kids.' He glanced away. 'I don't understand why he'd do such a thing...'

'None of us do.'

'Anyway, we'll talk about the future tomorrow. Don't worry, we'll manage.' He walked away, shoulders slumped, and Beth knew how devastated he was about her dad. He had worked for Rob Beaumont before Beth was born, they'd worked side by side for over twenty-odd years. Reggie would feel the loss as much as the family.

Inside the warm kitchen, Aunty Hilda sat at the table, still laden with food. She held Ivy on her knee opposite Joanna while Peggy stood adding coal to the fire and Freddy was asleep in his pram.

'What was that letter Jane gave to you?' Aunty Hilda asked, looking old in her severe black dress. Her wrinkles seemed to have doubled within a year, and she moved much slower now.

'Will has been recognised as a prisoner of war. The Red Cross have had confirmation.'

'Poor Will,' Joanna murmured, her face chalk white in contrast to the black mourning she wore.

Beth hated seeing everyone in black, herself included.

'I'll get away home, Beth, before this one wakes up,' Jane said, wheeling the pram to the door. She gave Beth a kiss on the cheek. 'You know where I am if you need me.'

'Thank you.' Beth hugged her friend and watched them leave before sitting at the table.

Joanna reached out and grasped Beth's hand, her eyes red from weeping. 'I might stay the night.'

'Yes, I'd like that,' Beth answered and smiled her thanks as Peggy placed a cup of tea before her.

'Are you hungry, love?' Peggy asked, going back to the range.

'No, not really. Tea is enough, thank you. I've the accounts to work on. I might have something a bit later.'

'Can't the accounts wait?' Joanna frowned. 'Today isn't the day for accounts.'

'Will the bills wait to be paid? I think not.'

Aunty Hilda sighed deeply. 'I'll never forgive Rob. I've loved that man like a son ever since your mam married him and more so when he said I could live here when I became a widow, but to do this!' Aunty Hilda shook her head, emotion in her eyes. 'It's a betrayal.'

'Don't…' Joanna whispered.

'Why shouldn't she?' Beth defended. 'Aunty Hilda is right. He's betrayed all of us. He was our dad and was meant to look after us. Instead, he took the easy way out.'

'How could that have been easy?' Joanna shouted. 'He made a decision to take his life. None of that would have been easy. He must have been considering it for months, probably since Mam died.'

'Yes, maybe he'd been thinking about it,' Beth shouted back, 'but not once in all that time did he come to any of us and tell us how he was feeling. And it wasn't as if I didn't ask!'

'He wasn't like that and you know it. Dad wouldn't burden us with his grief.'

'But he *did*! Every day I saw it, *we* lived it, and still he'd not speak about it.' Beth sucked in a breath. Her chin wobbled as tears threatened. 'Not once did he say he couldn't go on. If he had… If he had, then maybe I could have helped him somehow, but he never gave me the chance.'

'It wasn't his way,' Joanna whispered.

'No?' Beth's sarcastic tone hid the hurt. 'Well, his way has left us in a mess, hasn't it? On top of everything else *I've* got to run the farm now. Unless you want to do it?'

'I don't know how. He taught you, not me.' Joanna sniffed. 'He didn't confide in me at all about anything. In the year since Mam and Ronnie died, not once has he come to my house. I only saw him if I came here and even then, he hardly spoke more than a few words.' Joanna looked at Beth. 'I am the eldest. Yet, it was you he trusted.'

The weight of the responsibility felt heavy on Beth's shoulders. She pushed back the chair and stood, feeling tired and sick at heart. 'Then I'd better get on with it.'

CHAPTER 14

The greenhouse and yard was a hive of activity as Beth supervised the lads carrying out trays of onions to be planted in the field behind the orchard. On Reggie's advice, Beth hired a few more village lads to help with the planting of the vegetables and they were in the fields with Reggie learning how to sow potatoes in straight lines.

March had ended as a cold and wet month, delaying much of the work that needed to be done. Usually they counted on a warmer March to get a head start on the planting, but heavy rain prevented the normal work and put them behind. Beth used the time to sow seeds in the greenhouse.

Beth informed Leah that the stall would be closed over Easter and then only opened two days a week selling what flowers had opened in the garden and the fast growing salad crops from the greenhouse.

Easter had come and gone without much celebration in the house. Beth and Peggy had gone to the church services, but being heavily pregnant Beth had made the excuse to not attend the village Easter parade. With her time taken up by the farm, she didn't have the energy to socialise as she'd done in the past.

Her dad used to call April the 'hungry time' when the farm was in a busy state of planting but not much harvesting as the winter crops were finished and the new crops not yet ready. Until the new vegetables had grown enough to be harvested and sold on the stall, Leah worked the rest of the weekdays at the farm.

Beth was glad of Leah's company, for her friend worked hard and efficiently and kept the lads in line. With the baby due in a few weeks, Beth knew Leah could be counted on to help Reggie with all the tasks.

As food prices rose and the war didn't look as though it was to end soon, Beth worried about keeping the farm profitable. Demands from the government to increase food production combined with the lack of skilled labour gave her many sleepless nights. The village lads although useful were not skilled farm labourers and rarely turned up if something else proved more exciting to do. Frequently Reggie came into the kitchen cursing under his breath at the lads for disappearing to play football or go fishing. The pull of earning higher wages in munitions factories or down the pits also became a challenge for Beth to keep them.

She kept most of her concerns from Noah, not wanting to worry him. She wrote to him every second day, long letters of Wrenthorpe gossip or Wakefield news. She filled pages of how the munitions factories were working shifts around the clock to meet demand, how conscription had taken more men and some businesses had closed in town. How Lofthouse Park Internment Camp was rapidly expanding and many of the locals felt the wealthy German nationals interred there were living a life of luxury compared to the poorer people of the area.

She gave Noah as much news as she could, hoping it would help him feel connected to home. Of herself she said very little but always assured him she was well and missing him. The truth that she barely slept and apart from her stomach she was skin and bone through work and worry would only cause him anxiety. How could she burden him with her worries when he lived in such unsafe conditions?

'That's the last of the trays, Mrs Jackson,' Davy said, breaking into her thoughts.

'Excellent. The others can plant out the onions, but I have another job for you.' Beth walked out of the greenhouse with him, rubbing her back, trying to lessen the ache that throbbed at the base of her spine. 'Have the old bales of straw in the barn loft taken over to the strawberry field that was hoed yesterday. You know how to put the straw around each plant, don't you?'

'Yes, Reggie showed me how to do it.' His mop of blonde hair fell over his eyes.

'Good. I want that smaller field finished by the end of the day, so no messing about. Take someone to help you. And where's your hat?'

'I lost it, Mrs Jackson.' Davy ran off.

Leah came out of the barn as Davy ran in. 'Beth, I've stitched the hessian sacks that had holes in them and piled them in the corner. What's next?'

'Could you finish the sowing of the late summer peas, please? I've the trays ready in the greenhouse and the seeds are in a marked bucket on one of the tables. I'll join you in a minute.'

'Why don't you have a rest? You've been on your feet since dawn.' Leah gave her a gentle smile. 'We can manage without you for an hour or two, you know.'

'I know you can, but there's so much to do.' Beth rubbed her back again. 'The cucumbers and tomato seedlings need watering and tying to stakes. I've placed the bean trays on the bottom table on the left-hand side of the greenhouse and kept the window closed to keep it warm, and the carrot seedlings need thinning out, too.'

'Beth,' Peggy called her from the herb garden, waving a piece of paper.

Leah put her hand on Beth's arm. 'Me and the lads will see to it. Go sit down for a bit. You're looking dark under the eyes. Have a rest. I insist.' Leah headed up the yard before Beth could protest.

'What is it?' Beth walked over to Peggy.

'It's from Melville House. An order of vegetables.'

Frowning, Beth read the list. 'We don't have all of this.'

'Well, we'll just have to give them what we do have. Hilda is having a nap and I'm cracking on with the rabbit pies to feed this lot.'

'I'll take this order over on the bicycle.'

'What?' Peggy's eyes widened in surprise. 'You'll do no such thing. Get one of the lads to do it.'

'They are busy, and Reggie has Snowy in the fields. I can ride the bicycle over.'

'Are you mad? You're ready to drop with a baby!'

Beth laughed at her shocked face. 'I'll be fine. I'm not due for weeks yet. And since Reggie built the little trailer for the bicycle, it's much easier to ride. It has four wheels now instead of two, making it completely stable. Though Lord knows how Will is going to react when he eventually sees it. His old bike is now a vegetable transport machine.'

'Please, Beth. We'll get someone else to ride the thing, I beg you.' Peggy folded her arms over her thin chest. 'I'll worry to death over you on that.'

'I can do it. Besides, there's no one else.' Beth remained determined. 'I'll take it slow and easy. It'll be good exercise for me, and I'll be out in the fresh air.'

'You have plenty of exercise running this farm, and fresh air to boot. I'm not happy about this. I'll find Davey.'

'Good heavens, no, not Davey. He's not responsible enough to take a delivery yet. He'll end up spending the day riding around the lanes visiting his friends. If one of them asks him to play, he'll be off that bicycle in a flash. We can't afford to lose the manor's custom. They always pay on time and have repeat orders.'

'I don't want you riding that thing,' Peggy objected. 'I'll go instead.'

Beth grinned. 'You've never been on a bicycle in your life. I promise I'll take it steady. Nice and slow.'

'You're a stubborn one, that's for sure.' Peggy shook her head.

Walking back into the barn, Beth wheeled out the bicycle from where it stood in one of the old horse stalls. Reggie's idea to add a trailer on the back for ease of carrying produce on short journeys to the village or to other farms was genius. Beth often had one of the lads on it to go on errands into the village, but she'd not ridden it herself yet.

In the wooden sided trailer, she placed a sack of potatoes, wincing as her back spasmed as she lifted the heavy sack.

At the far end of the barn was the root cellar, the below ground wood-panelled cellar which stored all the vegetables. The coldness of the cellar hit her as she opened the door. At the top of the stairs, a shelf held matches and a lap. Once lit, the lamp shone enough light for Beth to carefully make her way down the stairs to the racks and straw-packed crates of vegetables. It took her several trips, but finally she had most of the list ticked off and shut the cellar door.

The bicycle trailer was full. Along with the potatoes she'd added a net of onions, turnips, bunches of rhubarb, a bag of Brussel sprouts, beetroots, parsnips and the last two cauliflowers.

Retying her straw hat under her chin so it didn't blow off as she rode, she hitched her skirts up a little and mounted the bicycle. She pedalled out of the barn and down the drive as the sun poked out between grey clouds.

Pedalling down the lane, she waved to Reggie and the lads in the field, feeling happy as the breeze swept past her cheeks. She'd not ridden Will's bicycle since before she was pregnant and had forgotten the feel of freedom it gave her. With the trailer giving it more stability, she cheerfully made her way along the lane, taking the long way around, so as not to have to peddle up the hill into Wrenthorpe. Instead, she headed along Beck Bottom Road towards Kirkhamgate.

Waving to farmers and children she passed, she soon felt out of breath and slowed her pedalling. The pain in her back grew sharper with each turn of the wheels. The road to Kirkhamgate and Melville Manor seemed to stretch forever. What had possessed her to hop on a bicycle when she was due to give birth in a few weeks?

Her progress slowed further, and she cursed her stupid stubbornness. The sensible thing to have done would have been to get someone else to take the delivery. Why had she insisted? Had she been that eager to get away from the farm and all its problems and memories for a few scant hours? She was a fool.

At last she reached the tall iron gates at the beginning of the drive to the manor. Puffing, she climbed down from the seat and holding the handle bars pushed the bicycle up the gravel drive, her legs as wobbly as jelly.

Since being turned into a convalescence home some months ago, Mrs Handry, the manor's cook, had placed an order with Beaumont Farm for a supply of vegetables every week. At the time, her dad had wondered why they'd now buy vegetables from them when they had their own garden, but they soon learned that all the manor's male staff had enlisted, leaving no one to work in the gardens except for one old head gardener brought out of retirement.

At first, Beth had been wary of any dealings with Melville Manor, but knowing Louis wasn't at home and the manor was now under the control of the army and used as a place for soldiers to recuperate after being wounded, she felt churlish to refuse their orders. Besides, it was an extra income, and she couldn't afford to refuse money on principle. She was helping wounded soldiers, and it had nothing to do with Louis.

The grounds looked the same, albeit a little untidier. The fountain was green with mould and there was no sign of the peacock that usually strutted the lawns. A small blue motor car parked out the front of the wide doors stood next to a motor ambulance. She could faintly hear a piano being played, but other than that the manor and grounds were quiet.

Beth wheeled the bicycle around to the back of the house to the staff and tradesmen entrance and knocked on the green door, rubbing her back as she did so. The service courtyard seemed deserted. Beth thought to see soldiers strolling the park or sitting out for fresh air, but today everyone seemed to be indoors.

A young woman answered the door with a cheeky smile. She glanced behind Beth at the vegetables in the little trailer. 'You're from Beaumont Farm?'

'I am. I'm Mrs Jackson.'

'Come away in, Mrs Jackson.'

Entering a long narrow scullery, Beth turned right into a large room with a vaulted ceiling criss-crossed with darkened beams. A wide wooden table dominated the centre of the room, and along the far wall a black range hosted a collection of copper pots and pans. A fire glowed in an enclave on another wall where another young woman was turning a spit to roast several chickens.

'Would you like a cup of tea, Mrs Jackson?' Mrs Handry, the manor's head cook and a woman well into her sixties asked, coming into the room from a side door, which Beth took to be a larder. She carried a small marble slab full of ham slices and her eyes grew wide as she noticed Beth's round stomach.

'Thank you, Mrs Handry, that would be most kind.' Beth grimaced as a stitch throbbed in her side. She'd known of the head cook for some years, but they'd never spoken. Mrs Handry was famous for winning ribbons at the fairs for her delicate and tasty baking.

'Nora, bring in those vegetables,' Mrs Handry instructed,

spooning tea leaves into a white porcelain teapot before adding boiling water. 'I expected Reggie to bring the delivery, as he usually does. He often stops for a natter with me. I miss having a chat to familiar faces. It's not the same here now Mr Staines and the other men have gone.'

'Reggie will probably come next time. We're busy on the farm and I thought to have a ride out myself, but I wished I hadn't now. I've not ridden a bicycle in a long while. It's taken the wind from me.'

'I'm not surprised in your condition. Sit down and have a rest. When are due?'

Beth pulled out a chair from the table and gingerly sat down. She ached all over. 'Oh, not for three weeks or so.'

'Really? You're not very big. My sister was the size of an elephant with each one of hers and she had five.' Mrs Handry took a square tin from a shelf and opened it. 'Shortbread?'

'Thank you.' Beth's hand shook as she accepted the cup and saucer. The ride had exhausted her. She'd have a long walk back wheeling the bicycle, for she didn't think she could ride it.

'Are you all right, Mrs Jackson?' Mrs Handry asked. 'You've gone a bit pale.'

'I think I've made a mistake riding here.' Beth felt foolish but overriding that was the pain in her back which spasmed.

'Well, you stay there and rest a while. You're welcome to take a breather here if you don't mind us working around you.' Mrs Handry turned to the woman turning the spit. 'Jennie, stir that white sauce.'

'Thank you. A few minutes will see me right again,' Beth said with more confidence than she felt. 'I was silly not to send a lad. My stubbornness and independence has always got me into trouble.'

'Yes, I've heard a few tales about you and your wild streak, and I remember the day Master Louis brought you here in the storm. We all wondered what would come of it, but soon after he was sent for by his father…'

Beth remembered coming here all too clearly, of Louis trying to impress her with the grandness of the manor. He'd wanted to marry her, make her mistress of Melville Manor, and she'd run from him.

'But you're a married woman about to have a baby and all that nonsense should be in the past,' Mrs Handry declared.

Beth huffed. 'You'd think so, wouldn't you?'

'How's your husband doing over there in France?' Mrs Handry asked.

'As good as can be, I suppose. He writes often.'

'I get a letter each week from Mr Staines, and he sometimes mentions the men from the area.'

'How is he? I saw him before he enlisted.'

'He's doing all right. I suppose it's something they have to get used to, isn't it?' Mrs Handry sat opposite and ate a shortbread biscuit. 'I hear from Master Melville quite often, as he knew he was my favourite ever since he was a boy. His sister in London sends the odd letter to make sure we are coping now the army are in residence, but she never visits now.'

'How is it with the army lodging here?'

'Different, but not too bad. The doctor is Captain Scott, a lovely older man from Kent and as kind as can be. He was in the Boer War, you know? One or two of the nurses can be a little demanding, but he's not. To be honest, I'm glad they are here to keep us busy. I'd be bored senseless if the house was closed up. We had a taste of it when Master Louis left, and I didn't like it. Nothing to do and I enjoy being active.'

'How many wounded soldiers do you have here?' Beth nibbled at the shortbread but wasn't particularly hungry. The pain in her back grew worse, although she tried not to show it.

'Twelve at the moment, but the numbers change weekly. The most we've had is twenty-one, and the other week we only had four. They leave here when they're healed and go home for a spell before back to their units. Every man has always come and said thank you to me and the girls before they left. I cry every time.' Mrs Handry shook her head sadly. 'Those brave men going back over there after being wounded. Bless them all.'

'At least for a time they are well looked after being here and eating your delicious food.'

Mrs Handry beamed at the compliment and sipped her tea. 'The soldiers do seem to like my food and being here. After all, it would be paradise in comparison to the battlefields. I'm pleased we can do our little bit for the war effort. I never expected we'd be chosen to care for convalescing soldiers. It was a surprise when Master Louis wrote and told us that the army wanted the house. His father, Sir Melville, knew some officials in the war office and offered the house immediately. Still, it took weeks for us to get the house in order. Furniture had to be stored away and with all the manor's men enlisting, we had to rely on scout lads from the village to help until the nurses came and started cleaning.'

Nora brought in the last of the vegetables. 'That's a handy little transport you've got there, Mrs Jackson. We should get one, Mrs Handry. It'd come in useful when running errands.'

'Don't be daft, Nora.' Mrs Handry rolled her eyes at the girl. 'A bicycle indeed.'

Beth went to speak when suddenly a gush of water spurted between her legs and over the chair. 'Oh!' she gasped in horror. She had wet herself.

Mrs Handry jumped up quickly for someone of her age. 'Ye gods, lass.'

'I am so very sorry. I don't know what's happened.' Beth tried to stand, only to cry out as a pain gripped her stomach.

'Your waters have broken!' Mrs Handry looked aghast as though Beth had done it on purpose.

'No. They can't have. It's not time.' Appalled and frightened, Beth stared at the older woman. 'I've got to get home.'

'I'll call for Captain Scott. He has a motor car. Nora! Go and fetch Captain Scott.'

'Thank you.' Beth winced as another pain gripped her. She bent over double, holding onto the edge of the table. A throbbing pressure pushed down between her legs and she groaned, not comprehending what was happening.

The blue baize door leading to the principal part of the house opened and an officer walked in. 'Mrs Handry! I'm home. Isn't this a surprise?'

'Master Louis!' Mrs Handry cried in alarm. 'Oh, my heavens! I wasn't expecting you. I received no word.'

'Beth?'

Panting, fighting to control the pain, Beth glanced up, dazed. It took a moment for her to realise that it really was Louis Melville standing before her. His shock was as great as her own.

'Good God. What is happening?' Louis demanded, coming quickly to Beth's side.

'Mrs Jackson's waters have broken. She's in labour.' Mrs Handry dithered on the spot. 'I didn't know you were due home, Master Louis. Forgive me for not being prepared. Are you home long?'

'I'll explain later. Now isn't the time. We must help poor Beth.' He placed a hand on Beth's shoulder, a look of pity on his thin face.

Beth had a sudden thought. 'If you're home does that mean Noah is, too? You're his officer. Are they all home?' Her heart hammered at the prospect of Noah being at the farm right now. She had to get to him.

'No. I'm sorry. They are still in France.' Melville held out his hand but dropped it to his side. 'I've been in London on officer training and also for private business. But come, sit down.'

The news that Noah wasn't home crumpled Beth into the

chair. All she wanted at that moment was Noah. 'I must get home,' she whispered, fighting the urge to moan loudly as another pain came.

Melville squatted down in front of her. 'I'll take you home. I'll look after you.'

She didn't want Melville's help. She wanted Noah. The pain increased. Why was this happening so quickly?

'Beth, just this once, trust me, please. I'll do whatever you want me to.' His dark eyes were sincere.

'I can't have my baby here. I need my aunt and Peggy.'

'Shall I go and collect them from the farm and bring them here?'

'No. Take me home.' A pain stabbed her so sharply she cried out.

Melville held her arms and she groaned, alarmed at the pressure between her legs. Was the baby coming out already?

Another contraction had her reaching out for something to hold on to. Melville took her hands and she squeezed them tightly, fighting the agony pulsing through her body. 'Help me, please...' she ground out through clenched teeth.

'Where is Scott, God damn it!' Melville demanded. 'Mrs Handry, help me make Beth more comfortable.'

Beth concentrated on catching her breath and dealing with the pain as the kitchen came alive with people rushing about, all talking at once.

Abruptly, a bespectacled older man in uniform knelt before her. 'Mrs Jackson, I'm Captain Scott, a doctor.'

Beth gripped his hands like a lifeline. 'I need to get *home*.'

'We'll take you in the motor car. Can you stand?'

With his help, Beth stood and took a step, but something large descended between her legs. She whimpered. 'Stop. Stop. Help!'

'Is the baby coming, Mrs Jackson?'

Wide-eyed, Beth stared at him. 'No! It can't! Not here. I won't have it here.'

'How far apart are your pains?'

'I don't know. All the time.' Beth panted. 'I thought labour took a long time with the first? Joanna took hours…' She groaned again.

'Not necessarily.' Scott's smile did little to reassure her. 'I'm afraid labour is out of our control,' he said gently. He turned to Melville, who hovered behind him. 'Lieutenant, we must get Mrs Jackson to a bed.'

Beth reared back. 'No! I *must* get home.'

'I don't think we have time.' Captain Scott took her elbow. 'I need to examine you.'

'Then I can go?' she begged.

'Do you want to deliver this baby in a motor car, Mrs Jackson?'

Beth moaned as more pressure throbbed between her legs.

Captain Scott guided her gently towards the blue door. 'You're not alone. I'll stay with you. Though I confess it's been many years since I've delivered a baby.'

Another cry escaped Beth before she could stop it. 'I need a midwife.'

Captain Scott glanced at Mrs Handry. 'Is there a local midwife about that you can send for? It might ease Mrs Jackson's worries.'

'Aye, in the village,' she replied. 'Jennie get along to the village and find Mrs Baxter. I'll get some blankets warming and a pot of hot water on to heat.'

With Scott and Melville on either side of her, Beth stepped into a wide hallway. She had to waddle as her legs wouldn't come together properly. Doors leading into service rooms dotted the length of the hallway, but it was the stairs at the end that made Beth baulk. 'I can't get up them.' She held onto their arms as another pain brought her to her knees.

'I'll carry her.' In an instant Louis swooped her up into his arms and carried her up the stairs, across another hall to the main staircase.

The pain grew so intense, Beth cried out. She was vaguely aware of some men gaping and talking and of Captain Scott reassuring them all was well. Beth didn't feel well. She was going to die of this pain; she was sure of it.

Louis laid her down on a wide soft bed and Beth relaxed a little into the thick pillows. She didn't know where she was nor cared. Having this baby was all she focused on.

'You'll be fine, Beth.' Louis's touch to her forehead made her jerk into awareness. She didn't want him near her.

She stared at Captain Scott as a sudden urge to push gripped her. The noise she made sounded like an animal, but she didn't care.

'You must leave now, Lieutenant,' Captain Scott commanded, washing his hands in a bowl of water Nora brought into the bedroom.

Louis stood close to the bed. 'I'll be right outside, Beth.'

She didn't care. When the door closed behind Melville, Beth let out a breath. 'I need to push.'

Captain Scott, at the end of the bed, smiled as he examined her. 'Then let us get you comfortable, my dear.'

Two nurses entered and in a few moments a canvas sheet was placed under Beth and they stripped her from the waist.

'You're doing excellently, Mrs Jackson,' Scott encouraged as she held her knees to push the baby out. 'I can see the head.'

Puffing, Beth strained, wincing at the burning sensation between her legs.

'That's it. Nearly there,' Scott crooned. 'Getting the shoulders out now... Another push please, Mrs Jackson.'

Beth gripped her legs and then suddenly felt a fast relief as the baby slipped out.

Sucking in air, Beth laid back against the pillows, panting, sweating.

A baby's cry filled the room and goose pimples rose on her body at the sound of her baby. She'd done it.

'A girl, Mrs Jackson.' Scott beamed, wiping the baby's head and tying the cord. 'She's a little small but looks to be in perfect health if her crying is anything to go by.'

'A girl.' Beth grinned, overjoyed that she'd given birth to a girl. 'Noah wanted a girl.'

One of the nurses, a small woman with blonde curls, wrapped up the baby in a towel and handed her to Beth. 'Here you are. Meet your daughter who was in a terrible hurry to enter the world.'

Through blurred vision, Beth gazed down at the little pink face and felt a fierce love twist her heart. 'My, you *were* in a rush, weren't you, little one?'

Half an hour later, Beth had been delivered of the afterbirth and washed by Ada, the blonde nurse. The baby slept on the bed beside Beth and she couldn't stop staring at the precious bundle.

'There, all done,' Ada said, tucking in the freshly made bed. 'Captain Scott will be back to check on you in a little while. He's just checking on one of the men and then we must make our rounds. I'm assisting him, but Ginger, the other nurse, will be about if you need her.'

'Thank you.' Now feeling more herself, Beth smiled at the nurse. 'You've been very kind.'

Ada grinned. 'It's not every day I assist a baby being born. It makes a welcome change. I'll have something exciting to write home to Mother now. Shall I go and fetch you a cup of tea?'

'Thank you that would be wonderful.'

Ada scooped up the soiled bedding and left the room.

Beth gently picked up the baby and held her close. She gazed around the room, noting the masculine furniture and colours. The navy blue curtains matched the lighter blue silk wallpaper. An open door led off to a dressing room, for she could see the wardrobes and a standing mirror. Beth wondered whose room it was, perhaps Sir Melville's since he no longer lived here.

When a knock sounded, Beth glanced up as the door opened slightly and Louis poked his head around.

'I don't want to disturb you.'

'You aren't.' Beth watched him enter the room; the man she had once hated with such intensity, but now felt nothing. When had she stopped loathing him? When had he ceased to matter? Probably the day she married Noah. That same night she became a woman in Noah's arms. The effect of Melville's attack had lessened with every loving look Noah gave her. He couldn't hurt her, and she instinctively believed he no longer wanted to.

'Captain Scott said you did marvellously, and you and the baby are healthy.' Louis stopped a few feet from the end of the bed. 'You look well. Glowing in fact.'

'Hardly. I feel tired,' Beth answered truthfully. It seemed a little surreal to be in bed talking to Louis after their history. Was it time to put the past behind them? Then she remembered his treatment of Noah and stiffened.

'What have you decided to name her?' he asked, staring at the baby.

'Ruby Margaret. I liked the name Ruby and Noah wanted a little girl to be called after his mam who is Peggy, but her first name is actually Margaret.' Beth smiled down at her perfect daughter. 'So, she's Ruby Margaret Jackson.'

'Ruby. I like it.' Louis gave her a long searching look and then stepped to the window and stared out. 'I never would have believed that you would have a baby in my home, my bedroom.'

'*Your* bedroom?' Beth blushed. 'I'm sorry.'

'Don't be. I'm terribly pleased by these turn of events and that I was home to witness it.'

'I should have stayed at home today. My independence and stubbornness are my downfall as I told your cook earlier. Forgive me for the intrusion.'

He glanced over his shoulder. 'You've nothing to be sorry for.

I'm glad of it. Your independence has always been something I've admired.'

'Well, I'm a mother now. I must rein it in. I just hope my daughter is more placid like her father and not have my temper or wilfulness.'

'Your spirit was what drew me to you in the first place.' He kept staring out of the window as he talked. 'To me, you outshone every woman in the district. You became my obsession. I've loved you for so long, Beth. How I have wished that I'd done things so differently.'

'Louis…'

He still stared out of the window. 'My jealousy has been… out of control. I have loved and loathed you with equal passion. But I'd be deeply grateful to you if you could forgive me, if you can find it in your heart to do so.'

The baby stirred and made a small noise. Beth dragged her eyes from the man by the window and down to her tiny daughter. Emotions warred in her head. 'Why do you treat Noah so terribly? My brother Will used to write and tell me of the extra duties you gave Noah at training camp. Noah doesn't tell me much, but I'm assuming your nastiness towards him hasn't dwindled in France? How am I to forgive that?'

Melville turned to face her; his expression haunted. 'I don't deserve your forgiveness. I'm not a nice man, I know that. My father wasn't either when he was young, but he's changed his ways. My grandfather was hated, too. He died being hated by everyone in the area. It is a dreadful legacy to continue. I'm ashamed that I have done so. After some time in Amsterdam, I believed I had changed, as my father has done. In that city I became a new man, or so I thought. I studied books written by eminent men, philosophers, and such like. I did charitable deeds, spent my time with my father's friends who were humble and faithful to their religion…'

'What are you saying?' Beth gently rocked the baby as she made little noises.

Melville sighed. 'I thought I had changed until I came home and saw you that day in Wakefield. All my old feelings for you resurfaced. I became angry again for losing you. I'm afraid I've been taking it out on your husband.'

A shiver went through her.

'I've abused my position as his officer. Every hateful job the army has, I give to him if I can. I have wanted to break him, punish him.' Louis had the grace to look shamefaced. 'I haven't improved at all really, have I?'

Anger rose in Beth as she stared at him. She wanted to shout but dared not.

He walked back to the bed. 'I learned nothing in my time in Amsterdam. I've reverted to the man you hate. I can see it in your eyes.'

'What do you expect? You hurt my husband and for what?' Beth's tone was dangerously low with suppressed rage. 'What does that achieve? Tell me, I wish to know.'

'It achieves nothing. I can never have what he has. I look at you now holding *his* child with such love and wish with all my heart she was mine, that *you* were mine.' His voice broke.

'But I'm not and never will be, Louis. If you were to *kill* Noah, I'd still never be yours.'

'Yes, I understand that.' He stared at Ruby. 'She is exquisite, like you.'

'Louis...'

He exhaled deeply. 'I will leave your husband alone, Beth. I promise you on my father's life, on anything you like, but believe me, please. I will be a better man for you.'

Beth glared at him. 'No, not for me. Do it for yourself, leave me out of it.'

Louis nodded. 'I have many regrets, Beth. I'm sorry for all of them, especially those that turned you away from me. I once said you weren't good enough to be married to me. I was utterly wrong. I am not good enough for you.'

She glanced away at the sorrow in his eyes. 'I need to dress and go home.'

'You've just given birth.'

'I want to be with my family.' As much as she ached, the thought of leaving here spurred her on.

'Of course.' He took a step, then stopped. 'I'll take you in the motor car.'

'I'd rather someone else do it.'

'I'm sorry to hear that, but only Captain Scott and I can drive and he's busy with the soldiers.'

'Then I'll walk!' Frustrated, she sounded angrier than she was. In fact, she was simply tired and sore and needed Aunty Hilda's embrace and her own bed.

Louis frowned and then slowly smiled. 'What were you just saying about your independence and stubbornness?'

Beth stopped fussing with the baby and glared at him.

Suddenly, she chuckled, wondering if she was losing her mind. God, what was she doing arguing with this infernal man?

Melville's grin widened. 'We seem to rub each other up the wrong way at every opportunity, don't we?'

Another wave of tiredness washed over her. 'I wish it weren't that way. It's exhausting, and I've too much else to worry about.'

He held out his hand. 'A truce?'

Beth hesitated. 'Does that include Noah?'

Melville flushed with embarrassment. 'It does. You have my word.'

Awkwardly, she shook his hand.

'I'll leave you to dress and wait for you in the motor. I'll send in a nurse to help you.'

When he'd left the room, Beth gingerly climbed out of the bed and found her skirt, coat and shoes. Her ruined underwear wasn't to be seen and Beth cared less that she'd be going home without wearing any.

The door opened and Ada hurried to help her.

Finally presentable, Ada carried the baby down the main staircase and Beth followed to a chorus of well wishes from the soldiers waiting at the bottom.

Captain Scott came out of what was once the drawing room but now a hospital ward and gave her a severe tut. 'I'd advise more rest, Mrs Jackson.'

'I will, Captain, the minute I'm in my own home.'

'May I call on you tomorrow?'

'I'd like that, thank you. Beaumont Farm, Trough Well Lane, Wrenthorpe.'

'I'll find it.'

On the drive, a shining red motor car was parked beside the little blue one. Mrs Handry stood beside it with Jennie and Nora. 'Mrs Baxter was delivering another baby and sends her apologies.'

'Thank you anyway for everything.'

The cook stepped aside as Louis opened the door for Beth to get into the motor car. 'Take care of yourself, Mrs Jackson,' the cook said. 'I'll have one of the scouts ride the bicycle over to your place.'

'Thank you, Mrs Handry.' Beth smiled as she sat in the back seat and took the baby from Ada. 'Goodbye.'

Driving slowly along the lanes, Beth felt it was a lifetime ago since she'd pedalled away from the farm.

'I was sorry about your brother being taken, and your father's… accident,' Melville said from the driver's seat.

'Thank you.' Beth stared out of the window, sad that her father would never see Ruby, and when would Will be home to cuddle his niece?

'We treat German prisoners well. We must pray that the Germans treat ours the same.'

Beth gazed down at Ruby. 'My father believed they wouldn't do so. That they'd execute allied soldiers at random so as not to feed and look after them. Do you believe that also?'

'There have been stories regarding that, yes. But I truly believe not all of our men will be killed by the Germans. The Red Cross monitors the camps and check that conditions are suitable. The German can't kill them all.'

'The Red Cross can't be everywhere at once though.'

'No…'

'But my brother will return home. I know it,' she said with conviction.

'How are you managing on the farm?' Louis asked, changing the subject.

'We are getting by. We are at our busiest time with all the planting.'

'If you ever need help, or money…' His words drifted away.

'I'd never ask you.'

'No.' He nodded. 'Despite my behaviour, I would hope that if you ever do need me, you'd swallow your pride and come to me.'

Beth didn't answer and as he pulled into the farm's drive, the built up tears spilled over as Leah came striding down to the motor car, calling for Peggy and Hilda as she did so.

Within minutes, her family surrounded Beth as they all talked at once on seeing the baby in her arms. 'I'm fine and so is she.'

'A girl,' they declared.

'We've been so worried, and Reggie is out looking for you.' Aunty Hilda hugged Beth as tightly as she could with the baby between them.

'I told you, you weren't to go,' Peggy cried, kissing her cheek, and then coughing harshly as she fought her tears.

'As stubborn as a mule!' Aunty Hilda proclaimed, ushering Beth towards the house. 'Let me take a look at that baby. My, she looks like you! Look at the little mite, Peggy, your granddaughter.'

Peggy cried even harder, which made her cough worse. Leah helped Peggy to catch her breath while Aunty Hilda leaned closer to Beth. 'Tell me exactly how Louis Melville happens to be the one to bring you home?'

In all the excitement, Beth had forgotten Louis. She glanced over her shoulder to see Louis drive away without a word.

CHAPTER 15

*N*oah strode alongside his brothers and fellow men to the beat of shelling. The sun peeked out behind the clouds every so often, but the end of June weather was warm on his back as they marched along the dusty lanes of Northern France.

He and the men had grown used to the ruined villages they passed, the deserted farms, but as they marched further south, the damage was less intense and the French civilians were determined to stay in their homes and live as normal a life as possible.

Noah smiled at waving children lining the road, and was grateful when women brought out small items of food they could ill afford to part with, but such was their gratitude at the allied soldiers they shared what little they had. Old farmers tilled the soil churned by bombs, eager to get a crop in the ground to save them from starving.

Sometimes they'd march through areas totally untouched by war. Beauty could be found in wildflowers and bird song. Trees remained whole and in full leaf, cows bellowed to be milked and rivers ran clean.

Walking through towns not littered by war reminded Noah

that there was life outside of bombs, guns and destruction. Seeing white curtains blowing in the breeze or hearing a church's organ playing or watching children running to school gave him a reason to keep fighting.

Yet, beyond this normality was the backdrop of noise. Constant shelling from enormous guns performed its own symphony.

For days they'd trudged along dirt roads and the bombing continued day and night. His head throbbed with the drumming of it. Miles and miles of cloud plumes clouded the horizon.

Something big was happening and they were headed straight for it. Soon, he'd be a part of it. The German advance had to be stopped, so they didn't wipe out France and then turn their attention to Britain. He had a wife and child to protect, and for them he would die for.

'Fall out. Fall out,' the call drifted up the columns of men and with a small cheer the men fell onto the grass lining the road and opened their packs to find their food rations.

'I'm sick to death of bully beef,' James whined, opening a small tin of the meat. 'Wouldn't Mam's stew and dumplings go down a treat right now?'

'Don't talk about it,' Alfred groaned, lying back and closing his eyes against the sun. 'The other day I dreamed of hot custard and jam roly poly. I was right ticked off when the sergeant bellowed and woke me up.'

'Were you on watch?' Sid laughed.

Alfred shrugged. 'I might have been.'

Noah nibbled on the hard tack biscuit, careful not to break a tooth. Unless soaked in tea, the biscuits were so hard they could snap a tooth with one bite.

Stretching out on the grass and using his kit bag to lean against, he took out Beth's latest letter that arrived yesterday and re-read it as he ate.

· · ·

DEAREST DARLING,

I hope this letter finds you well and safe as can be. I'm pleased you received my parcel I sent last week. I wasn't sure if you needed more socks, so I was pleased to read that they came in useful. Tell Sid that Peggy has nearly finished another pair for him, though why Meg doesn't send him socks is beyond our understanding. We never see her. How Peggy finds the time to knit or do anything I don't know for she never has your daughter off her knee.

Ruby is still small, though she feeds well. I think she'll be a dainty little thing like Joanna and unlike me! She is a contented sweet soul and never a minute's trouble. It's as though she understands her mam is busy and she must make less work for me. At night, when it's peaceful and just the two of us alone, I talk to her all the time about her brave daddy. I promise the minute I find some spare time I'll go into Wakefield and have a photograph taken of us both and send it to you.

We've been rushed off our feet trying to keep the snails, slugs and insects off the crops. The weather has been terrible with much rain and cool days, which the snails and slugs thrive on. It's a constant battle to fight against them. The lads are running a tally as to who catches the most. So far, Tom is winning.

The crops aren't growing as well as they should. As I mentioned in previous letters May was warmer than June, which had been damp and cool. We are hoping July gives us more sunshine and hotter days so the fields can produce healthier crops. Reggie isn't liking the current situation. You know how in tune he is with the nature. He feels the harvest this year will not be as good as in previous years and prays daily that we'll get better summer weather in July and August. Still, we mustn't complain.

I will post your next parcel in the next day or two. I need to add some more items to it like the chocolate you asked for, but getting into town is a challenge. I have to go between feeding Ruby or send someone else. Leah has been wonderful and often comes each evening to see us and brings the things we've ordered from the shops.

Joanna heard that Jimmy was slightly wounded. Do you have any news on that? She's been told the wounds aren't life threatening and he is currently at a British hospital in France. Naturally, she is worried and waits for a letter from him daily.

We have heard no further news about Will. The Red Cross are trying to find what prison camp he is held at and to start communication with him. All we can do is wait.

Is there any chance of you getting leave soon?

Stay safe and well, my love.

Your wife and daughter love you most dearly.

Beth

June 28th, 1916

Beaumont Farm

NOAH TUCKED the letter away into his breast pocket. How old would his daughter be before he saw her? He had no idea what she looked like. Did she resemble him or Beth or neither of them? When Beth wrote to him that she was safely delivered of a daughter, he'd been overjoyed, and celebrated well into the night at a little village bar. Beth's note had been short to give him the news, but a lengthier letter arrived the following day describing the events leading up to the birth, and in it she dealt him a blow he still reeled from. He couldn't get his head around the fact that Beth gave birth to his daughter in *Melville's* house. That *Melville* drove her home and had seen *his* daughter before Noah. At first, he'd been too angry to reply to Beth. Riding a bicycle while so heavily pregnant has been irresponsible in his mind. However, what angered him the most was that the one man he hated got to witness everything Noah did not.

In the weeks that followed, Noah couldn't rejoice in being a father. It seemed too unreal. His letters home were short and factorial. He kept his emotions out of them, and he knew this upset Beth, for her replies begged him for more of his thoughts.

She sent parcels weekly full of his favourite things and he replied with notes of thanks and not much else.

Of Melville, he saw very little since his return from England. As an officer, Melville moved around more than the rank-and-file men. Melville had officer training, was often recalled to HQ for debriefings and lectures. Although glad to see less of him, Noah was burning to question the man. His brothers cautioned him, knowing he was spoiling for a fight. Melville wasn't to be touched, they warned him constantly, or he'd end up on a charge or worse.

Still, the less Noah saw of Melville, the deeper his anger burned. He waited for Melville to taunt him, to throw it in his face that he had helped Beth, that Noah's daughter had been born under his roof. Yet, not a word had passed between them. The odd times Noah had seen Melville they'd been surrounded by men listening to Melville while he gave them new orders.

In the weeks following, Noah tried to catch his eye, but each time Melville turned away, which only puzzled Noah even more. Usually Melville was eager to tease and poke him into a reaction, but nothing. Noah didn't know what to make of it.

Another column of men from a different unit marched past and soon after they were ordered back on to the road again.

The boom of the big guns became clearer, louder. The ground shook beneath their feet.

'Something is going on,' Sid said, walking beside Noah.

Alfred, on Sid's other side, cursed. 'And we're walking right into it.'

Road signs were long gone, and Noah didn't know where they were, but asked the question to Sergeant Bourke as he came alongside him.

'Doing all right, Corporal?' Bourke asked.

Noah nodded. 'As well as can be, Sergeant. I wouldn't mind knowing where we're headed?'

Sergeant Bourke scratched his head under his cap. He was a

homily looking man who treated the men well. 'All I know is we are heading for Albert. I don't get told a lot more than you do, I'm afraid. I just give the orders I'm given.'

Scanning ahead, Noah searched for Melville. 'Lieutenant Melville hasn't mentioned much to you?'

Bourke frowned. 'Not likely. The man has been a pain in my backside for weeks, ever since he returned from home. God knows what's wrong with him. Hardly two words are said to anyone unless it's an order. I don't like it when officers go quiet, for it usually means news I don't want to hear.'

'You think that's all that's wrong with him?' Noah persisted.

Bourke gave him a queer look. 'He's leaving you alone, isn't he? Be grateful for small mercies.'

Noah remained quiet, intrigued that even Bourke had noticed Melville's odd behaviour.

Bourke spat to the side of the road and then from behind his ear pulled out a half-used cigarette and lit it. 'I've a spot on the map that we have to reach by tonight. I'm to get you lot there and that's all I know.' He turned and walked further down the line to chivvy up some stragglers.

The thunder of shells grew louder the longer they marched. The men grew quiet, the lively chatter and singing ebbed away as refugees from the towns and villages started to flood towards them.

'I think we are going the wrong way,' Alfred joked. 'We need to be with them lot.'

'Poor buggers,' Albie muttered.

In silence, they headed towards the booming guns while men, women and children carried their belongings and travelled the other way.

The roads became congested with army personnel and vehicles. As they approached the mobile HQ and stores, Noah gazed around at the camps set up behind the lines. Casualty Clearing Stations, tents with a red cross on a white flag dotted the fields amidst a jungle of ammunitions depots, cooking facilities, communication huts and stores of sawn timber duckboards, rolls of barbed wire, sandbags and hundreds of men.

'Christ, they're throwing a party, aren't they?' Sid laughed, puffing on a cigarette.

Tired and hungry, the officers led Noah's unit into the reserve trenches as night fell on the last day of June. Hot stew was brought into the line and the men ate ravenously. Flickers of lit cigarette tips twinkled like stars along the trench. Sleep was impossible with the earth-shuddering shells exploding less than a mile from their trench.

'Bloody hell, there are a lot of men around here,' Albie stated, filling his bottle from a large water tin.

'Word is that there's ten British divisions for this battle,' Alfred told them.

'If that's correct, then this must be important to them,' Noah added. 'Write a note to Mam, all of you.'

Without complaint they all wrote quick notes home, not one of them voicing their thoughts that it might be the last letter their mam will receive.

After midnight they were ordered into the forward trenches. As quietly as possible, they walked along the duckboards into sandbagged trenches, to join the various other battalions.

Sergeant Bourke and Lieutenant Melville came along the trench at dawn.

Although exhausted, the men straightened and listened as Melville spoke.

'Right, men. The whistle is at 0730 hours. Over the top we go. We've been told that the artillery has smashed the barbed wire and destroyed the first line of German trenches. Our task is to take that trench line and continue on under rolling artillery attack. The guns will blow away the Germans before we reach them, and we are to mop up what is left afterwards. Clear?'

'Yes, sir,' they chorused enthusiastically.

'You are to carry all of your kit in preparation of a large advancement. Check your weapons and ammunition supply. It'll be a long day so take enough rations, conserve your water. The British people will be proud of our efforts. Good luck and may God be with you.' Melville stared at Noah in the darkness, lit by the flashes of the exploding bombs.

Noah stared back. Tomorrow Melville could be dead, or he could be. What would the fates decide?

They ate again by the rising light and then fell into position along the trench before seven o'clock just as a new heavier bombardment started, cutting visibility over no man's land with shrouds of smoke.

'Well done, fellas, tell them we're coming,' Sid grumbled, standing beside Noah as the earth shook with the explosions.

'They know we're coming,' Alfred spat. 'Let's get it over with, for Christ's sake.'

Gut clenching, Noah looked at each of his brothers. 'Listen to me. We stay side by side. It's going to be madness out there.' He had to yell to be heard. 'Keep each other in sight. No bloody heroics, understand? We go into this together and we come out of it together. Got it?'

They nodded and shook hands and patted each other on the shoulders.

Noah's heart thudded in his chest as they turned and readied themselves for the whistle. Nervous with anticipation, he clutched his rifle, trying to clear his mind of only the task ahead. He closed his eyes momentarily and sent a whispered message of love to Beth and Ruby.

When Melville blew the whistle, Noah's unit surged out of the trenches to be hit with a wall of smoke from the shelling. The heaviness of their packs made it hard work to run over ground so uneven it seemed impossible to run two steps without turning an ankle.

Noah jogged alongside his brothers, eyes focused on the

swirling smoke, rifle in hand, his senses on high alert. This is what they were trained for. It'd be no different to any other battle they'd been involved in. They'd make it through, and tonight be sitting together nursing cups of warm tea.

They reached the first line of barbed wire unscathed, but instead of the wire being blown to bits as reported, the rolls were largely intact.

'Christ Almighty!' Alfred yelled, searching for a gap in the wire.

'Hurry!' Noah urged as the smoke rose, exposing the barren crater-filled landscape ahead. He could see the bobbing helmets of the Germans as they ran along their trenches to man their machine guns and get into position.

'Here! Here!' James, a little further down, found a gap and they quickly ran to him.

Noah used his rifle butt to push the wire aside, then turned back to make sure his brothers were able to scramble alongside. Suddenly, the rat-tat-tat roar of the machine guns started. A storm of bullets burst from the German trenches, spinning men around as they were hit. Some fell within yards of Noah, but there was no time to help them. Frantic, soldiers pushed through the uncut wire, becoming tangled and stuck, the perfect target for the enemy.

'Get in a crater!' Noah yelled as bullets whizzed past his body, the sound frightening him to jump into the nearest crater.

He landed next to Albie and Alfred. Sid and James were in the shell hole to their right.

'We can't stay here,' Albie panted. 'We've got to advance.'

'Listen to me,' Noah urged. 'Run from crater to crater. Weave as though you're playing football, don't make it easy for the bastards,' Noah instructed.

'Come on!' Alfred yelled, crawling up the muddy side.

Climbing out of the hole, they ran ahead with bullets pitting the ground as they ran. Noah rolled into the next shell hole, before climbing up the other side of it and kept going. He felt a sting in his shoulder and dropped to the ground. Crawling several feet, he dived into another crater to catch his breath. His shoulder stung, but he ignored it. The smell of smoke and gunpowder and dirt filled his nose. He tasted grit in his mouth.

He laid against the side of the hole, sucking in deep breaths just as Albie jumped down beside him.

'What a shit fight this is,' Albie grunted. 'I thought the artillery blew away the Germans?'

'Seems they got that bit wrong.' Noah glanced over his shoulder as James scrambled into the crater. 'You all right?'

James nodded, breathless. 'Can't get a shot at them though, I'm too busy running. They're well dug in.'

'We've got to try and breach that first trench. Ready?' Without waiting for a reply, Noah scrambled up and over the rim of the crater and ran towards another roll of barbed wire.

To his right, he saw Sid frantically cutting the wire to make a hole for him and Alfred to forge through. Running in a weaving pattern to dodge the bullets, Noah made for them. He turned his head to yell for Albie and James to help.

He was within ten yards when a machine gun opened fire. Noah fell to the ground as bullets pinged past him, one clipping the edge of his tin helmet. Shocked, he lay still for a moment.

Albie fell down beside him. 'Are you hit?'

'No, I don't think so. You?'

'Not yet!'

Noah peered over a lump of earth. 'Let's go.'

In what felt like slow motion, Noah ran towards Sid and Alfred. Bullets sprayed from the machine gun, pitting the dirt around him. He tripped, landed on his knees and then got up again with help from Albie.

'Shit!' Sid swore, dropping his wire cutters as a bullet hit them.

Noah was only yards from them when abruptly Alfred jerked

several times. He staggered once, a look of surprise on his face, then he slumped forward over the barbed wire, arms out like a scarecrow.

'No. No. No! Alfred!' Noah screamed.

His feet felt like lead and wouldn't move fast enough. He yelled again as Sid pulled Alfred down from the wire and crumbled to the ground.

Noah skidded to his knees besides Alfred. In horror, he stared at his brother, riddled with bullet holes. Blood seeped out alarmingly fast from his uniform, covering him like a red cloak.'

'Bandages!' Albie cried, frantically searching through his kit. 'Help him!'

Noah didn't know what to do first. His medical kit was limited, the bandages he carried too small for the amount of blood and holes puncturing Alfred's chest. 'Stretcher-bearers!' he screamed, gazing wildly behind them, but the stretchers-bearers weren't close enough to hear him.

'Oh God,' Sid moaned, his hands hovering over Alfred's face. 'Oh, God.'

James's anguished cry as he ran closer brought them to life. The bullets slammed into the surrounding ground.

'Get down! Get down!' Noah yelled at James. His mind whirled. How could he fix this? He cradled Alfred's head. With shaking bloody fingers, he felt for a pulse, but he knew his brother was dead.

A bullet pierced Noah's kit and another pinged off Sid's helmet.

'Go!' Noah urged. 'Get to a crater. We're sitting ducks here.'

'Alfred!' James cried, tears running down his face. 'He can't be dead.' James pulled at Alfred, trying to lift him. 'We have to take him back.'

'Leave him. Go, damn it!' Noah pushed his youngest brother ahead of him as they crawled and shuffled along the rough ground to the crater.

The four of them lay at the bottom of the crater, deaf to the carnage going on around them. Alfred, their brother, was dead. It didn't seem real.

'I'm not leaving him over there,' James had a murderous expression on his face.

'We can't take him back to our trenches. The machine gun has us in their sights.' Noah rubbed a red and filthy hand over his face.

Albie closed his eyes. 'We have our orders to advance.'

'How the hell can we?' James spat. 'There's nothing but machine guns mowing us down! We have to get Alfred back!'

'He's gone, James,' Noah murmured. 'He'd not want us to risk our lives trying to get his body back.'

'We'd all die,' Sid added. 'That gun out there is focused on the gap in the wire, knowing it's the only place we can get through.'

'This is bullshit!' James fumed, his chin wobbling. 'He's our brother! We have to take him back.'

'We've not been told to retreat, and if we do, we'll be shot for deserters,' Noah snapped.

'Stuff you then. I'll do it on my own. I'm taking Alfred's body to the trenches and the doctors!' James made a dive for the other side of the crater.

'Hold him!' Noah yelled to Sid and Albie. They pinned James down as he struggled.

'Look to me!' Noah slapped James's face. 'We'll come back for him. We'll not rest until we find him and can bury him. I promise you. First, we have to follow our orders.'

'Listen!' Albie suddenly shouted. 'The artillery...'

They paused and listened to the shelling growing less intense.

'It's moving further away,' Albie said.

'Christ! We are meant to be right behind the artillery. It's our cover.' Noah yanked James up. 'We're going now.'

Before Noah could react, James climbed up the crater and

197

over the top. He was sprinting as fast as he could towards the German trenches.

'Not that way, for Christ's sake!' Sid ran after him.

A slight breeze drew the bomb smoke towards them. Noah lost sight of Sid and James as he and Albie ran through the gap in the wire and headlong into the smoke, hoping the Germans wouldn't be able to see clearly either.

Dodging around yawning shell holes and leaping over dead bodies, Noah stumbled and tripped over the uneven ground. Machine gun fire separated him and Albie. He swore profusely as he fell into a crater, landing heavily onto a body.

He scraped his way up the steep side of the hole and paused to take a deep breath. British soldiers were running in and out of the smoke, up and down the shell holes. Broken men hung on barbed wire like skewered roasting meat.

His brothers were scattered. He had to find them.

Racing on, hearing nothing but machine gun fire and exploding shells, he felt a bullet nick his calf. He stumbled, the pain sharp. Another bullet twanged off his water bottle.

Was the next bullet the end?

He couldn't think straight.

He kept running, his throat dry, his chest heaving.

When he fell again, he landed next to a British soldier, lying face down. Noah lay panting. When the officer moaned, Noah reached over and pulled the man onto his back. Shocked, he stared at Melville's pale face.

'Where are you hit?' Noah asked, scanning Melville's chest, which had a stain of red near his ribs on the left.

'My leg,' Melville moaned.

Noah glanced down at Melville's legs. His right one was intact, but the left had a bone sticking out of his thigh. Blood soaked his trousers. Quickly, Noah sought his medical kit from his pack.

'Leave me,' Melville groaned.

'And if I do, you'll bleed to death.' Noah bandaged the wound roughly with bandages until he ran out. Using Melville's own medical kit, he tried to stop the bleeding.

'Don't move,' Noah warned. 'I've got that as tight as I can, but I don't know if I've stopped the bleeding enough until we can get you some help.'

'I'll be fine.' Melville winced in pain, sweat breaking out on his face.

'Here, drink this.' Noah helped Melville drink from the water bottle. 'Stretcher-bearers will be along soon.'

'No, they won't.'

Noah paused in wiping the blood off his hands. The irony of the situation wasn't lost to him, even in these circumstances.

Melville gave a small grin. 'You've probably saved my life, Jackson, if I can get back to our side.'

'That's a big if,' Noah grunted. 'I've got to go and find my brothers.'

Melville nodded, but gripped his sleeve, stopping him. 'I know Beth must have told you about having the baby at the manor.'

Noah stiffened.

'I also know you must be wanting to kill me for being there…' Melville sucked in a breath, pain showing on his face. 'Part of me wanted to taunt you about it…'

'I'm surprised you didn't. I've been waiting for you to say something.'

'I couldn't.' Melville winced again. 'I promised Beth. I owe her.'

'That hasn't stopped you before.' Noah frowned, seeing more blood seeping from the wound in Melville's chest. He didn't have any more bandages. 'Keep still. I've got to go.'

Melville's grip tightened on his arm. 'Seeing Beth… in agony and then afterwards seeing the love for her baby… your baby… She's so tiny and beautiful… Beth is an amazing woman. I love her.'

Noah fought the urge to punch him.

'I know she isn't mine…' Melville grimaced as shellfire from the Germans grew closer to their position, drowning out his words.

Noah stared around the top of the crater. No more men were running past. Shells were landing close now as the German artillery returned fire. He had to find his brothers. A shell burst twenty yards away, showering them with soil and small rocks.

'I've made provisions…'

Noah glanced back down at Melville. 'What?'

'For the baby. If I die. Ruby is to get something from me for her future.'

Enraged, Noah grabbed Melville by the front of his jacket and shook him. 'We don't want anything from *you*, understand? Nothing. Ruby is *my* daughter, *mine*. Beth is *my* wife, *mine*. You are nothing to us.'

Noah's shaking caused Melville to cry out in pain before passing out.

Rage blinded Noah as he let go of Melville's jacket. 'Don't you dare die, you bastard. I'm not having you leave something to my daughter in your bloody will.'

Noah dragged Melville by the shoulders to the top of the hole. Under fire from machine guns and exploding shells, he dragged Melville back towards their own trenches until two stretcher-bearers ran to help him.

'We've got him, Corporal,' said one of the soldiers. 'You've been nicked a few times yourself.'

'I'm fine. Keep him alive.' Handing him over, Noah took one last look at Melville then ran back into the smoke and the pit of hell.

CHAPTER 16

*R*uby's little murmurs came from the pram where it stood in the shade with a net over it to stop the flies bothering her. Beth continued to hoe along the garden beds, dislodging the weeds and aerating the dirt around the rows of lettuces and carrots. The chickens pecked at the soil, feasting on worms and insects.

She paused for a moment, seeing the postman walk up the drive. Her heart leapt at the thought of a letter from Noah. Since she'd written to him of Ruby's birth happening at Melville Manor, his replies had been cordial, and she knew instinctively he was hurt by the fact Melville had been there at such a special time when Noah had not. She didn't know how to soothe his hurt. Letters weren't enough.

In the herb garden at the back of the house, Peggy and Aunty Hilda sat on chairs. Peggy was shelling early peas while Aunty Hilda was creating net bags for the onions. The postman walked around the side of the house and into the yard and Beth heard him say good day to the two women and hand Peggy a small bundle of letters before walking away.

Standing in the middle of the vegetable garden, looking down into the herb garden at the two woman she loved dearly, Beth hoped that Noah had written to her.

Peggy leapt to her feet, the other letters falling to land on the path.

Instinctively, Beth dropped the hoe and scattering the chickens rushed along the rows and out of the garden.

Peggy stared at her as Beth reached her side. In her hands was a brown buff envelope. 'I can't open it. I know it's not Noah, or you'd be notified, and it can't be Sid as Meg would get the telegram…'

'Which ever one it is might only be wounded,' Aunty Hilda said gently.

'Open it, Beth,' Peggy whispered.

Taking a deep breath, Beth took the envelope and opened it. She drew out the note inside. 'It's from the Infantry Record Office. Army Form B.104-82.'

Beth's hands shook as she skimmed the note.

'Tell me,' Peggy murmured.

She didn't want to say the words out loud. She swallowed. 'Madam, it is my painful duty to inform you that a report has this day been received from the War Office notifying of the death of Private Alfred Jackson, West Yorks Regiment, which occurred on the 1st of July 1916, and I am to express to you the sympathy and regret of the Army Council at your loss. The cause of death was Killed in Action.'

'Alfred…' Peggy swayed.

Beth took her in a tight embrace. 'I'm so sorry.'

'My poor boy.' Peggy sobbed, which brought on a bout of coughing that had her wheezing like she used to do last year but which had lessened of late. Now though, she gasped for breath and Beth's heart broke at the pitiful sight of her crying for her son and wheezing.

'Come away inside,' Aunty Hilda urged. 'I'll put the kettle on.'

'Why have the boys not written and told us?' Peggy wept, staying where she was. She gazed at Beth. 'Surely they'd know?'

'I don't know. Yes, they're serving in the same unit but maybe they were split up or something?'

Peggy's face paled. 'What if they're all dead? That's why they've not written?' The alarm on her face and another fresh bout of coughing had her bent double.

'Don't say that!' Frantically, Beth read the note again. Especially the date. 'This was written on the third of July, today is the fourth. They say Alfred died on the first. Perhaps letters are coming? The boys might be in the thick of things still?'

'Aye,' Aunty Hilda nodded eagerly. 'I bet letters will arrive any day from them. What are those on the ground? Who are they from?'

Scooping down to collect the rest of the post, Beth scanned through them. 'Bills, produce flyers and a seed catalogue.'

Peggy wiped her eyes with a handkerchief. 'My poor Alfred.' Fresh tears rolled off her lashes. 'He was always such a cheeky lad. My naughty one.'

'He was a good and loyal son to you.' Aunty Hilda nodded. 'Come inside now.'

'I'll get Ruby.' Beth hurried up the yard to where Ruby slept peacefully. Beth gazed at her daughter and prayed that Noah was safe. Pushing the pram towards the house, Beth paused as Reggie came up the drive with several of the lads.

'Reggie.' Beth halted them from noisily coming into the yard, joking and chatting. 'Peggy's had a telegram. It's Alfred, he's been killed,' her voice faltered.

'Oh, no. Now that's a sad piece of news,' Reggie said and the lads behind him fell quiet.

'Take everyone up to the pub to grab a bite to eat, will you? Now isn't the time for us to be dishing out a meal. I need to focus on Peggy.'

'Aye, aye. I'll keep the lads out of the way for the rest of the day. We'll work in the far fields this afternoon, just come and get me if you need me.'

'Thank you.' Beth smiled gratefully.

Inside the kitchen, Beth pushed the pram into the corner and sat at the table beside Peggy. 'Is there anything I can do?'

Peggy dabbed at her eyes with a handkerchief. 'I need to visit Reverend Simmonds and ask him to mention Alfred in Sunday's service as we can't have a funeral, can we?'

'I can do that for you.'

Peggy turned tear-filled eyes on Beth. 'Would you, love?'

Beth grasped Peggy's hand. 'I'll go right now, shall I?'

'Thank you. What would I do without you?'

'Ruby will be fine with us,' Aunty Hilda said, pouring out two cups of tea.

'She's not due a feed for a couple of hours.' Beth changed her work boots for shoes.

'Oh, and Beth,' Peggy said, halting Beth as she stepped to the door. 'Will you buy me some black crepe material from Mrs Davies, please? I threw out my black mourning blouse last year. It'd worn thin after wearing it for Leo.' Her chin wobbled.

Beth's heart sank as she nodded. 'I'll see to it.' She collected her purse from the dresser. Calling into the little haberdashery shop in the village would mean a long chat with Mrs Davies, who liked to gossip, and Beth wasn't in the mood for it.

'We could do with more black ribbon for armbands, lass,' Aunty Hilda added.

Beth left the house and walked up the lane, her straw hat shielding her from the summer sun, which they'd seen less of this summer than in previous years. She eyed the crops as she passed the fields, willing them to grow strong and healthy and that the weather would stay dry for another few months so they could bring in the harvest.

'Beth!'

She stared up the lane and waved as she recognised Joanna

pushed Ivy in the pram. 'I've not seen you for two weeks,' Beth said as Joanna hugged her.

'I know I'm sorry,' Joanna apologised.

'Hello, sweetheart.' Beth tickled Ivy under the chin and then frowned, noticing the black armband Joanna wore over her white sleeve. 'What's that for?'

'Jimmy's dad died five days ago. A heart attack. It's been awful. Jimmy's mam isn't coping with it at all and I've had to organise the funeral which is tomorrow.'

'I didn't know. I'm so sorry.'

'It's been terrible and well I only wrote and told Jimmy about his dad yesterday. I couldn't face doing it. He'll be devastated and the newspapers are full of this big battle that's gone on. Apparently wounded are steaming into London in their thousands, the hospitals can't cope. I don't know if Jimmy has been involved with it or not.'

'They have,' Beth said sadly. 'Alfred's been killed.'

'Peggy's Alfred?' Joanna gasped.

'Yes. We got the telegram today. I'm on my way to see Reverend Simmonds and to buy black crepe.'

'Oh, heavens, that is terrible. I'm sorry to hear it, really, I am. The Jackson boys are such laughs. I had a dance with Alfred at your wedding. Peggy must be inconsolable.'

'She's worried they've all died because no one has written.'

Joanna's eyes widened. 'No! Surely not.'

'I'd know if Noah was dead.' Beth lifted her chin in defiance of such a thing ever happening. 'If this battle is as big as you say then there's bound to be confusion and… and…' Beth ran out of words, feeling angry at being so out of touch and useless.

'I've today's newspaper under the pram. You can read it if you want.'

Beth nodded. 'I've been too busy to read the newspapers much. I'm too tired at night to read. They are still delivered… I've not had the chance to stop Dad's order yet.'

Joanna rubbed Beth's arm. 'You can't do everything. You're running a farm and have a new baby. Don't be too hard on yourself.'

'I'd best go and see Reverend Simmons.'

'I'll stay the night if you want, extra support and all that.'

'I'd like that.'

'I'll have to leave early to go home and get ready for the funeral in the morning.'

'You can leave Ivy with us. Saves you worrying about her and Peggy loves her to pieces. It might help her take her mind off Alfred if she has Ivy and Ruby to fuss over.'

'I think Ruby will do that more than Ivy.' Joanna smiled.

'We need noise in the house. Peggy isn't used to the quiet after raising five boys.'

'Well, it's never quiet when Ivy is around. She takes after her Aunty Beth, that's for sure.'

'Hey you.' Beth chuckled and sighed. 'I'd best go. I'll be as quick as I can.'

In the village, Beth opened the little gate to St Anne's Church, hoping the reverend would be about and not on visits.

'Mrs Jackson.' Reverend Simmons, a slender man with receding black hair and a kind face, was closing the church door as she approached along the path.

'Good day to you.'

'This is a pleasant surprise.' He held a small black leather bible and his straw boater hat he was known for wearing.

'I'm sorry to call unannounced and I know you are busy.' For some reason seeing the reverend choked her up. He was always so kind to her and the family and having buried three of her family within a year of each other, he'd been full of kindness and support.

'Never too busy for you. How may I help you?'

'It's about Peggy…'

'Ah, Mrs Jackson. How is she?'

'Not too good, I'm afraid. We've just learnt that Alfred has been killed in battle.'

His expression fell in sympathy and he shook his head. 'That is dreadful news. Today, all I've received is bad news. Alfred adds another name to my list to pray for. I attended Melville Manor this morning due to an ill soldier trying to take his life due to being considered fit enough to return to France. Such a sorry case.'

'Poor man.'

'Then Mrs Handry told me that Lieutenant Melville had been seriously wounded and may not make it. He's in a London hospital.'

'Louis Melville?' Beth blinked in surprise.

'Yes. The poor fellow is in a bad way. Wounded in the chest and leg.'

'I didn't know.' Beth didn't know what to think or feel about that news. Was Louis close to death? It seemed unbelievable.

The reverend tapped his bible. 'Mrs Jackson must be terribly upset. I shall visit her at once.'

'You will?' That surprised Beth, knowing how short for time the reverend was with his many duties.

'I was on my way to visit Mr Chambers on Sunny Hill, who's been brought low with a bad chest, but I think Mrs Jackson needs me more.'

'Thank you, Reverend. I think a visit from you will be a comfort. She asked me to come and see you as she'd like Alfred's name mentioned in Sunday's service.'

'Well, I'll go and talk to her now and assure her that will be done.'

'Thank you. I'm off to buy some black material from Mrs Davies if she has any left...'

'Mrs Davies keeps a good stock.' He grimaced. 'Such are the times we live in.'

Beth didn't know what to say.

'Perhaps soon we will talk about your daughter's christening?'

Beth nodded. 'I've been putting it off in case Noah can come home on leave.'

Reverend Simmons patted her arm. 'I understand.'

At the gate, the reverend put on his hat. 'Thankfully, in my little parish, I've not had to make many of these calls, but after reading about the current battle going on in the Somme area of France, I fear I may have to do many more.' He walked away, heading for Trough Well Lane, while Beth turned the other way to the few shops that catered for the village. She hoped the reverend would never have to make that call again to Beaumont Farm.

CHAPTER 17

*H*olding a lantern high, Beth walked carefully between the rhubarb in the darkened forcing shed. Bright yellow-green stalks creaked in the silence as they grew in the warmth of the shed while outside a biting cold November wind blew.

As a child she'd been enamoured by the sound of the squeaky rhubarb growing and still was. She'd squat low beside her dad and listen for the sound and marvel at the colour of this magical crop that grew inside during the dark winter days. Rhubarb had been her dad's passion, and although she wasn't as passionate about it as he was, the crop remained an important part of the farm's income, especially since the harvest hadn't been an enormous success this year just as Reggie predicted.

Leaving the shed, she secured the door tight against the wind. Despite it only being four o'clock in the afternoon, the light was fading fast, shortening each day, much to her dislike. She never wanted to say goodbye to the summer months. Winter always felt like it lasted longer every year.

As she made her way across the yard to the house, voices carried on the wind. Beth paused, wondering who'd be out in this weather with night descending rapidly. She listened for a moment but heard nothing more, only the banging of a loose board in the barn.

As the wind howled through the orchard, Beth quickly entered the house and shut the scullery door behind her. Hanging her coat up and taking off her boots to replace them with house slippers, Beth grumbled at the amount of washing that awaited her in the morning. The copper tub was filled with clothes soaking in caustic soda.

She hated washday. She grabbed the washing stick and gave the clothes another poke and a twirl in the water. Her mood grew more despondent as she saw some stains still hadn't lifted from the clothes. However, it wasn't just the dirty washing which made her feel low in spirits. Over the last few months since Alfred's death, Noah's letters were less jovial, conveyed less information, and even became less frequent. She feared for his peace of mind. She wrote to him of Ruby and everyone, gave him news of the farm and the village, but he barely responded to anything she wrote.

Sighing, she put the stick down and entered the kitchen. 'That wind is awful,' she told Aunty Hilda and Peggy.

'Aye.' Peggy coughed. The wintry weather aggravated her chest as normal.

Aunty Hilda creaked to her feet. 'You need a hot lemon and brandy, Peggy. The nights are drawing in and it'll ease your chest. I'll make you one.'

'And have one yourself too, Aunty?' Beth teased, checking that Ruby still slept in her pram in the corner of the kitchen.

'Prevention is as good as a cure, they say.' She sniffed haughtily, but there was laughter in her eyes.

'At your age you can do what you like,' Beth added. 'I think I'll heat some water for a bath before we eat.'

'Good idea,' Aunty Hilda agreed. 'I'll get in after you.'

Beth took the tin bath down from the hook in the scullery

and placing it in the front room before the fire, she began the laborious task of filling it with buckets of hot water she heated on the range.

By the time the bath was half full, Beth was trying to figure out if they could afford indoor plumbing that was becoming more and more in fashion. How wonderful it would be to turn one of the bedrooms into a proper bathroom with piped hot water.

Naked, she slipped into the steaming water, her mind full of figures at the expenditure of such extravagance.

The entire house needed updating. She believed it must be ten years or so since any of the rooms had seen a lick of fresh paint or a roll of new wallpaper. Her bedroom walls were still covered in the floral pattern of her and Joanna's childhood. The kitchen needed an upgrade, too. Perhaps they could install one of those fancy new ranges she'd seen in catalogues?

Behind her, she heard the door open. 'I've only just got in, Aunty. Can I have five minutes more?'

'You can have as long as you like,' the male voice replied.

Beth squealed and swished around, sending water over the sides and soaking the towels laid over the floorboards. Heart racing, she stared at Noah standing in the doorway. 'Noah!'

His grin brightened his dirty face. 'Hello, my lovely.'

Beth jumped out of the bath and flew into his arms. 'You're home.'

He kissed her soundly. 'Only for six days, my darling, and I've already spent one of them travelling.'

She kissed away his words, unable to believe he was standing in her arms at long last. 'I can't believe it.' She kissed him again and then pulled away. The sound of male voices came from the kitchen. Beth knew the brothers would be consoling Peggy as Alfred wasn't among them and would never be coming home.

'You're all here?' she asked as his hands roamed her wet body.

'Yes, except Alfred, of course...'

'Such a tragedy. Peggy hasn't been the same since.'

'It's been five months and I still can't take it in. I still look for him in the lines even though I was there when he died.'

'We were so worried when we didn't hear from any of you for over a week. Peggy was adamant you'd all gone.'

'Get in the bath,' he ordered gently. 'You'll catch your death from cold.'

She did as he ordered and sank into the warm water.

Noah took the cake of soap and began rubbing it over her legs. 'The first week of that battle was beyond insane. We had to hold our positions, such as they were, for days until the reserves could reach us.' He smoothed the soap over her calves in a leisurely motion. 'Our brigade lost so many men. It was chaos. I couldn't find Sid or James for three days. Albie got sick and my wound became infected. It was madness. I don't know how any of us survived.' He picked up one of her feet and ran the soap over it. 'Eventually, we found Alfred's body and buried him...'

'What you must have gone through, my love. I can't tell you how relieved we all were when the letters started arriving.'

He switched to the other foot. 'I wrote as soon as I could. I did explain.'

'Yes, I know you did.'

Beth took a moment to study him. He'd lost weight, but it was the drawn look on his face that broke her heart. His beautiful blue-green eyes appeared haunted, lost. 'I think you need this bath more than me.' She quickly stood and wrapped a towel around her, eyeing up the filthy state of him. He smelt of sweat and dirt and something else she couldn't identify. 'Get in.'

'I don't think I have the energy, darling.' Now the surprise of being home had worn off, Noah seemed to deflate before her eyes.

'I'll help you.' She kissed his lips and then piece by piece stripped the army and the war from him. She poured another jug of scalding water into the bath. She hurriedly dressed in her nightgown and robe, pushing her feet into her house slippers.

Lying back, Noah sighed and closed his eyes as she washed him from head to toe. Dirt was ingrained into the creases of his neck. Lice crawled through his brown hair, which had a sprinkling of grey through it.

'You need delousing.'

'I'm sorry. I'm in a bit of a state.'

'I'll be back in a moment.' Beth hurried into the kitchen, only to stop and embrace each of her brothers-in-law and welcome them home. From under the sink she found the delousing powder and took the kettle of boiling water.

Once back in the front room, she continued washing Noah who was half asleep. 'Did you have a peek at Ruby when you came in?'

He smiled. 'A small one. I didn't want to wake her, and my brothers were loud enough greeting Mam. She's beautiful like you. I knew she would be. I can't wait to hold her.' Tiredness closed his eyes once more.

'I'm so glad you're home. It's been too long. I scan the newspapers for battles, but also dread the thought I might find your name listed in the lists of wounded and the dead.'

He gazed at her and took her hand to play with her wedding ring on her finger. 'After the worst week of my life, they took us out of the front line.'

She reached over and kissed him and then continued washing him.

'Since then we've been consolidating our positions and fighting the odd battle they throw at us. The conditions are appalling. The trenches are full of mud and water and rats...' He gave himself a small shake. 'Enough of that. No more talk of war.'

'I want to hear what you go through.' She noticed the little scars here and there on his body. He had a wound on his shoulder that still looked red and sore. 'You don't tell me much any more and you said you'd tell me everything.'

'And I will tell you some of it, but not all of it, and not tonight. I'm here with you and Ruby, finally. I want to forget the war for a few days.'

'I'll fetch you some fresh clothes. This water is getting cold. Besides, Ruby will be awake soon and wanting food.' She nudged his discarded uniform with her toe. 'That lot needs scrubbing.'

'It needs burning, but it's all I have at the moment,' he said ruefully.

'I'll wash it tomorrow.'

'You'll have the others as well. We are in an awful state, sorry. Lice is rampant.'

'You're home, that's all that matters.'

An hour later, with a meal of rabbit stew and a pudding of apple pie and custard devoured, they all sat sipping tea. Every pot was on the stove heating water as each brother went and had a bath in turn.

Noah sat at the table with Ruby on his lap. He couldn't stop gazing at her and kissing the top of her head. He grinned as she tried to grab at whatever was closest. Happily, she sat and let Noah feed her and the sight brought tears to all their eyes when she blew bubbles at him and gave him the biggest smile. Ruby was an innocent, clean and whole, to her father and uncles who'd seen too much devastation and destruction.

'We must have a photograph taken, the three of us,' Noah said as Ruby was passed around his brothers.

Beth nodded. 'I was happy with the photograph studio I went to with Ruby a few months ago. He was very patient and under-standing.'

Noah put his arm around Beth's shoulders. 'Getting that photograph made me so happy. I don't think there's one soldier in my brigade who hasn't seen it.'

'Yes, whether they wanted to or not!' James teased, holding Ruby and stroking her plump little cheek with his finger.

'I'm allowed to be proud of my daughter,' Noah defended, yawning.

'Are you lot off up to the pub?' Peggy asked, clearing away the plates and bowls.

'Nope, not tonight.' Albie also yawned. 'I just want to sleep.'

'We all do.' Sid nodded. 'I'm too tired to walk into the village and go to Meg.'

'Save it for in the morning, lad.' Peggy patted his shoulder. 'Meg isn't expecting you, is she?'

'No, I've not written and told her. We don't write much.' Sid shrugged as though it didn't matter.

'There's talk she's been spending a lot of time in Wakefield. Young Walt is left with her parents, mostly.'

Sid scratched his head. 'I'm not surprised. Being a mam wasn't all Meg thought it would be.'

'Flighty, that's what she is,' Peggy announced sourly.

'Leave it, Mam.' Sid yawned.

Beth stood. 'I'll go up and put clean sheets on the beds. There's Will and Ronnie's beds and Dad's... We'll fit you all in.'

'I'll help you,' Noah said.

'You're half asleep.' Beth pushed him back on the chair. 'Stay with Ruby. I can manage.'

It wasn't even nine o'clock when everyone went to bed. Ruby, as though knowing something different was happening, decided to stay awake and she lay on the bed between Noah and Beth, playing with a little peg doll that Reggie had made for her or trying to suck her toes.

'I've missed nearly seven months of her life.' Noah sighed, playfully tugging Ruby's toes out of her grasp.

'It can't be helped, my love. She's too little to understand or even know.'

'Let's hope that the war is over before she grows much older.'

'Do you think that's likely?'

'It can't go on forever. Countries will run out of money. Mr Grimshaw explains many things to me in his letters. He's studying the war in fine detail. Economics will play their part.'

'Well, I hope it's soon. I want you home.'

Noah reached over Ruby to cup Beth's cheek. 'I've missed you so much. I live through each day praying I'll not get hit so I can return home to you.'

Tears filled her eyes, but she blinked them away. 'I've been so frightened of so many things. Yes, the real danger of you being killed is always at the front of my mind, but since Ruby's birth you've been so distant… Your letters are so formal… It's like I'm losing you even more than just physically, but mentally, too. Does that make sense?' She glanced away from him to her baby, who was blowing bubbles.

'I'm sorry. I didn't handle the news well of you giving birth in the manor. After everything that happened to you at the hands of Melville, it was the last place I expected you to have our baby. Then Alfred was killed and the constant struggles of living with hundreds of men and the danger... It's difficult.'

'It wasn't planned, you know, me being at the manor. I explained that to you.'

He rubbed his eyes. 'I know.'

'Did Melville speak of it to you?'

'No, not really. I barely spoke to him from the time he returned from England to the day of the battle when he was wounded.'

Beth leaned back against the pillows, knowing he was exhausted, yet needing to clear up any misunderstandings between them. 'So, Melville treated you better than he did?'

Noah glanced at her. 'Did you have something to do with that?'

'No, Melville told me he'd leave you alone. That he was

working on being a nicer person. His jealousy always made him evil and he was trying to overcome that.'

'It seems he had much to say the day you had Ruby.'

She played with the edge of the blanket. 'I think he was trying to make amends.'

'You honestly believe that?' Noah sounded doubtful.

'I actually do. He was very taken with Ruby and the whole experience of seeing me in pain. I think it affected him.'

'The man loves you,' Noah grunted.

'But he knows I love you.'

'Well, he left me alone, and then shortly after his return the battle happened, and he was wounded. I've not seen him since. We've been told his injuries will take some time to heal. It's doubtful he'll ever soldier again. Listen, I don't want to talk about him or the war. Let us simply be together, yes?' Noah yawned, his face grey with fatigue. He plucked Ruby from the blankets and laid her on his chest. Within minutes they were both asleep.

Beth took Ruby from him and placed her in her cot, then adjusted Noah's pillows better and covered him with the blankets. He didn't stir.

Watching him sleep, Beth felt relieved he was home and a little annoyed he had returned a slightly different man. She wanted her loving Noah back. Not this man who couldn't talk to her. He hadn't even wanted to make love.

CHAPTER 18

*B*eth finished feeding Ruby and with her washed and changed and fast asleep, she went downstairs to the front room where the others had gathered after the evening meal.

'Come on, it'll be fun,' James was saying to his mam.

'I don't know...' Peggy sat by the fire, knitting in her hands. 'Take Beth with you for an hour.'

Beth stooped to add more coal to the fire. 'What's going on?'

'We're off to the theatre and then a few drinks. We want Mam to come with us, but she won't.'

'You know if I start coughing, I'll ruin it for everyone,' Peggy protested.

Albie came into the room dressed in his clean and pressed uniform and his hair neatly combed. 'Come on, Mam. It'll be a treat for us all to go out. Beth go and get dressed. Your aunt said she'll mind Ruby. Leah is meeting us at eight.'

'Really?' Beth beamed. It'd been so long since she'd been on a night out.

'I'm not going.' Noah looked up from a book he was reading. One he'd got from the library that day when they were in Wakefield having their photograph taken. 'You go, Beth. I'll mind Ruby.'

'I don't want to go without you,' Beth said, going to sit on the arm of the sofa where he sat.

He took her hand. 'I don't mind, honestly. I don't want to sit with a load of people. I'm with men every single day. I'd just like some peace and quiet.'

'You're an old man!' James snorted.

Noah gave him a stern look. 'No, I just like the idea of sitting by the fire reading my book. Something I've not done for a very long time.'

'We've been home three days, Noah, and we've done nothing but sleep and eat,' James objected.

'What's wrong with that? We get little enough sleep in France.'

'It's time to have some fun,' James persisted.

'I'm not stopping you.' Noah chuckled.

'I'm also ready for a bit of entertainment and having the lovely Leah on my arm is just the ticket.' Albie adjusted his cuffs. 'I'm not waiting for you two to argue about it. Let him stay home, James. Sid said he and Meg will meet us in town.'

'Have a good time.' Noah glanced up at Beth, still perched on the arm. 'Go, sweetheart. Enjoy a night off, you deserve it. You work so hard.'

'You know what,' Aunty Hilda said, standing with a creak in her knees. 'I think I might go, too.'

Beth stared wide-eyed at her. 'You never go to the theatre.'

'I'm seventy-nine years old next week. Let's celebrate it in case I don't reach eighty!'

'Don't say that,' Beth chided. 'I've lost enough family recently.'

Aunty Hilda patted Beth's shoulder as she went past. 'We will all go out. Yes, we will, Peggy,' she added as Peggy went to protest, 'and we'll leave Beth and Noah alone for a few hours. Something you've not had for a long time.' She gave an exaggerated wink, then pushed James gently out the door. 'Get Snowy harnessed to the cart, I ain't walking into Wakefield, lad.'

Noah grinned, and for once looked like the old Noah.

For ten minutes the house was chaotic as everyone got ready and left. When silence descended, Beth felt a little anxious.

'Shall I put the kettle on?' Noah said, standing.

'I can do it.' Beth jumped to her feet.

Noah took her in his arms and kissed her. 'Let *me* spoil *you* for once. Since I've been back all I've done is eat and sleep and take walks with Ruby. You've run about looking after all of us as well as seeing to everything on the farm. Tonight, it's going to be just you and I and I have a plan. Do you have any wine in the house?'

'There are a few bottles in the larder that Aunty Hilda brings out for special occasions.'

His grin returned. 'Go upstairs and wait until I call you down.'

'Why?'

'Just do it.' He tapped her bottom as she turned for the door.

Upstairs, Beth paced the bedroom floor while Ruby slept in her cot. Twenty minutes went by and then half an hour. Beth wondered if Noah had fallen asleep, something he'd done regularly in the past couple of days. Months of being in the trenches and sleeping rough in villages had caught up with him. The first night he'd slept in until after ten o'clock the next morning. He'd done the same again for the next two days.

She stepped out onto the landing to listen for his movements.

'Beth,' he called softly from the bottom of the stairs so as not to wake Ruby.

'I'm wondering what you've been doing for the last half an hour.'

'I'll show you.' He took her hand as she reached him. 'Close your eyes.'

'Noah, really.' She giggled like a young girl, and at that moment she felt the giddiness of when they first met over three years ago.

He guided her into the front room and then stopped. 'You can open them.'

Beth opened her eyes and gasped. The tin bath sat before a blazing fire, steam coming off the water. All around the room were lit candles, casting a golden glow and flickering shadows. Two glasses of wine sat beside the bath on a tray.

'Oh, Noah.'

'Do you like it?'

Tears burned hot behind her eyes, tears she tried never to shed, no matter what the circumstances. 'It's wonderful.'

'Shall we bathe, madam?'

She laughed. 'How will we fit?'

He gave her a saucy raise of his eyebrows. 'Where there's a will there's a way.'

Slowly, in the glittering light, they undressed each other. Beth's fingers trembled with anticipation. She saw the desire in Noah's eyes and knew hers reflected the same.

'You are beautiful.' He sighed, kissing her exposed neck, his hands running gently over her breasts until she arched into him.

It'd been so long, so very long since they'd made love and she was desperate to feel him.

Carefully they eased into the bath and she revelled in his erection, teasing it further with her fingers until he moaned. She had to kneel as he lay back, his legs over the side of the bath and his hands roaming her body while she kissed his chest.

'I've been waiting for this for so long,' he murmured.

'Me too,' she whispered against his mouth.

'I've not had the energy until today. Then suddenly I felt more my old self. I'm sorry for making you wait.'

'Don't apologise, you were exhausted.'

'And now I'm eager for you.' He grasped her by the hips and with water dangerously close to spilling over, he drew her on top of him.

Beth shivered with an aching need only he could fulfil.

Together they moved as one, slowly at first, then faster until water splashed over the side of the bath, soaking the towels.

Satisfaction came quickly for them both and she laid her head on his shoulder, panting.

'I'm so pleased you didn't go to the theatre,' Noah murmured, kissing her palm and her fingertips of one hand.

'I nearly did go, too.' She raised her head and smiled at him. 'This is *so* much better.'

She climbed off him and squashed as they were; she turned to lie against his chest, their legs hanging over the side.

Sipping the wine, Beth relaxed completely. 'Aunty Hilda will have a fit when she sees all these candles being burnt.'

Laughter rumbled in Noah's chest. 'I doubt she'll mind very much at all.'

'I don't want this night to ever end.' Beth ran her fingers over Noah's thigh.

He kissed the side of her head. 'With a house full of people, I can't promise you another bath like this,' he joked, 'but we'll spend every moment together until I have to go. I think I'm over the worst of my sleeping around the clock.'

'Talk to me,' she whispered, stroking his arm.

'What can I tell you that I've not already mentioned in my letters?'

'I never know where you are because of the censors,' she prompted. 'The newspapers aren't always accurate in what they report.'

'Well, after landing in France, our first battle was Loos, near the Belgium border. From there we went into Belgium and near a town called Ypres.' Noah drank his wine and put it back on the floor.

'What is Belgium like?'

'Aside from the destruction brought by the war, the country-side is flat with many farms, and beautiful in its own way. We only saw a small part of it and the Germans had smashed it up quite a bit. We stayed in that area over the winter and into spring.'

'And after Ypres?'

'We travelled south over the border into northern France and the area around Albert. That's where we launched the big attack in June.'

'I read about it in the newspapers. Such losses. Jane's Alfie was wounded again, a week after Alfred died.'

'Yes, I heard. Our brigade is vastly reduced, many of them are. We've been stuck around the Somme for months. In and out of the trenches. We take a mile from the Germans and then they take it back again. It seems pointless in many ways, but I suppose the chief commanders know what they are doing. However, I hope we don't go back to that sector. It's a dismal place.'

'I think we should go to bed,' she suggested, climbing out of the bath. The water was becoming cold. Grabbing a towel from the back of the chair, she wrapped it around her, and they collected the wet towels from the floor. 'These floorboards have never been so clean with the amount of water spilt on them lately.' She chuckled.

'Good thing I rolled up the rug. What about all this?' He indicated the bath.

'Leave it. I'll sort it out in the morning. Tonight is about us being together.'

'There's nothing I want more.' He kissed her gently. 'I can't bear leaving you again.'

She placed a finger on his lips. 'Don't talk of leaving, not yet. We'll think about that later.'

Hand in hand, they walked upstairs to the bedroom.

CHAPTER 19

*E*ntering the kitchen after spending the morning updating the account ledger and writing cheques to pay invoices, Beth smiled as Ruby grinned up at her. Her daughter was growing fast, and at nine months old was the joy of Beth's life. Ruby and Ivy had made Christmas a little more cheerful with their laughter and antics.

Giving Ruby the last spoonful of mashed potatoes, Peggy cleaned her granddaughter's face. 'My look at the state of you, missy.'

'I'll take her for a walk in the pram. It'll get her off to sleep and I need a walk. I've spent too many days cooped up inside with all this rain we've had,' Beth said, plucking her daughter from Peggy's lap and placing her in the pram. 'You need a break from her, too.'

'I never need a break from Ruby.' Peggy turned away and coughed. The winter air always returned the chill to her weak chest, and she coughed most days. 'But I might have a lie down.'

'You didn't sleep much last night,' Aunty Hilda said, coming in from the scullery. 'I'd be surprised if you got a few hours' sleep all night.'

'I feel bad keeping you awake.' Peggy washed up the bowl.

'I manage fine with what I get, don't worry.' Aunty Hilda put the post on the sideboard. 'That lot was just dropped off by that new post office lass. Margery Lynch's girl. I don't have my glasses on me, so I can't see who it's from. I don't think she's right in the head. She smiles too much, it's not right.'

'Who?' Beth pinned on her black felt hat, which had material blue forget-me-nots stitched onto the brim.

'Margery Lynch's girl.'

'What's wrong with smiling?' Peggy asked, drying her hands.

'She shouldn't be grinning like a gormless fool when she might be delivering mail from the War Office.' Aunty Hilda tutted.

Beth pounced on the mail. When Noah and his brothers finished their leave in November, Noah promised Beth he'd write more often. The week at home with her and the family had helped the old Noah to resurface. By the time she said goodbye to him at the train station, Beth's love for him had deepened even further, as his for her. No matter how long they'd be separated for, they would handle it, knowing they had each other.

'Any for me?' Peggy asked, putting a little woollen jacket on Ruby and an extra blanket in her pram.

Beth flipped through the envelopes. 'A letter for you, Peggy, from James.' She handed it over.

'How lovely.' Peggy stroked the letter, coughing at the relief of not receiving bad news.

Skipping the business letters, Beth's stomach clenched at the last envelope with a Red Cross stamp. She glanced up at Aunty Hilda. 'It's from the Red Cross.'

Aunty Hilda sat down at the table and Peggy grasped her hand in comfort.

Anxious, Beth slit open the envelope and pulled out the scrap of paper.

. . .

Dear Mrs Jackson,

It is with great pleasure I write to you with information about your brother, Private William Beaumont. He has been located in a prison situated over the French-German border. A colleague of mine has visited the camp and found your brother in good health mentally, though he is a little undernourished as to be expected as a P.O.W.

Private Beaumont asked for us to convey his love to his family and to tell you not to worry. He is doing all right.

I hope this brings you some peace of mind at this difficult time. We will endeavour to stay in contact with your brother and send correspondence accordingly. You may reply to your brother through me at the address on the envelope.

Yours respectively,
Mrs Eileen Hodge.
January 15ᵗʰ 1917.
Brussels, Belgium

BETH HELD the letter to her chest, smiling at Peggy and Aunty Hilda. 'Will is alive and well. Can you believe it? He's sent his love and told us not to worry.' Beth couldn't believe it. After so long to actually hear words from Will was such an enormous relief.

Aunty Hilda wiped her eyes with the edge of her apron. 'Our lad has been so brave, so brave…'

'If only Dad had waited to hear this news,' Beth murmured, still unable to forgive her dad for leaving her.

'Shall we send Will a parcel via Mrs Hodges?' Aunty Hilda suggested.

Beth nodded, liking the idea. 'We can try, that's for sure. I'm certain Mrs Hodge would do her utmost to get the parcel to Will.'

'Let's hope the Germans don't take it!' Peggy muttered.

Aunty Hilda sniffed. 'It's perfect timing for that to arrive only a week after the second anniversary of Mary and Ronnie's deaths. It's fitting, as though the fates are giving us some hope.'

Beth placed the post on the table. She'd found the second anniversary of her mam and Ronnie's drowning hard. They never got to see Ruby. 'I'm going out for that walk. The rain has thawed the snow and Ruby sleeps better once she's been outside.'

'It'll be mucky in the lanes,' Aunty Hilda warned, pulling herself together and filling the kettle with water. 'Reggie is checking the traps for rabbits. He's taken Davy with him. Tom and the others are cleaning out Snowy's stall. I heard that Tom talking to the other lads saying he's going to enlist next week.'

Beth paused as she pulled her coat on. 'He's only sixteen.'

'Aye, well, he's going to lie about his age. Apparently, one of the lads in the village got accepted just after Christmas by lying about his age and Tom's thinking of doing the same.'

'We need to tell his mam,' Peggy said, still holding James's letter. 'He's too young to go.'

'Reggie says Tom's mam will likely support his lie,' Aunty Hilda told them as she added tea leaves to the teapot. 'His mam is a right one for money, she'll welcome his army pay. You know her, don't you, Peggy? It's Jilly Forsyth from Sunny Hill.'

'That's Tom's mam?' Peggy frowned. 'When he said he was a Forsyth, I thought he meant the family from near Silcoates Mill.'

'No, that's a cousin.' Aunty Hilda nodded wisely.

'Well, we start harvesting the first crop of rhubarb next week,' Beth added, checking that Ruby was warm enough for the outdoors. 'And none of those boys will have the time nor energy to think about enlisting. I'll see you both later.'

Pushing the pram down the drive, Beth stopped at the gate and decided which way to go. Either up the lane to the village or down the lane towards Beck Bottom Road. She turned right and headed down the lane, not in the mood to stop and talk to people in the village. A quiet walk to clear her mind from the accounts was needed and she wanted to think about Will being found and what she'd send to him.

By the side of the lane, snowdrops flowered along with the

odd polyanthus. Puddles still dotted the lane from the overnight rain shower, which had melted the remaining snow. A flock of starlings flew overhead, silhouetted against the pale grey sky.

'Look at the birds, Ruby.' She pointed upwards but when she looked at her daughter, she was asleep snug and warm under a thick woollen blanket.

Beth gazed at her daughter, still in awe of the little creature she had made with Noah. Her baby had to be the prettiest she'd even seen, though she was careful not to say that in front of Joanna and Ivy.

Although it was mid-January, the snow that month so far had been in fits and starts, not sticking around for long, which gave them a boost to start ploughing the far fields ready to plant seeds in the next few weeks.

Beth was eager for spring to arrive and to feel the warm days again. She knew how difficult Noah and the men had it in France, wallowing in trenches inches thick with mud and water. Noah filled his letters with how they coped with everyday life during winter on the battlefield. He mentioned how happy they were for the respites they received when they were rostered out of the lines and sent to nearby villages for a few days' rest.

Every week she sent parcels to Noah and his brothers, lovingly put together by herself, Peggy, and Aunty Hilda. His heartfelt thanks and appreciation was written in every letter. The men shared their parcels, so everyone benefitted. Aunty Hilda's fruit cake was a hit, and they couldn't get enough of meat paste or herrings in a can, tins of condensed milk and bags of sweets. Newspapers were passed around until they became tattered and torn. It gave Beth such pleasure to send him the things that helped make their lives a little better.

Throughout the long dark nights, she, Peggy and Aunty Hilda knitted socks and scarves, mittens and mufflers, knowing their time and efforts were gratefully received.

Beth hoped that with spring's arrival the war might draw to a close. She'd also hoped that she'd fallen pregnant again from Noah's leave in November, but that hadn't happened, and despite a few days of sadness that she wasn't pregnant, Beth had soon cheered up over Christmas as Joanna and Ivy came to spend a week with them and Ruby started crawling.

In truth, she was too busy to have another child, and perhaps it'd been a blessing she hadn't fallen pregnant.

Turning onto Beck Bottom Road, Beth pushed the pram close to the verge as a horse and cart went by. The driver dipped his hat, but Beth didn't recognise him and wondered at it. Before the war she'd known nearly everyone within a two-mile radius of the farm, but now with the local men gone, strangers had come to take their place and those who were rejected by the army came to take up the work positions previously done by people she knew.

Concentrating on manoeuvring around puddles, she wasn't aware at first of the long sleek cream-coloured motor car with a black roof pulling up alongside. She turned to stare at it, hoping they didn't want her to move over any further or she'd be in the ditch.

The window was wound down and the driver, a woman, gave her a warm smile as she stopped the vehicle.

Beth didn't know her and was about to keep walking when the door opened, and Louis Melville's head appeared.

Smothering a small groan, Louis awkwardly climbed out of the motor car, leaning heavily on his cane. He wore a black suit, not his uniform.

'It's good to see you, Beth,' he said, straightening up, his face pale.

'I didn't know you were home,' she answered, then thought that was a foolish thing to say. Why would she know?

'It's been a long time coming. I cannot tell you how happy I am to be back in Yorkshire and familiar surroundings.'

'Have you been in hospital all this time?'

'I was in several hospitals until just recently. I was released from the latest hospital a few weeks ago on the condition I stayed in London. Thankfully, my family's townhouse isn't too far from the hospital and my sister was an excellent nurse.' He gave a brief smile. 'But I was hankering after a change of scenery. My sister's noisy friends become a bit tiring after a while.'

'So, you've come home.'

'I have. The doctors agreed since the manor is a convalescent home with a residing doctor and his team. As soon as he said I could travel, I hired Miss Green here to drive me home.'

'From London?' Surprise widened her eyes. 'Why didn't you take a train?'

He glanced away to the pram and back again. 'My injuries prevent me from sitting for long periods of time. With Miss Green driving me we could stop overnight along the way and whenever I felt the need to stop and rest.' He limped a step closer to the pram and carefully peered in as though movement caused him great pain. 'My, she has grown. She's beautiful.'

Beth swelled with pride. 'She's nine months old now.'

Melville stared at Ruby for a moment. 'Nine months. I remember the day she was born. How tiny she was.' He glanced at Beth. 'So much has happened since then.' He straightened up again and winced at the effort. He looked in agony.

'Are you home for long?' she asked.

'Until I heal, which maybe some time. My leg isn't the only problem, and that is bad enough. I also received a chest wound and it's proven rather difficult to heal. Anyway, I should be going and not keep you standing still in the cold.' He glanced again at Ruby. 'I would very much consider it a marvellous thing if you would come and visit me sometime?'

'Visit you?' Her tone rose in surprise. 'Why?'

His lips moved as if to smile, but didn't quite manage it. 'I would like us to be friends.'

'Why?'

'So, I can make it up to you, what I did in the past.'

'It's done, forgotten. I am married and I have Ruby. We can't be friends.'

'Do you know that your husband saved my life?'

Beth took a step back in shock. 'What did you say?'

'Noah Jackson saved my life.'

She stared at him, trying to work out if he was lying or not, but he'd know she'd only have to ask Noah for the truth. A quick spark of anger ignited in her chest towards Noah for not telling her. How could he have not mentioned this to her?

'I see he didn't tell you.' Melville shrugged. 'I'm sorry. I do not mean to cause trouble.'

'It's what you do though, isn't it? You are always causing me trouble.' She wasn't angry at him.

He looked up at the scudding clouds, the wind was picking up. 'I have lost friends in this war.' He stared at Beth before glancing at Ruby. 'There are things I must tell you. Can you meet me somewhere?'

She started to shake her head, but he held up his hand.

'It can be at a tea room or restaurant, somewhere surrounded by people, or a walk in Thorne's Park, perhaps? I only want to talk.'

'I don't think so.'

'Please, Beth. I have no right to ask anything from you, but I have something I wish to discuss with you.'

She couldn't help but be intrigued. 'Very well, I'll meet you at Thorne's Park next Saturday at midday, weather permitting.'

He smiled, a look of gratitude in his dark eyes. 'Thank you. I'll see you then.'

Beth turned the pram around and headed back to the farm as the motor car pulled away. What on earth was she doing meeting him of all people?

* * *

BETH HAD HOPED the weather would be inclement for her meeting with Louis Melville on Saturday, but as luck would have it, the sun shone in one of those rare bright winter days.

From the tram's window, she spotted Louis standing by the gate at the Denby Dale Road entrance. Beth took a deep breath and gripped her bag tighter as she stepped down from the tram and walked towards him.

Although still cold, requiring Beth to wear her warm black coat and velvet hat, the lack of wind made the day pleasant. Many people took advantage of the clear sky to parade around the park, and the tram from town was packed with families.

'I'm glad you came,' he said in greeting, doffing his hat while leaning heavily on his cane.

'I nearly didn't.' That was the truth. She'd worried for days about meeting him and what it would achieve. Such was her anxiety over it, she didn't tell Aunty Hilda or Peggy what she had planned. Instead, they thought she was at the stall with Leah. She *had* gone to see Leah, but only for half an hour for a quick chat with her and Fred before catching the tram.

Without speaking, they turned and entered the park. An avenue of trees cloaked in tight green buds stretched before them as children ran about, excited to be free of restraining hands.

Not knowing how to start a conversation with this man, Beth gazed out over the lawns, keeping a few feet apart from him as they strolled, or rather as Louis limped along leaning on his cane.

'It is a fine day,' he said.

'It is.'

Minutes passed and Beth adjusted her stride to compensate for his disability. 'Are you up for this walk?'

'I need exercise. I refuse to sit around all day. Captain Scott says walking will strengthen my leg wound.'

'You look in pain.'

He gave a snort. 'There are times when I wish I was dead, such is the agony. It is those times I curse Noah Jackson for saving me.'

A few more minutes went by and Beth sighed. 'I don't know why you wish to talk to me, Mr Melville. We have nothing in common, nor do we mix in the same circles.'

'I'm not asking you to dinner at the manor, Beth,' he said mockingly.

'I wouldn't attend.'

That made him smile. 'No, you wouldn't.'

'Then why this meeting?'

'Once before I explained to you that I am a changed man, or continually trying to be. I am not totally converted yet and can still lose my temper occasionally.' He gave a wry grin. 'But I feel I am improving my manner. War soon commands a level playing field and teaches you to be humble. Bullets and shells do not distinguish between private and officer, rich or poor. I have survived the battlefield, but I'm not out of danger.'

'What do you mean?'

'The doctors in London do not give me hope that I shall live to be an old man. Indeed, they wonder how I'm still breathing. Shell fragments are still lodged in my chest, close to my heart and lungs, apparently.' He tapped his injured leg. 'This, as infuriatingly painful as it is, is the least of my worries.'

She noticed he was becoming slower with each step. 'Do you want to sit for a moment on that bench over there?'

He nodded, his face showed the strain of the walk.

When they were seated and he stretched his bad leg out in front of him, he rested his cane between them on the bench.

'I do not wish to see you in pain,' she said stiffly, finding it difficult to be friendly with him. 'I know we were once enemies, but I've grown up a lot since then. I am no longer the girl who worked on a market stall. Rather, I'm a married woman, a mother, and I run a business.'

'You've always been above every other woman I know.' His appraising smile seemed genuine. 'You're the only woman who has given me such moments of insane madness and yet, one smile from you and I come completely undone. You are like a drug, Beth Beaumont.'

'I'm Beth Jackson.'

He bowed his head. 'Forgive me, but you'll always be Beth Beaumont to me.'

She watched some small boys playing ball. 'What did you want to talk to me about?'

'Ruby.'

Snapping her head around, she glared at him, instantly defensive. 'My daughter has nothing to do with you.'

He raised his hand in surrender. 'Please, I only wish the utmost best for her.'

'I don't understand.'

He paused, took off his black hat and wiped the sheen of perspiration from his forehead with a handkerchief, and Beth realised how much of an effort this meeting was for him.

'When I lay wounded on the battlefield and Jackson rescued me, I told him that I'd made provisions for Ruby.'

'What? Provisions?' Shocked rendered her unable to say more.

'I will try to explain.' He shrugged, a little flustered. 'My feelings for you are complex, they always have been. I have always wanted you. Even when you turned me down for a miner, I still wanted you. My pride, my rage, my desperate yearning to be loved by you made me act like a monster. I cannot undo that. Naturally, you'd take nothing from me, but the moment I saw your daughter, the day she was born, only an hour old, I instantly wanted to make everything right between us.' His fingers ran down the pleat in his trousers. 'I felt I could make good some wrongs. So, I have made an account for Ruby with my solicitors. I've freed up some money to be invested on her behalf and the dividends will be hers at the age of twenty-one.'

Beth could only stare at him.

'It is highly unlikely I will marry and father children. The shrapnel in my chest doesn't give me a long future and besides, there is no woman I feel I could love. My father is desperate for me to give him an heir, but it won't happen, unfortunately. My sister has no plans to have a family either. She is one of those independent women of London who is a little too free with herself, if you get my meaning. I have several cousins who I cannot stand and who are rich enough in their own way. I have no need nor inclination to have them included in my will.' He gazed up at the sky. 'I want Ruby to benefit from my wealth as an eternal apology to you for my actions.'

'I don't know what to say.' And she didn't she was utterly gobsmacked.

'Your husband had plenty to say.' Louis chuckled. 'He dragged me back to our own trenches to save me from dying out in no man's land. He told me he didn't want me to die and leave anything to his daughter.' Louis looked Beth in the eyes. 'In his shoes, I would have done the same. However, this is more than just our feelings. What you and your husband think about me isn't the issue. This inheritance is for Ruby, to give her a life without financial hardship. Surely you as her mother cannot deny her that?'

Beth rubbed her face with both hands, chuckling.

'You think this is amusing?' he asked, astonished.

'I think that once again you've had the last word. You've done something, which I think in your heart is genuine and decent, for Ruby, and which I cannot refuse for her sake, but it'll also cause trouble between Noah and me.'

Louis leaned forward eagerly. 'I have done it for her. Not you nor Jackson.'

'Yes, and you know Noah will never agree to it.'

'It's not up to him to agree. When Ruby reaches twenty-one she can decide what she does with that money. She can spend every penny of it or give it away or do whatever she wants with it. It'll be her choice. Not yours and not Noah's.'

'But you must understand that Noah and me will argue about

this. Is that what you want? To cause discord in our marriage? Are you hoping we'll argue so much we'll end up hating each other and I'll come running to you and your money?'

He grabbed his cane and jerked stiffly and painfully to his feet. 'My thoughts were only for Ruby. She is the child of the woman I admire above anyone else. She is the child I wish I had with you. I've said all I've come to say. Good day, Mrs Jackson.' He stepped away as Beth rose to her feet.

She didn't call him back or run after him. He'd dropped a bomb of his own, and the fallout would be just as disastrous as any on the battlefield.

CHAPTER 20

*A*s well as actual rain, a shower of dirt and small stones poured down upon Noah and the men of his unit as they waited in the assembly trenches. Dawn was an hour away and their order to attack the German trenches situated near the village of Tilloy was planned for seven o'clock.

During the night, they'd marched from the cellar they'd been billeted in on the edge of Arras to take up position at two o'clock without incident. The men snatched minutes of sleep at a time despite the enemy's bombardment of the forward trenches and the light rain that fell.

Noah yawned, tired and cold. The April morning was frigid, their breaths misting in the air. He longed for summer, warmth and sunshine. He took the photograph out of his pocket, shielding it from the raindrops and dirt.

Two beloved faces gazed back at him in sepia. Beth sat straight-backed on a wooden chair, holding Ruby on her lap, wearing a frilly white dress. Beth had sent it as a present to celebrate Ruby's first birthday. Soon it would be Beth's birthday. How many more special days would he miss?

He tucked the photograph away, and pulling up the collar of

his coat, he squirmed against the earthen wall and closed his eyes. Another hour of sleep would be welcomed.

Whispered voices carried along the trench. James and Sid were laughing softly at something and beside him Albie snored gently. Noah thought to write a letter to Beth later, even though he only wrote one yesterday after spending hours as a member of one of the carrying parties taking supplies up to the lines.

The drone of a falling shell, which then landed and exploded thirty yards away, shook the ground, vibrating through his body. He swore as dirt pelted him, tinging off his tin helmet like hail.

'For God's sake,' Albie murmured. 'I can't get a bloody minute's rest.'

'The sun's rising. Have we enough light to play cards by?' James asked them.

'It's too cold to concentrate,' Noah mumbled.

Sid chuckled. 'You just don't enjoy losing, our kid.'

Noah went to speak when the droning sound came again. In the second for him to realise it was closer than the one before, he pushed Albie to one side. He screamed at them to take cover. The explosion shuddered ground like an earthquake. His teeth rattled in his head and a pain seared through his ears. The air seemed sucked out of his chest. His lungs wouldn't work. He couldn't breathe.

Dazed, he lifted his head where he lay at the bottom of the trench with Albie pinned underneath him.

'Noah,' Albie croaked, moving his arms. 'Noah?'

He sucked in a lung full of air thick with dust. 'I'm all right. I think. You?'

'Aye.'

Ears buzzing as though a thousand bees were trapped inside his head, Noah shook his head to try and clear the confusion. Something held his legs down and he twisted to see the earthen wall of the trench had collapsed, pinning Noah's feet.

Albie slithered out from under him, coughing.

Noah yanked hard on his legs.

'Wait a minute.' Albie helped by pulling off sandbags that had fallen from the top of the trench.

Along the trench the walls had tumbled inwards, creating mounds of dirt, sandbags and timber slats that had once held back the soil. The smoke cleared slightly, but as another bomb fell close by, Noah ducked down and covered his head with his arms.

'You're free,' Albie said, placing the final sandbag back up onto the side of the ruined trench wall.

Suddenly, Noah saw a leg and an arm sticking out from under the collapsed pile of earth and sandbags further down the trench.

'Sid!' He scrambled over the broken duckboards on his hands and knees, screaming their names. 'James!'

Albie was instantly beside him, dragging at the dirt with his hands, trying to free their brothers. Other soldiers not injured helped, while Sergeant Bourke gave frenzied orders to clear the debris and watch for an attack.

They uncovered Sid first, but he lay with his eyes open and Noah recoiled. 'No... No...'

'Stretcher-bearers!' Albie yelled, digging out the soil around James's head. 'Stretcher-bearers!' His frantic calls for help brought a young stretcher-bearer running into their part of the trench, but the damage was done. The shell had landed too close to Sid and James for them to survive the blast.

Noah wiped the muck from Sid's face, smearing the mud across his cheeks. Gently, he closed his brother's eyes and cradled him against his chest.

Distraught, he didn't hear Sergeant Bourke's command to release Sid to the stretcher-bearers. He snarled like a dog when someone grasped his arms to take Sid away.

'No!' Noah rocked, stuffing his fist into his mouth to stop from raging as he watched the medics take Sid and James down the trench to the casualty clearing station. His mind was shattered.

'Go with them, quickly now.' Sergeant Bourke grabbed Noah and Albie's arms, thrusting them down the trench. 'Be back in ten minutes. Go!'

Stumbling over men's legs who sat on the fire step or pushing past those who were clearing space from the damage of the shells, Noah hurried along the narrow trench. He ducked instinctively as another shell fell just short of the trench, sending up a fountain of earth, knocking him sideways.

'We're sitting ducks here!' one soldier shouted to no one as they ran past.

Down another narrow trench and past a line of soldiers making their way forward, Noah and Albie dodged men and supplies.

Carrying parties forced their way through the tight walkways to the forward trenches. To Noah, it felt like swimming against a tide. Another shell burst nearby, making every one pause and duck down.

Every second Noah had to wait to pass someone was another second too long. The crowded supply routes finally opened into a wide area behind the support and reserve trenches. Carriages, horses, motor ambulances, piles of supplies and units of waiting soldiers were spread across the fields.

A tent with a large red cross on the side had been erected for the casualty clearing station. Around it, hundreds of stretchers were piled in readiness for the battle. Two stretchers-bearers stood smoking, awaiting the carnage they'd soon have to retrieve. Two nurses were opening crates of supplies, their white aprons stark against the drab of the khaki tent.

Inside the tent, Noah found Sid and James still on stretchers on the grass. They both looked like they were sleeping. There didn't seem to be a mark on either of them.

Were they only unconscious? Had he got it wrong? Hope swelled and Noah took half a step forward.

A doctor came and bent over to examine the Jackson brothers. A nurse took the second identification disc off the long cords that hung on each of their necks, leaving just one disc remaining. The doctor murmured something to the nurse as she wrote on square-shaped identification cards she'd tie on their bodies. She paused and nodded in response to the doctor's instructions.

In silence, Noah stood with Albie as the doctor pronounced his brothers dead. The nurse kept writing without looking up. In her hand she held the two discs. Noah couldn't stop staring at them, knowing that before long, his mam would be holding those discs and crying over two dead sons. He should be there with her to support her. He needed to write to Beth and warn her, but the officials would have telegrams sent quicker than his letter would arrive. It would devastate his mam. Three sons dead. How would she deal with it? How would any of them deal with it?

The doctor came over to them, taking his glasses off to clean them with a cloth from his pocket. 'I'm sorry. It seems it was instantaneous. There's nothing I could do. They were already dead before they arrived here.'

Albie staggered. Noah grabbed his shoulder to steady him but didn't look at him or speak. He couldn't. To see his own pain reflected in Albie's eyes would bring him undone, and to speak would mean he'd have to acknowledge the loss…

A stretcher-bearer rushed past, bringing in another wounded man. Noah pushed Albie outside into the weak morning sunshine.

Slowly, as though sleepwalking, they made the return journey through the trenches to their own position.

Sergeant Bourke didn't ask any questions. He didn't have to as Noah and Albie slid onto the fire step.

Albie bowed his head while Noah rested back against the trench wall, unable to think clearly.

'They were damn good soldiers.' Bourke swore softly and made a note in his little book. Then he stormed along the trench, barking orders. 'Check your weapons, men. Look lively, damn you. Why aren't you wearing your helmet, soldier? Are you a fool? Is your head made of steel?'

Noah let the sergeant's voice swirl over him. He felt frozen, numb.

'We can't die, Noah,' Albie whispered hoarsely. 'It wouldn't be fair to mam to lose us all.'

Noah stared at the dirt wall opposite him. Shortly, a whistle would blow, and he'd be clambering over that wall and into the pits of hell. If he were to die today along with Sid and James, he prayed it would happen quickly.

* * *

'WHAT DO you mean Louis Melville's leaving you money?' Jane's shocked face stared back at Beth.

'Keep your voice down,' Beth hissed, glancing around the packed tea room. 'It's not for me, it's for Ruby when she's older. It's in a trust or something and I or Noah can't touch it.'

'Even so, you can't allow him to do it.'

Beth groaned in frustration and wished she'd not confided in Jane, but she had to talk to someone about it. '*I'm* not taking it. I'll not see a penny. Ruby will get it when she's twenty-one, apparently.'

Jane tilted her head, eyes narrowing. 'Do you believe him? Do you think that he's just saying this to get to you and it all could be a lie? Because, really, it sounds ridiculous that he would give your child a small fortune.'

Stirring her tea, Beth shrugged. 'I don't understand it either, but that's what he said he's done for her. He told me he wished he'd treated me better, and if he had, perhaps I might have felt differently about him. He likes to think of Ruby as the daughter we would have had.'

'He's delusional. That's dangerous.' Jane's eyes widened. 'You have to stay away from him.'

'I don't think he's dangerous. Not any more. He's riddled with pain.'

'Do you really think he's changed?' Jane seemed doubtful as she pushed away a strand of red hair that had come loose from under her hat.

'In some ways, yes. There seems less arrogance about him.'

'How many times have you met him in the park now?'

Beth glanced out the window at the drizzling rain, which had spoilt the sunshine of the morning. May was proving to be a month of mixed weather, warm one day and cold the next. 'Twice. The first time back in January and just recently he sent a note asking for me to meet him last Saturday.'

'Why did you go? You hate him.'

'I don't hate him, not any more. I did, naturally, for a long time, but well… I've matured and perhaps so has he.' Beth played with her spoon. 'Louis is more humble than before.'

'*Louis?*' Jane glared at her. 'You're calling him by his first name?'

'Jane, I can't keep being nasty and holding a grudge. Life's too short. He's doing all the right things. He's trying to undo the wrongs of the past. He wants to be my friend.'

'A friend?' Jane raised an eyebrow. 'And what does Noah think of all this?'

'I've not told him.'

'Are you mad?' Jane tutted. 'Noah will lose his head over this, and rightly so.'

'He knows about the money Louis has put aside for Ruby. He doesn't know about the two meetings in the park.'

'Then tell him, for God's sake.'

'I can't. He's taken James and Sid's deaths hard. It'd be cruel to burden him with this when he's out there.'

'So why do you keep meeting Melville?'

'I've done it twice, Jane. It's been two meetings in a public park. I'm not having a torrid love affair with him.'

'Do you want to?'

'No!' Beth gasped. 'How can you say such a thing to me? You know Noah is my life.'

Jane shrugged. 'We're in a war. People act strangely in a war, you know that.'

'I'd never do that.' Beth sipped her tea.

'Maybe Melville is hoping Noah gets killed. He's probably softening you up so that if you become a widow, he can scoop right in and save you.'

Annoyed, Beth glared at her. 'I don't need saving.'

'And the farm? Last year's harvest wasn't the best, was it?'

Sighing, Beth leaned back in the chair. 'While it's true the farm profits aren't great, I'll keep it going somehow and without any help from Louis Melville. I have to keep it going for Will's sake.'

'Just be careful of Melville.'

'I am always on guard with him, have no fear about that.'

'Will you see him again?'

'I'm not sure. He wants to see Ruby.'

'I hope he's not becoming obsessed with her as he was with you.'

'He still has feelings for me,' Beth admitted.

'You're playing with fire, Beth. I'm worried.' Jane sipped her tea.

'Don't be. I can handle him.'

'You couldn't last time, remember?'

'That was nearly four years ago, Jane. It feels like a lifetime ago. I'm not the same person and I don't think he is either.'

'I don't understand why you are being friendly with him. It makes no sense to me at all. If he wants to give Ruby some money, then deal with that in twenty years' time. Until then, leave well alone.'

'I'm not encouraging him, if that's what you think. I have enough to do at home.'

'Then stop meeting him.'

Beth rubbed her forehead. 'He wants to see Ruby next Saturday.'

'Say no. I'm telling you, Beth, as your dearest and longest friend, this will end in tears if you don't stop seeing him. Think of Noah.'

'Lord, you're making it sound so sordid.'

'Answer me this then. *Why* are you meeting him?'

'Truthfully, I don't know. Curiosity perhaps, definitely on the first meeting in the park. But when I saw him last Saturday, we just talked. He told me about Amsterdam and the other places he's travelled. His father's health isn't good, so Louis wants to visit him as soon as he's fit enough to travel himself. He spoke a little of the war and the effects it's had on him. I found that interesting as I was able to learn about it from another perspective besides what Noah writes in his letters.'

'An enemy to a friend,' Jane murmured. 'Would Noah be so understanding?'

'No, of course he wouldn't be.'

'Maybe if Melville had shown that side of himself to you four years ago, your life might be very different by now. You might be mistress of the manor and not a rhubarb farm.'

Beth gave a small grin. 'I'd still have chosen Noah.'

'I hope so.'

Sipping the last of her tea, Beth collected her bag. 'I'd best be off. I've got to visit the bank and then the post office.'

Jane stood and picked up her shopping. 'Yes, and I'll go home and give my mother-in-law a rest from the kids. Freddie's a right handful at the moment. He's two next month and he runs about and makes demands as though he's five.'

They walked out onto Westgate, noticing the rain had stopped.

'Bring Freddie over to the farm and let him run with Ivy in the fields. Joanna is often over these days. She's tired of being in her house all the time with just Ivy, so she comes every second or third day now. She's thinking of getting a job, too.'

'I'd go mad if I didn't have my job.' Jane grunted. 'A noisy mill is still quieter than all those Taylors!'

Beth kissed Jane's cheeks. 'Come over for Sunday dinner. Joanna will be there, too. Peggy will enjoy seeing Freddie, you know how she is with babies.'

Jane's expression turned sad. 'How is Peggy coping?'

Beth sighed deeply. 'She's not, not really. She just gets through each day. To lose three sons, well, how do you recover from that?'

'It's so tragic.'

'Peggy is beside herself with worry that she'll lose them all...' Beth shivered at the thought of Noah never coming home.

'She doesn't even have their graves nearby to visit.'

'Will you come on Sunday? It'll be lovely to have you and Freddie at the table.'

'I will, thanks. See you then.' Jane headed off to the tram stop while Beth went along Westgate towards the post office, putting off the visit to the bank a little longer. Funds were dwindling in the farm's account and Beth hoped they'd have a good harvest this year and that the prime minister, David Lloyd George's incentives for farmers would stabilise the markets.

Seed prices grew more each year, which effectively made the crop more expensive to produce and sell and the higher prices at the markets were not welcomed by the buyers. The shortage of male labourers working the fields also caused headaches and although Beth was willing to hire women to replace the men who'd enlisted, she found the few village women she hired either didn't turn up each morning or disappeared during the day and went home.

Last month Tom and two other lads had joined the army, leaving only Reggie, young Davey and one other lad called Arthur to work on the farm with Beth.

Another problem was that Leah struggled each day to sell the vegetables at competitive prices. Encouraged by the government, people all over the country dug up their own gardens and planted vegetables. Allotments became the word on everyone's lips. The government also made it illegal for people to consume more than two courses for lunch and three courses for dinner in a public place. So, Beth's regular customers, the owners of restaurants and cafes, no longer bought as many vegetables from the Beaumont stall as before.

Only three months ago, the Royal Family endorsed a government incentive for people to *voluntarily* reduce their eating and to begin *rationing* themselves on their food intake. Beth feared for the farm's income.

With her mind on the problems of the farm and the Melville situation, she wasn't at first aware of the commotion further along. Was it an anti-war demonstration for they were growing in popularity now?

A group of people stood gathered and a policeman was running across the street towards them.

Passing the crowd, Beth peeked between the people to see what all the fuss was about. She glimpsed what seemed to be a man lying on the ground. A cane with a gold top lay abandoned beside his legs.

Beth knew that cane.

She squeezed through the murmuring people to see the man better.

Surprised that Louis Melville lay on the ground beside the road, she knelt down beside him. 'Louis?'

'Do you know him, madam?' the constable asked, kneeling opposite.

'He's Louis Melville from Melville Manor, Alverthorpe Road, Kirkhamgate.' She held his gloved hand, noticing his hat lay further away. He looked unconscious. 'What happened?'

The constable glanced around at the crowd. 'Anyone see what happened?'

'He came out of that shop,' an older woman announced, pointing to the men's hat shop behind her. 'He kind of fell down the step and knocked into me. I was about to give him a right tongue-lashing, but he fell to the ground and didn't move. Is he dead?'

Beth stared at Melville's pale face. Good Lord, *was* he dead?

The constable felt for a pulse on Louis's neck as the people leaned closer, all talking amongst themselves, eager to witness the drama.

'I think I can feel a pulse, but it's weak. This man needs an ambulance and to be taken to the hospital. Thank you for your help, madam. I'll have someone go to his home and inform them.'

Beth nodded as the constable blew his whistle to a colleague riding a bicycle further up the road.

Still holding Louis's gloved hand, Beth knelt on the hard ground, not knowing what to do and feeling utterly helpless. She couldn't leave him alone. No one deserved to lay ill and alone on the street.

The time seemed to drag by as they waited for an ambulance, but at last one came trundling along and they quickly loaded Louis into it and shut the doors. A moment later it was trundling away again.

The gathering drifted away, the excitement over. Traffic continued going past while Beth stayed rooted to the spot.

Should she go to the hospital or go home?

Would Melville recover or die?

How would she explain her long absence to Peggy and Aunty Hilda? Ruby would be missing her.

Would someone from the manor go and sit beside Melville's hospital bed? Mrs Handry or Captain Scott? Why did she care? She owed him nothing. Yet, something tugged at her brain. If Melville was being honest and intended to leave money to Ruby, then surely she should at least find out if he was all right?

She took a step, then faltered. What if she was seen sitting beside his bed? Gossip would race like wildfire. How would she explain her actions?

Such a risk could destroy her reputation, even her marriage. No, Melville had people looking after him at the manor. Mrs Handry or the kind Doctor Scott would surely visit him in hospital.

Decision made, Beth hurried on to the post office. Then she'd go home to her daughter where she belonged.

CHAPTER 21

A month went by before Beth plucked up the courage to venture to Melville Manor and visit Louis. She took Ruby with her in the pram, telling Aunty Hilda and Peggy she was going for a walk and would call in at the manor to see Mrs Handry and ask if she needed a new order of vegetables.

In the last month, the farm kept Beth fully occupied as she dealt with the everyday issues of running a business during wartime. She'd taken on two women in their thirties, Esther and Joyce, both from Stanley and neighbours of Joanna.

Beth had asked Joanna to work on the farm, but Joanna decided she'd get more money in the munitions factory, while Jimmy's mam took care of Ivy. Beth wondered why Esther and Joyce didn't work in the factories as well for she couldn't match those high wages, but Esther said she preferred being outside and Joyce had a weak chest from working in the mill for years and didn't fancy being stuck in another building all day breathing in noxious fumes.

Both women had taken to farm work like they were born to it, and Reggie treated them no differently to the lads and taught them all he knew. As the summer progressed and the weather became warmer, the farm grew busier and Beth worked long hours.

Noah's letters arrived routinely, full of love and longing. She replied the same, missing him terribly. Working hard helped, but special occasions were difficult. Ruby had taken her first steps and Noah hadn't been there to see it. She told him everything Ruby was doing, and he replied full of questions, but she always sensed his disappointment to be missing out.

Determined to no longer keep secrets from Noah, Beth had even told him that Melville had collapsed in the street and she'd been there to help in a small way. After her visit today, she would write and tell him about that, too. The manor was one of their customers; she was only being polite by calling to ask how he was.

Although that *was* the truth, she still felt a little intrigued by Louis and his insistence to bequeath money to Ruby. Somehow, he'd got under her skin. Each time she saw him, and he behaved decently and kindly, she felt more relaxed and less anxious around him. Four years had marked a lot of changes in them both. She just needed Noah to understand that Louis Melville was no longer a threat to her, or them as a couple.

As she pushed the pram in the June sunshine, it was easy to forget the country fought a war and that just across the English Channel men were fighting and dying. The recent anniversary of Alfred's death had been a sad day, but with the sun shining and Ruby making baby noises in the pram, Beth could believe today was a simple summer's day like those in previous times before the war.

It was only when she turned into the manor's driveway and saw the soldiers playing a gentle game of cricket on the front lawn, and others strolling about or sitting in the shade reading, that she was drawn back to reality.

She was tired of missing Noah, tired of doing everything herself. She wanted Will home and safe to run the farm so she could return to being Noah's wife and concentrate on being a mother to Ruby and future children. Was that so much to ask for?

'Mrs Jackson,' Captain Scott called from where he bowled to a batsman. He quickly gave the ball to another solider and walked over to her.

'It's good to see you, Captain.'

'And you.' He bent to grin at Ruby. 'And look at this beautiful baby I delivered!' he boasted, pleased as punch. 'Isn't she just smashing?'

'She certainly is,' Beth agreed. 'Those soldiers seem to be doing well.'

He glanced at the players. 'Yes, they have recovered enough to be sent back to their regiments. They are due to leave in the morning. I'm expecting another batch of men next Tuesday. Six in total.'

'That'll keep you busy.' She paused as one man yelled catch it and another ran and successfully caught the ball. She brushed a fly away from Ruby's face. 'I've come to see Mrs Handry, but also to inquire after Mr Melville.'

Captain Scott's expression saddened. 'Ah, yes. It's not looking good for him, I'm afraid. Clayton Hospital has released him into my care, merely days ago, but basically there is nothing more that can be done for him.'

Beth jerked her head up to stare at him, not expecting to hear such dire news. 'When Reggie told me last week that Mr Melville was home. I presumed he was well again to leave hospital.'

'Unfortunately, it is the opposite. They operated on him after his collapse, but they found the shrapnel too close to his heart. To remove them would cause severe bleeding. They nearly lost him on the operating table. He's been terribly weak since then.'

'I had no idea he was so ill. I assumed he'd rally…'

'They've allowed him to come home to die. I don't expect him to last another week.'

The news was so unexpected Beth blinked in shock.

'Would you like to say a few words to him? He only has days.'

Beth nodded, not knowing what she'd say to him.

'I'll go inside and see if he's awake. I'll come to the kitchen for you after you've spoken to Mrs Handry.'

Beth thanked him and, pushing the pram, walked over the gravel drive and around to the back of the house and the scullery entrance. A peacock called from somewhere, but Beth couldn't see him.

In the warm kitchen, Mrs Handry turned from stirring a simmering pot and smiled a welcome. 'Mrs Jackson. This is a surprise.'

'I hope I'm not disturbing you, Mrs Handry?'

'Not at all, dear. Come in. Oh my, will you just look at that little beauty.' She beckoned Nora and Jennie to admire Ruby. 'Reggie said she's a bobby dazzler and he wasn't lying.'

'Reggie loves her. He's the closest she'll get to a grandfather. She thinks the world of him. She's always putting her arms up for him to pick her up the minute he walks into the kitchen.' Beth pushed down the pram's hood so Ruby could see more.

'Can she have a piece of shortbread, Mrs Jackson?' Mrs Handry asked.

'I'm sure she'd devour one.' Beth chuckled as Ruby clapped, smiling and showing off her little front teeth.

The blue door opened on the far wall and the captain came down the steps. 'He's awake, Mrs Jackson, and would like to see you.'

Faced with seeing him, Beth baulked.

'We'll look after Ruby, Mrs Jackson. She'll be perfectly fine with us,' Nora said, cooing over the baby.

Mrs Handry sighed. 'He's spoken about you, Mrs Jackson. The

pain medicine makes him talk when he's half asleep. He's always saying sorry.'

Beth didn't know what to say. 'I'll go up for a few minutes. I won't be long.'

'Do you want me to come in with you?' Captain Scott asked at the bottom of the stairs.

'No, I'll be fine.'

'Prepare yourself for change, Mrs Jackson. He isn't as he once was.'

'And he'll definitely not recover?'

'No. The shell fragments have damaged his heart far too much. It's a wonder he's survived this long.'

'Does he know he's dying?'

'Indeed. He made me tell him the truth.'

Beth nodded and slowly went up the wide staircase, remembering the time four years ago when Melville had shown her around the manor to impress her, back when he wanted her to be his wife…

She stopped at the bedroom door, the same room in which she had given birth to Ruby. It felt surreal.

Opening the door, she stepped lightly across the carpet rug to the side of the bed.

Louis watched her approach. He gave a weak smile. 'You came.'

'Yes.' A chair was placed beside the bed and she lowered herself down onto it, trying not to show her astonishment at how different he was. The flesh was stripped from his bones, leaving grey skin pulled tightly over his skeleton. Always a thin man, he now looked half the man he used to be. His dark eyes were sunk deeper into his skull and his lips were a strange shade of blue.

'I'm very glad you are here…' His voice lacked depth and strength.

'Is there anything I can do for you?'

'Just talk to me.' He swallowed, pain made him wince.

'Is your sister here?'

'No... My father died last week... She's gone to Am... Amsterdam...'

'Oh, I'm sorry. I didn't know.' How many more surprises would be sprung on her today? Sir Melville dead.

'Kept it out of the... newspapers.' He took shallow breaths. 'I'm lord of the manor now... though not for much longer...' His voice grew fainter. 'Ruby?'

'She's downstairs in the kitchen, eating Mrs Handry's shortbread.'

He smiled. 'Good. I always want her to be happy...'

'I'll do my best to make sure she is. I have a feeling she's going to be headstrong though.'

'Like her mother...'

Beth grinned. 'Possibly. Already she has everyone at her beck and call. One cheeky smile from her and everyone is doing their best to make her happy.'

'Wonder if she'll have your temper...'

'Heavens, I hope not!' Beth laughed gently.

'Is Jackson well?'

She nodded. 'As far as I'm aware. His last letter said they were billeted in a village somewhere. They weren't expecting to be back in the trenches for another week or so.'

'Good men. All of them.' His eyes closed.

Beth waited, wondering if she should leave him to sleep. She half rose when he opened his eyes and held out his hand.

Tentatively, she took it.

'I have loved you from the first moment I saw you...'

'Louis.'

'Let me finish... Running out of time...' He paused as though gathering strength. 'Solicitors... will write... to you... my will.'

'About Ruby?'

Louis nodded slightly. 'I'm sorry I was mean... nasty...'

'It's forgotten, honestly. It was a long time ago.'

'Tell Noah… He was the better man…' He gave her a tiny smile. 'Don't hate me…'

Beth leaned forward. 'I don't hate you. I haven't for a long time. I forgive you, Louis.'

'Thank you, Beth…'

CHAPTER 22

January 1919.

Beth held onto Ruby's hand as they struggled through the crowds of people on the station's platform. Leah held Ruby's other hand, for the child was wanting to escape. They'd left Reggie outside in the cart while Peggy and Aunty Hilda had remained at home because the cold of winter had flared up Peggy's chest again and Aunty Hilda was looking after Ivy.

Jimmy had returned home sick with the influenza that was sweeping the country, indeed most of Europe, and had been admitted to a London hospital. Joanna had caught the train last week to stay in London and be close to him. She'd sent a telegram yesterday saying he was over the worst and gaining strength.

'Beth!' Jane waddled to her side, pregnant again from a leave Alfie had last year. 'When is the train due? I thought I'd missed it.'

'Any minute now,' Beth told her.

'What a grand day this is.' Jane was already sniffing with emotion. 'Have you heard from Joanna?'

'Aye, she's fine and Jimmy's getting better each day.'

'That's a relief. Any word from Will?'

'A telegram came this morning. He's been discharged from the hospital in France and declared fit enough to start to make his way home in the next few days. The army and the Red Cross are assisting him.'

'I can't believe they are finally all coming home. Well, not all, obviously.'

Beth nodded, remembering the three Jackson brothers who wouldn't be coming home to Peggy's embrace. She thought of Will and how he'd be coming home to only her and Joanna. No parents would enfold him in loving arms. The army telegram this morning had filled the house with joy. Will had survived the prison camp, the starvation and beatings. He'd only written twice in the last year, small notes to say he was well.

After so long, they'd have Will home safe and where they could care for him and return him to the healthy young man he once was. Unlike the serving soldiers, who once the armistice had been declared, were safe in allied territory, the prisoners of war were released into Germany without care or thought to their wellbeing. The Germans were starving, they wanted rid of the extra mouths to feed.

Beth feared that the Germans might retaliate for losing the war by shooting the prisoners. It had been a nightmare trying to find out what was happening with Will, but Mrs Hodge had done wonders in sourcing information when she could and relaying that to Beth.

The Red Cross were helping the army get the prisoners back home, but they were so malnourished they needed medical help, but at least they knew Will was safe.

Red tape between countries had held up the repatriation of all the troops. Demonstrations in London about the length of time it was taking to get the men home were reported in the newspapers, but finally after the election in December, a revised plan brought in by the new Secretary of War, Mr Winston

Churchill, had sped up the process of bringing the soldiers home.

A roar went up from the waiting families as they spotted the train coming down the track.

'The train's coming, Ruby.' Beth could barely talk, such was the excitement in her throat. 'Daddy's coming home.'

Ruby looked up at her with Noah's blue-green eyes. She was a mixture of them both and such a pretty child it made Beth's heart ache to look at her sometimes. How had she produced such a beautiful child?

The noise of the train pulling into the station and the cries of the crowd made Ruby put her hands over her ears. Beth pulled her in close to her skirts as she scanned the train's windows for a glimpse of the man she'd loved and missed for so long.

Doors sprang open all along the train and names were yelled as the crowd surged to find their beloved men returning from the war. As much as Beth wanted to race forward, she knew Ruby would be trampled, so she hung back and waited.

Tears filled her eyes as she watched sweethearts embrace. Mothers and fathers hug their sons. So many men, all in suits, having given up their khaki uniforms on returning to English shores. She couldn't make out anyone she knew.

Then suddenly she saw Albie. 'Albie!' she yelled making Ruby jump. 'Sorry, darling. Leah there's Albie.'

Leah ran forward and threw herself into Albie's arms. They kissed and Beth's vision blurred at the sight of them. The relationship between the pair had blossomed with every letter and card, every note and photo exchanged. Beth was so happy for them.

After kissing Leah, Albie let her go enough to hug Beth. 'Oh, Beth, it's so good to see you!'

'And I'm so happy to see you, too. Welcome home. Where's Noah?'

'He was behind me, but there's such a crowd. We could hardly get out of the carriage.' He turned and being taller scanned over the heads of others. 'Noah! Over here!' He waved.

Beth still couldn't see him.

'Alfie!' Jane cried out. She spotted her husband and hurried over to be smothered in his arms.

Beth had held back her tears for years. Never wanting to break down in fear she'd not stop crying if she started. However, seeing Noah walk towards her, knowing he'd not be ever walking away again, she finally let them flow.

He was home. The man she adored with every heartbeat gathered her into his arms.

Grinning, his eyes filled with tears. He held her so tight she thought she'd break a rib, but she didn't care.

After a moment, he loosened his hold enough to kiss her soundly. 'I've missed you,' he whispered.

'Don't ever let me go.'

'I promise I won't, even under threat of death.' He smiled, looking a little older, a little thinner, but still her Noah with love in his eyes.

'Are you my daddy?' Ruby's sweet little voice piped up.

Noah squatted down and wiped his eyes full of tears. 'I am, darling. I'm your daddy.'

Ruby stared at him for a long moment. 'Will you buy me an ice cream?'

'It's too cold for ice cream,' Beth said, sniffing into a handkerchief.

A tear fell over Noah's cheek. He cleared his throat. 'Sweetheart, I'll buy you ice cream for the rest of your life.'

Ruby smiled her father's smile and took his hand with complete trust.

Beth choked on a sob.

With his other arm wrapped around Beth's waist, they walked out of the train station and into their future.

ACKNOWLEDGMENTS

In the first book, The Market Stall Girl, I acknowledged my ancestors from the Wakefield area so I won't repeat myself again.

However, I will mention certain things again to ward off any confusion. From Wakefield Council I was able to obtain a map of Wakefield and surrounding villages for the years 1907-1919, which helped me enormously, as it showed the original names for roads and lanes. In the last one hundred years many places have ceased to exist or have changed and been renamed.

Potovens Road is now called Wrenthorpe Lane.

There was a Potovens Lane, which Noah's family lived on and a Potovens Road which went over Sunny Hill and towards Alverthorpe. It confused me at the start I can tell you!

Alverthorpe Road is now called Batley Road.

Brook Street outdoor market is no longer. The area of Brook Street has been redeveloped into a shopping mall. I do remember walking around both the indoor and outdoor markets in the early 1980s with my mum.

In the 1950s, my parents went courting in the lanes around the fields of Wrenthorpe as both families lived on Sunny Hill. My parents married in St Anne's Church in Wrenthorpe.

My father left the pit and worked as a farmer, including helping out at Asquith's Rhubarb Farm in Brandy Carr. The current owner, Ben Asquith, remembers my dad. Sadly, Ben is the last in his family to own the family farm which has been going since 1870s. http://www.brandycarrnurseries.co.uk/history/

Wrenthorpe Mine is no longer in use and the land is now the Wakefield Metropolitan District Council offices. My father, grandfather and great + grandfathers all worked at a local mine in Newton between Wrenthorpe and Outwood.

I'm a huge fan of genealogy and spend many hours finding ancestors on ancestry.com and when I do find these generations who ultimately created me, I am always intrigued by their stories, and wished someone had written down what they were like, where they worked, not just a note on a census. It is through tracing my family tree that I found five brothers. The Ellis brothers who were my 2nd great uncles on my maternal grandfather's side - they were his mother's brothers. The five brothers all fought in WWI. Benjamin, Charles, Alfred, James and Arthur. Arthur died in 1916 on the first day of the Somme battle. Thankfully, the other four came home as I've found out recently!

The First World War holds great fascination for me and through my research I have learned so much and gained a huge respect for those who lived through it, especially my own ancestors who were simple hard working people and who ultimately answered the call and made sacrifices we can only imagine.

Thank you for reading The Woman from Beaumont Farm. I hope you enjoyed it as much as I did writing it.

I want to thank all the readers who support me and review my stories, it means a great deal to me. I love your messages!

A special shout out to Deborah Smith and her facebook group for their support, not just for me but for all authors they read and champion. I'm truly thankful they like my books!

Best wishes,
AnneMarie Brear
2021

ABOUT THE AUTHOR

Award winning & Amazon UK Bestseller AnneMarie Brear has been a life-long reader and started writing in 1997 when her children were small. She has a love of history, of grand old English houses and a fascination of what might have happened beyond their walls. Her interests include reading, travelling, watching movies, spending time with family and eating chocolate - not always in that order! She is the author of historical family saga novels.

To join her newsletter to hear more about her books please visit her website:

http://www.annemariebrear.com

Printed in Great Britain
by Amazon